Novel

William Baer

Southwell Press

Novel / by William Baer

ISBN: 978-1-956199-09-3

Library of Congress Control Number: 2025907742

Cover Image: *Man Sitting at Desk in Dark Room*, zef art (Shutterstock)

Cover Design: WB & Vanessa Jaramillo

Southwell Press, Wayne, New Jersey

southwellpress.com

For my family and friends
especially Debbie

I.

THE PREMISE

Chapter 1

The Box

Tuesday, September 25

I was reading, actually rereading, the initial thirty-five words of *Absalom, Absalom!* when I heard the crack at the picture window, felt the burn in my left shoulder, and realized I'd been shot.

> *From a little after two oclock until almost sundown of the*
> *long still hot weary dead September afternoon they sat in*
> *what Miss Coldfield still called the office because her father*
> *had called it that –*

I put the book down on my desk and slid the chair backwards, slightly to my left, which seemed safely out of the angle-of-trajectory for a second firing. Instinctively, almost stupidly, I did my best to hold my shoulder together, ignoring the pain, compressing the bleeding wound, and staring at the cardboard box on the desk in front of me.

Thirty minutes ago, there'd been a knock on my front door. With no reason to rush, I got up from my desk, walked down the staircase from my high office perch, opened the front door, and found the cardboard box lying on the ground. It was a standard 9x12x4-inch cardboard mailing box, but it had no USPS, FedEx, or UPS stickers, which meant that it had been hand-delivered. I looked around a bit, across Crow Trail at my neighbors' log cabin, then across Osborne Terrace and into the thick green trees that blocked out the lake in the valley below.

There was no one around.

Returning upstairs, somewhat curious, I opened the box.

It contained, oddly enough, a hairbrush, four photographs, a rifle manual, and a typed note with detailed instructions:

The hairbrush: an ordinary hairbrush, pinkish, girlish, with a few strands of blonde hair entangled.

The photographs: four long-distance shots of a young girl, maybe seventeen or so, trim, tallish, blonde, nicely dressed, attractive, fashion-conscious, elegant, stately, maybe athletic. All four of the photographs were taken in environments that I knew well from nearly two decades ago: (1) the young girl walking across St. Mary's Courtyard, (2) entering a student residence with another girl at Dean's Court, (3) sitting outside a café, The Doll's House, reading a book, and (4) sitting alone amid the ruins of St. Andrews Cathedral, which, in the foreground, clearly revealed the barrel of a rifle.

The manual: the standard Remington manufacturer's "Owner's Manual and Instruction Book" for "Models 700, Seven, and 673 Bolt Action Centerfire Rifles." Unmarked.

The note:

If you do not follow each of the following instructions, explicitly, your daughter will die:

1. *Write a novel within the next three months.*
2. *Give the completed manuscript to your agent on December 12.*
3. *Write about the experience you're going through.*
4. *Do not, under any circumstance, contact the police, but you can and should pursue the case on your own, with or without private investigatorial assistance.*
5. *You can travel to Scotland or anywhere else.*
6. *Do not, under any circumstance, inform your daughter about what is happening. Or anyone else.*
7. *In the novel, you should speculate about who's doing what and why. The novel* must *have a resolution.*
8. *The novel will consist of twelve chapters, being the same exact chapter titles from the "Novel" section of* Writing Fiction, *and the novel will describe your writing processes as you proceed, including the "Millarisms."*
9. *Arrange to have the novel published on February 24.*
10. *Dedicate the book to "WF" and arrange for any profits to be donated to the University of San Juan Medical School.*
11. *When all the conditions are met, and only then, the rifle will be forwarded to your home and the threat will terminate.*
12. *Now, right now, read the opening of* Absalom, Absalom! *up to the dash.*

Which I did.

Getting myself shot.

But I had no daughter.

No children at all.

Or did I?

I was a thirty-six-year-old widower, living alone in a log cabin in Packanack Lake, Wayne, New Jersey. My wife Marquita had died five years ago in a car crash on the Pacific Coast Highway near Topanga Beach, and I was doing my best to put it behind me. Needless to say, we never had children.

Despite my current predicament and the shock of the assault, I seemed oddly lucid.

I dialed 911, told them I'd been shot, and, in spite of their insistence that I *not* hang up the phone, I hung up the phone. Then I called Jack Colt, knowing that he never picked up his phone, and listened to his wiseass message:

"Since you're calling me, you obviously want something. So tell me what the hell it is."

"It's Bret Buchanan, Kyle's brother. I've just been shot, and I need your help. Come to Chilton tomorrow and don't tell my brother I called you."

The pain was accelerating, but I needed to hide the box before the cops arrived.

It was September 25.

Faulkner's birthday.

Chapter 2

Puerto Mosquito

Wednesday, September 26

H er clothes were off.

She smiled, slipping off the edge of our little pontoon into the warming waters near the southern shore of Vieques Island. As she did so, she was immediately engulfed, surrounded, embraced, by a photo-phosphorescent aura of blueish-greenish-whitish light that followed her every movement, everywhere, beneath the black surface of the water, beneath the black and moonless sky.

Mosquito Bay.

Being the brightest bioluminescent bay on the entire planet, being, according to *Travel and Leisure*, one of the fifty most romantic places in the world.

Being, tonight, the *most* romantic.

Eventually, her dripping wet face emerged from the surface, as the odd glow continued to radiate all around and beneath her.

"You're much too beautiful," I said. "What am I supposed to do with you?"

"Do you need an instruction manual?"

Earlier that day, we'd been married at the high altar of the historic Cathedral de San Juan Bautista in Old San Juan, and, tonight, this was her "special wedding gift" before we flew north tomorrow morning for a honeymoon in the Canadian Maritimes.

Later, she explained that the little bay off Vieques Island, ten miles from the main island, was an ecological peculiarity, saturate with microscopic Dinoflagellates that glowed in greens and blues whenever they were agitated, entirely dependent for subsistence on the red Mangrove trees that surrounded the bay.

"There's over 750,000 Dinos in every gallon, but don't worry, Jersey boy, they're harmless."

She smiled again.

From the water.

"Lose the clothes and get in here."

Which I did, and we swam, treaded water, and held each other close, bathed in the surreal underwater lights of Mosquito Bay.

I woke up.

I was flat out in a hospital bed in Chilton Memorial, and everything came back. Including the pain. I looked down at my left hand and tried to move my fingers. They all moved. Sometime late last night, before the IV drip, a young doctor told me the good news that the bullet had missed all of the bones, just missing both the clavicle and the scapular, and that it was, essentially, a flesh wound to the deltoid that should heal up nicely. Then I told him about the fire escape accident in the Bronx, when I was fourteen, and the subsequent nerve damage, and he looked thoughtfully noncommittal, saying:

"We'll have to wait and see."

In other words, he didn't have a clue.

Soon I was flushed with morphine and conked out cold.

It looked like I had a private room.

Kyle was gone, but Wendy was sleeping in a nearby chair, looking ever-so-lovely even within her worried sleep. I found the remote, raised the head of my bed, and looked at the clock. It was almost ten.

Despite our hyper-awkward break-up two weeks ago, which I'd handled as clumsily as humanly possible, despite Wendy's subsequent frustrations and irritations, when she got the news late last night, she immediately drove from the city to New Jersey. She was terrified, but we calmed her down.

Isn't there some kind of adage: "The writer who dates his agent is an idiot"?

If there isn't, there should be.

Then Jack Colt stepped into the room and took it over.

He always looked far bigger and far more menacing than his actual 6'2". Colt, who descended directly from Samuel Colt, was the most famous private detective in New Jersey, the most famous private detective in the whole NYC Metro area, having rescued the governor's daughter several years ago deep in the Pine Barrens, then, later, solving the famous "Little Girl Killings," etc. He was a Paterson-born hardass who always looked like a slicked-up mob guy in his dark Armani suits, his Ray-Ban Liteforce shades, and his jet-black greased-back hair. Everyone who'd ever met Colt was afraid of him, except for me, because he was an old pal of my younger brother Kyle, who *also* wasn't afraid of him, who was now the chief prosecutor at the Passaic County Courthouse.

"You don't look so bad," he said.

He looked over at Wendy, registered nothing, then looked back at me. Saying, without actually saying it, "What can I do to help?"

I told him.

In detail.

"By the way," I mentioned after-the-fact, "if I knew what kind of rifle it was, could you track it down?"

He didn't bother to ask how a sniper victim could possibly know what kind of weapon he'd been shot with.

"Tell me."

"A Remington 700."

"Useless. Much too common."

As I'd expected.

"By the way," I said, "this is between you and me," meaning that my brother was out of the loop.

"Yeah," he said.

Then he left the room, and it felt empty.

I picked up my cell.

There was a text from Vinny.

An Embracer 100 crashed in the Poconos. You want more info?

Vinny obviously hadn't heard about the shooting.

Wendy opened her eyes, pretty blue eyes, and looked at me sadly, and it broke my rotten heart.

Chapter 3

Cherry Valley

Wednesday, September 26

I was sitting on a ridge in the Poconos, in the Appalachians, high above Cherry Valley, not far from the Sorrenti Vineyards, seven miles southwest of the Delaware Water Gap. The remains of an Embracer 100 were scattered across the fields beneath me, surrounded by Vinny's NTSB go-team. Fortunately, there'd only been one occupant, thus one dead body, the pilot, whose remains were already gone by the time I arrived. Generally, with smaller jetcraft crashes like this one, it was pilot error of some kind, but I'd have to wait and hear from Vinny.

The truth was, I wasn't thinking about any of it. Not the crash below, not the family of the dead, not my afternoon release from Chilton, not the drive across New Jersey and the Delaware River, not even the pain in my shoulder.

I was thinking about Death Valley.

I was thinking about six years ago. Thinking about another plane crash. About a Cessna Citation, with four passengers and a pilot, traveling west from LA on some kind of business/party trip towards Las Vegas, with planned sightseeing flyovers at Yosemite, Death Valley, Area 51 (from a distance), and the Hoover Dam.

But they never made it to Nevada.

It was one of those rare and horrible hypoxia tragedies, a bit like the one that had killed golf champion Payne Stewart back in 1999. For some reason, the overflow valve on the Cessna had been left open, and the pressure dropped, and everyone on board got high on oxygen deprivation, as the pilot, descending toward the canyon, apparently lost consciousness and crashed.

All five had died: the pilot, the VP of LA Comtex, his HR assistant, and two young women.

The corporate jet had crashed into the salt flats at Badwater Basin, at the exact lowest elevation in North America, which is one of the weirdest places on earth. Two hundred square miles of blinding white salt, with a little borax mixed in. A plantless, cloudless, moistureless, broiling wasteland, fifteen miles south of Furnace Creek, one of the hottest places on the planet, which set the all-time hottest temperature – 134 degrees F – back in 1913. As for the aircraft itself, the undercarriage of the fuselage had shredded and buckled and broken, and its left wing had catapulted over two hundred feet away.

Markie and I sat on our little folding chairs in the 106-degree heat watching Vinny and the NTSB team sort through the wreckage. We'd driven out from Malibu, and I was glad that by the time we got there, the bodies were gone. I'd been to a bunch of these wrecks with Vinny, and the worst part was always the smell. The smell of death. The smell of burnt flesh.

Markie certainly didn't need any of that.

"Are we being morbid?" she wondered.

She wore a white straw hat, Gucci shades, and, even on the hellish floor of Death Valley, a light cotton de la Renta yellow flare dress, with matching yellow spikes.

She was looking for some kind of reassurance.

"We're writers, right? It's fine."

We drank gallons of Gatorade, and she took lots of notes, and, occasionally, Vinny would take a break and come over and fill us in:

There was lots of booze in the cabin.

Not to mention cocaine.

No, the women were *not* their wives.

The pilot was young, reasonably experienced, but he'd never trained in a decompression chamber.

The Citation, he explained, is a very reliable craft, being a low-wing cantilever monoplane with two excellent Williams International FJ-44-3A turbofan engines.

It can cruise over 400 mph, beneath a ceiling of 40,000 feet.

Despite common misconceptions, hypoxia isn't simply oxygen deprivation, it's actually insufficient oxygen pressure within the lungs.

Inducing drowsiness, euphoria, mental impairment, nonchalance, disorientation, overconfidence, and cluelessness. The victims have no idea that anything's wrong, as they lull into hypoxic stupor, then unconsciousness, then death.

Etc.

"Did they die from hypoxia? Or did they die from the crash?" she wondered.

"They were dead before the crash."

Which seemed like a good thing.

Later that night, the three of us went up to the top of Dante's Peak in the Black Mountains. To the west and the north. Beyond the wreckage in Badwater Basin, we could see the steep Panamint Mountains rising to Telescope Peak. Off to the north, beyond Furnace Creek, we could see the shadowy Funeral Mountains.

The night had cooled off to about 80 degrees, and we sat there, high above Death Valley, like Dante above the circles of hell, as Vinny patiently answered all of Markie's questions. We had a cooler with rum punch sangria and a little boombox that played Jose Feliciano's classic *La Historia* album over and over.

Vinny Erickson is my best and oldest Jersey buddy. We met in grammar school, went to high school together, where he played first base on my double plays from short at DePaul Diocesan. At least until I wrecked my shoulder in the Bronx. Nowadays, Vinny was, admittedly, a bit unathletically overweight and his reddish hair was thinning out. But nothing else had changed. *Everyone* loved Vinny, not to mention his wife Angie and their two little sports-crazed boys, but underneath all the congeniality and pleasantness, Vinny was, as he'd always been, on a mission. When he was twelve, his parents had died in a plane crash, so he went off to Rensselaer, became a pilot, went to Embry-Riddle Aeronautics in Daytona, the most elite flight school in the country, got his psychology PhD at MIT, then finally became what he'd always planned to become, an air crash inspector for NTSB.

His specialty was "human performance," including pilot-system interaction, and he was especially adept at interviews and in-court testimony. He rose quickly through the ranks and was now one of NTSB's senior Inspectors-in-Charge, running go-teams and overseeing all the specialized groups – weather, black box, systems, maintenance, air traffic control, postmortem, etc. – as well as the FAA reps, the union reps, and the manufacturer reps.

His only goal, being exactly the same as NTSB's primary objective, was to make air travel safer.

"Where's the black box?" Markie wondered.

"It's in the rear. On the big jets, there's always two, and they're not black. They're orange."

Markie smiled, writing down almost everything Vinny said. Then she asked more questions. Despite his endless responsibilities and an early get-out-of-bed-time tomorrow morning, he was ever-felicitous, ever-relaxed, and fully aware of Markie's "writing problem."

Glad to help.

Later, after Vinny took off, Markie and I walked over to the ledge and looked down into the moistureless cauldron that got its name because thirteen would-be miners once died of dehydration and/or heat stroke in the Mohave Desert's now-famous valley during their abortive journey to the California Gold Rush.

She took my hand.

"I can do this," she said, with confidence.

She was happy, *very* happy, which meant that I was happy.

"You OK, pal?"

It was Vinny.

He was standing over me in the darkness, somewhere in the middle of the Poconos.

"I'm fine."

"Maybe you need to go home and get some rest. You got yourself shot yesterday."

I didn't bother to argue.

"Maybe you're right."

Then I admitted:

"I was thinking about Death Valley."

"You know, given the circumstances back then, it might seem callous to say that it was a great time and a great memory, but it was."

"It was."

"I miss her too, Bret."

"I know. And just in case you're wondering, I wasn't brooding about it."

"Good, cause Jersey guys never brood."

I smiled and reassured him.

"I *never* brood."

He didn't disagree, so I changed the subject.

"What happened down there?"

Referring to the pulverized Embracer.

"There was a flash storm last night with tons of cloud cover and fog. He must have got disoriented."

That was that.

It happens sometimes. It's what they call "controlled flight into terrain." It's apparently what happened to John F. Kennedy, Jr., off the coast of Martha's Vineyard.

Chapter 4

The Premise

A man is forced to write a novel about writing a novel about being forced to write a novel.

II.

RESEARCH

Have fun! All *real* writers love to research, but don't let it take over your life. It's like booze; you've got to know when to stop and get on with things.

Chapter 5

Absalom, Absalom!

Thursday, September 27

S o I read it again:

> *From a little after two oclock until almost sundown of the*
> *long still hot weary dead September afternoon they sat in*
> *what Miss Coldfield still called the office because her father*
> *had called it that –*

I suppose someone was trying to say something about my life.

I was sitting at my desk again. It was two days after the shooting, and, needless to say, I'd been doing a lot of thinking. Maybe someone was trying to say that my life was essentially unproductive? That I was living off my wife's talents? Off the bogus Pulitzer? That by the age of thirty-six, I'd never written any of the novels that I'd planned to write. Like the radium girls novel, or the air crash novel, or my two current novels-in-progress, neither of which – not the one about the cryonics trial, not the one about the Tylenol murders copycat – had even a rough outline.

Instead, I was doing endless research and rereading Dante.

So what?

Why not?

I was enjoying myself.

I suppose someone was trying to say that my somewhat solitary life, in my old log cabin, was "still" and "weary" and "dead." Just like that September afternoon in 1909 when Quentin Compson was summoned by the elderly Miss Rosa Coldfield to hear her version of the bizarre history of Thomas Sutpen, as they sat together in the lifeless mote-filled office of her dead father.

I suppose someone was trying to say, what the hell are you doing with your life? You've won a Pulitzer for fiction, and yet you've *never* written any fiction. At least, not a novel. But *now* you will. You have no choice. Finally, you'll write a damned novel. I'll even tell you *what* to write about, and *how* to write it, and I'll force you to do it.

Well?

Was it true?

Was I excessively disengaged?

Was I lazy?

I really didn't think so, but someone seemed to believe I was. Yeah, I'll be the first to admit that I've often felt, ever since Markie died, that I wasn't doing much with my life. Even though I *had* edited her final novel, and I *had* written a textbook, and I *had* completed two screenplays. Nevertheless, there's no doubt, at the moment, that I was pretty bogged down in endlessly extrapolating research about both the cryogenics idea and the 1982 unsolved Tylenol murders in Chicago, but so what? That's what writers do, right? Research. Maybe I wasn't in such a big rush about anything because I didn't need to be. Money was no longer an issue, and neither, it seemed, was time.

But I will admit that I didn't feel like I was doing much with my life in other ways. My brother ran the insanely-frenetic Passaic County Courthouse, yet he still managed to spend lots of time with Angie and the twins, and he even, every Sunday afternoon, played tennis at the Packanack Lake tennis courts with Cindy and Mindy, an endlessly fascinating pair of mentally-challenged teenage twins that he'd met at the North Jersey Twins Club.

Of which he was president.

Vinny was more of the same. At the drop of a hat, the guy had to fly all over the country to oversee in-depth investigations of fatal air crashes, but he still found the time to coach both of his kids' baseball and tennis teams.

While I sat here at my desk, read my Dante, then watched tons of ESPN and *48 Hours Mystery*, occasionally leaving the house to grab some pickup at Vinni's Pizzarama or Zorba's Greek. I'm exaggerating, of course. After all, until recently, I had something "going" with Wendy, and I'm always a part of the family stuff at both Kyle's and Vinny's, and I still had a great bunch of old Jersey buddies to hang with, and talk about sports, etc., as well as a number of writer pals in the Apple to talk with about literary stuff, literary gossip, etc., but the truth was, underneath it all, I was essentially disappointed with myself, and maybe the schmuck who'd shot me felt exactly the same way I do.

As for that, the Wayne cops told me that the rifle had been fired from the roof of the Flannagan's old colonial, through a slight break in the trees' thick foliage. The Flannagans had been down at their place at the shore the past two weeks. In Manasquan.

There were no eyewitnesses, no earwitnesses, no evidence left behind at the scene, and no suspects. At least, that's what I was getting from the lead detective, Eddie Turasco, whom I knew through my brother.

"Any thoughts on who did it?" he asked.

"No."

"None?"

"None."

Even though I was absolutely certain that I'd been shot by the anonymous son-of-a-bitch who'd knocked on my front door and left the cardboard box.

But the truth was, I really didn't have any enemies. I'm not even sure that I *know* people who have enemies. Except for maybe Kyle. After all, he'd slammed the door on a lot of cretins at Rahway State Prison. Having enemies, most probably, was an occupational hazard. But I was just a "writer of sorts," and there was no one in my life whom I'd consider an enemy.

"Maybe it was just some kid jerking around," Eddie suggested.

"An accident?" I said, encouraging the idea.

"Yeah, maybe some peabrained kid took his old man's rifle up on the neighbor's rooftop and fired off a round for kicks."

"Yeah, I did some jackass stuff when I was a kid," I admitted.

"Me too."

If nothing else, I was strictly adhering to rule #4 about not, "under any circumstances," telling the police about the box. Or the note. Or the instructions. Or the threat.

And what about that?

The threat?

I didn't have a daughter.

But, then again, what if I did?

The girl in the picture looked like she was about seventeen or eighteen years old, and eighteen years ago I was an undergrad at the University of South Carolina. Which meant Bonnie McMillan. Then seventeen years ago I transferred to St. Andrews in Scotland. Which meant Skye MacAllister. So I spent much of the past two days reading over my old calendars, looking at old pictures, remembering as much as I could about those parts of my life, then searching for my two past lovers on the internet.

I suppose, in some ways, I was an odd kid. I can never remember a single moment in my life when I didn't expect to be a writer someday. Sure, it would have been fun to be a fireman, or an astronaut, or play centerfield for the Mets, but *nothing* took precedence over my dreams of being a writer. A storyteller. Which was definitely something that my mother had always encouraged when I was still a little kid in the Bronx, and it seems to me that the most important day in my early life was when I was five years old and my mother walked me over to Poe Cottage on East Kingsbridge Road, nine blocks from our apartment near Fordham Road, and we went inside the tiny house, and my mother pointed at the little bed, saying, "That's where Virginia died." Which I'd already read about, although it wasn't until several years later that I finally figured out that "consumption" meant tuberculosis. "And this is where he wrote 'Annabel Lee.'" So I sat down on the bed, and she sat down in the chair, and she recited the entire poem.

And so, all the night-tide, I lie down by the side
Of my darling, my darling, my life and my bride,
In her sepulcher there by the sea –
In her tomb by the sounding sea.

And all the rest of it.

And that was *that*.

I was soon reading Scott, another of my mother's favorites, and *The Count of Monte Cristo*, and Stevenson, and, later, when we moved to New Jersey, she bought me the Jack Burke trilogy, and I started reading the Brontës, Austen, Dickens, and lots of other stuff.

Then Faulkner.

Eventually, I fully expected to go off to college and study Faulkner. So when the time came, it seemed perfectly logical that I'd go to Ole Miss, given that both his house and his grave are within a mile of the campus, but, eventually, I decided on South Carolina because they had the Institute for Southern Studies, which was run by James B. Meriwether who also edited the annual Faulkner issue of *The Mississippi Review*. So at seventeen years of age, the Jersey boy went south to Columbia, South Carolina, meeting Bonnie Jean MacMillan near the end of the fall semester of my sophomore year, nine months before I transferred to St. Andrews, meeting Skye MacAllister, who, unsurprisingly, was from the Island of Skye in the Scottish Highlands.

Of the two possibilities, Bonnie seemed the most likely.

But Bonnie was dead.

According to multiple sources on the web, she'd died last year with her second husband in a small plane crash at Lake Moultrie in South Carolina. The obituaries claimed that she'd had two daughters: Faulkner, age seventeen, and Charleston, age twenty-six, which was obviously impossible because it meant that Charleston was born when Bonnie was seven years old.

What about Faulkner?

What about the girl with the suspicious name?

Was it possible that, once I'd left that summer, Bonnie had found herself pregnant and that, for some inexplicable reason, she'd decided not to tell me about it?

Then named the child Faulkner?

I suppose it was possible. Maybe it was more than possible. Maybe it's why there was a pink hairbrush in the cardboard box.

My email pinged. It was Irene Davis:

I told you I'd leave you alone.

I'd forgotten about Irene.

I guess I *did* have an enemy in this world, but ever since the restraining order, which her new email had just violated, she'd been behaving herself.

Out of sight, out of mind.

Irene Davis was a crackpot lawyer from Delaware who got it into her self-absorbed off-kilter brain that Markie's first book, *Aircrash*, was about her. That the novel was, as a consequence, libelous. Which set off a seemingly endless series of bogus lawsuits against Markie, then later, after Markie's death, against me, which were all promptly tossed out of court. Obviously frustrated, she started cyber-stalking and hacking my computer until I got fed up and requested, and was granted, the restraining order. In several of her old emails, Irene claimed that she was actually following me sometimes, but I'd never actually met her or seen her, except, of course, for the photo on her law firm's website.

Now she was back.

Was she bragging about her good behavior? Or was she taunting me about the box?

My cell vibrated.

It was Colt, wasting no time.

"She's your daughter."

"No doubt?"

"No doubt."

He hung up before I had the chance to say thanks. Colt was a guy with lots of connections, and I knew that he could finagle DNA tests quicker than anyone else. Then keep the results quiet. Yesterday, at the hospital, he'd swabbed the inside of my mouth and took the pink hairbrush with the yellow strands.

I think it's fair to say that the axis of my life had suddenly shifted.

I felt weak, faint, confused, and ashamed.

Markie was dead, and so was Bonnie, but I had a daughter some-where. I felt helpless, overcome, as if momentarily crushed into noth-ingness. Which was something that didn't happen very often in my life.

If ever. But now I was a father, an absent and lousy one, and someone was threatening my daughter.

When I came back to myself, I called Melanie Thompson on the Paramount lot and told her I wouldn't be there for the opening at Grauman's Chinese.

"It's a family problem."

She was obviously disappointed, but she was also sympathetic and understanding.

"We'll miss you, Bret."

"Thanks."

Now it was time to get my ass down to South Carolina.

Chapter 6

The Palmetto State

Friday, September 28

"Do you know who I am?"

"You're Faulkner's father."

As instructed, I'd been sitting on the lowest steps of the South Carolina State House, in front of the Washington statue, facing the flagless Confederate Memorial. Behind me, the Capitol building was looming majestically in Greek Revival style, with a Stars and Stripes waving from the top of its dome. In 1865, on February 17, after the "March to the Sea," General W. T. Sherman, made a point of marching through Columbia and shelling the foundation of the new State House. The thinking, both now and then, was that Sherman bore a special grudge against the South Carolina assembly which had initiated the Civil War following the bombing of Fort Sumter by voting to secede from the Union. Then the rest of the Confederate states followed, and, to this day, there are six bronze stars marking the places where Sherman's artillery shells struck the building.

Rebels have a long memory.

But their flag is gone.

In 1962, in remembrance of the Confederate dead, the state assembly voted to hoist the Stars and Bars on top of the dome along with the US flag. Some believed it was done less as a ceremonial participation in the Civil War Centennial than it was a defiant gesture against court-ordered desegregation. Whatever the motives of the individual state senators, it initiated a heated controversy that festered until 2000, when a compromise was reached, proposed by an African-American senator, along with one who was not, and the rebel flag was moved to the Confederate War Memorial in front of the State House.

Which some people felt was *even more* prominent.

Then sports got involved. The NCAA initiated an economic boycott of the state and called for a general moratorium. Over the next fifteen years, the state of South Carolina sacrificed over two hundred billion dollars in lost tourism revenues and cancelled conventions and sporting events. In 2007, the "old ball coach" got fed up and chimed in. Steve Spurrier, the legendary football coach of the South Carolina Gamecocks, had had enough of "that damn Confederate flag" and suggested that "we need to get rid of it." Nevertheless, it still took another eight more years as well as the horrific murders of nine black parishioners, including a state senator, at the Emanuel African Methodist Episcopal Church in Charleston, by a deranged racist named Dylann Roof.

In response, the Carolina Senate voted 37-3 to take down the flag on July 10, 2015, and hide it inside a local museum.

The monument, of course, is still there, and I was staring directly at it, unthinkingly, when I heard her spikes clicking down the steps, so I stood up, looked at Charleston MacMillan, and asked her if she knew who I was.

"You're Faulkner's father."

She was tall, with cropped dark hair, wary brown eyes, and very sharply dressed in a nicely cut gray business suit, with a two-button blazer, notch lapels, and a pink-tinted blouse buttoned at the collar. She looked, at least to me, like a taller version of the young Winona Ryder, before *Girl, Interrupted*, before the shoplifting, and I think it would be perfectly reasonable to say that she was strikingly beautiful.

Bonnie, of course, was beautiful as well, but in a very different way, and I didn't see any resemblance. Nevertheless, I could definitely hear the "South" in Charleston's voice, although her Carolina accent was much softer and more contemporary than Bonnie's, which was full (and proud) of endearing colloquialisms like "hush," and "bless your heart," and "fixin'," and "reckon'," and "kiss my go-to-hell." The latter of which she never said to me.

As for Charleston, she worked as some kind of personal assistant for one of the big-shot senators in the state house, and when I called her office earlier, she said to wait on the stairs outside. She sounded rather reluctant on the phone, and she didn't seem any happier to see me in person. Maybe she thought I'd abandoned Bonnie when she got pregnant.

Which might explain her coolish demeanor.

"I never knew about Faulkner," I assured her.

She didn't believe me.

"Then how do you know about her now?"

"An old friend told me," I lied. "Three days ago."

"Who was it?"

"I'm afraid that I can't tell you that."

She didn't like my evasiveness, but I had no choice.

She didn't bother to respond.

"Does she know about me?" I tried.

"She knows about her mother's relationship with some dumbass Yankee boy, and a few facts about her college days in Columbia, but she was never told exactly who you are."

"Why not?"

"You sure ask a lot of question for a never-been-there father."

"I didn't even know I *was* a father."

She was still suspicious, but, at least, she was thinking it over.

"What do you want?"

It wasn't quite as cold as it sounded.

"I want to know what happened."

She was wavering.

"Do you have a picture?" I wondered.

She hesitated.

Then she took out her wallet and showed me a picture of a young girl standing in front of the Capitol Building, standing on the same steps where we were both standing right now, smiling and waving at the camera. She was definitely the same pretty girl in the four photographs taken at St. Andrews.

"Can I meet her?"

"I'm not sure you deserve to meet her. Besides, she's in Scotland."

Which was no surprise.

"Look, I'm not sure exactly who you are, Charleston, but I want you to understand that I loved Bonnie very much back then, and that things would have never ended the way they did if I'd known she was pregnant."

She began to cry.

Unexpectedly.

Soft sobs.

Embarrassed, she leaned into me, resting her head on my right shoulder. I had no idea what was going on, so I waited patiently, trying to ignore the increasing discomfort in my other shoulder.

Finally, she got a hold of herself, stepped back, and looked at me directly.

"I'm sorry about that, but Bonnie meant everything to me. *Everything*."

"Would you tell me about it?"

She shrugged, then nodded yes.

We walked over to a stone bench, sat down, and she explained that she'd been orphaned at ten and that Bonnie, who was already taking care of her new baby, took her in and raised her like a daughter.

"Like a best friend, too."

"But Bonnie was only eighteen at the time," I said, stating the obvious.

"Yes, and she adopted me that same year. So I grew up like a big sister to Faulkner, although I was really more like an aunt, since I'm nine years older."

She thought it over.

"Now that Bonnie's gone, no one means more to me than sweet Faulkner, and I miss her terribly."

She stood up.

"Don't worry," she assured me, "I'm not about to cry again. I don't know where that came from. Besides, I need to get back to work."

"Can we talk some more? Maybe tonight?"

She deliberated a moment.

"Alright, seven o'clock on Palmetto Street in West Columbia."

"The same house?"

"The same house."

Charleston turned and walked away, as I watched her go.

Chapter 7

Elmwood

Friday, September 28

I was sitting on another stone bench, in front of five hundred dead Confederate soldiers, staring at a "fire rainbow" in the Carolina sky. Although I'd never actually seen one before, I knew that it wasn't actually a rainbow and that it had nothing to do with fire. Whatever it was, it was enflaming a perfectly blue sky with spectacular swatches and splotches of pinks, yellows, and radiant greens. As if the sky, as if the entire universe was showing off for Bonnie MacMillan, who was lying in her grave a few feet in front of me, with red and yellow roses lying against her simple tombstone.

Bonnie's favorite color was yellow, but the lady in the flower shop told me that yellow roses symbolized "friendship," which was certainly true in our case, but not enough. So I bought a bunch of red ones too.

I'd spent the long afternoon meandering around both the town and the university, where all kinds of memories, most of them good, many of them related to Bonnie, lingered everywhere. I'd been a student at South Carolina for over a year before we met, being, at first, a seventeen-year-old Jersey/Yankee in the heart of the rebel South, loving its history, the university, the parties, the Southern belles, the Chaucer classes with Bert Dillon, Gamecock football, Gamecock basketball, etc.

I was, at the time, it seems to me now, perfectly content. Then I met Bonnie MacMillan, and I got a whole lot more content.

It was a night in November. The night before the S.C.-Clemson game. The annual Battle of the Palmetto State. But now we had coach Lou Holtz, with soaring expectations, and the Columbia campus was combustible and rocking, as I was out club-and-bar hopping with my roomy Leroy and a few other guys, and we stopped off at the Palmetto Club, and I went up to the bar, ordered a Seagram's on the rocks, turned around, and there she was.

With her thick blonde hair, viridescent eyes, and an endorphin-inducing country smile. She was wearing a pretty white dress with pretty red trim, and she had the word "Kill" neatly marked in black on her right cheek, and "Clemson" marked on her left. She was tallish, ladylike, confident, and I could sense, almost instinctively, that she was an athlete as well.

Somebody put Mark Chesnutt's "I Don't Want to Miss a Thing" on the jukebox, which is about as romantic as it gets, and she looked me up-and-down and said, with her hyper-thick Carolina accent:

"Well, lookie here at the Yankee boy."

How she knew I was north of the Mason-Dixon, I had no idea. Maybe it was obvious.

I smiled, said nothing, sipping some rye off the rocks in my glass. Just like a Jersey guy would be expected to do under the circumstances.

"Does he know how to dance?" she asked, referring to me.

"Just with girls in white dresses."

So we danced to what she later told me was her favorite song. She also liked horror films, rhubarb pie, George Strait, teddy bears, ROTC, Darius Rucker, tennis (third singles), poly sci (her major), and British lit (her minor).

When the song ended, I certainly didn't want "us" to end as well, so I said:

"When I kiss you later, will I get 'Kill Clemson' all over my face?"

"Well, hon, let's find out."

She kissed me on the mouth, and it was like all the honeysuckle (whatever the hell that is) in all the Faulkner novels.

That was that.

Even the controversial loss to Clemson the next day, during the famous "Push-off" game, didn't slow down our North/South romance. But the truth was, I only had one more semester at South Carolina, and I let her know right up front, and we basically ignored it. By that time, I felt that I'd already gotten whatever I needed from the Southern Studies program, and I'd already been accepted to transfer to St. Andrews in Scotland. But even that ever-hovering problem never slowed us down, and it was, it would be fair to say, a pretty steamy fun-filled spring semester, and I believed that I was in love with her.

Looking back, I'm sure that I was.

As for Bonnie, she told me many times that when she saw me that first night at the Palmetto it was a LAFS thing, meaning "love at first sight," and that nothing, not even two years in Scotland, would mess things up.

Because, as Bonnie liked to say, she "didn't want to miss a thing."

Bonnie Jean MacMillan had grown up across the Congaree in West Columbia. Her father was an ex-Marine who'd married late and died when Bonnie was a little girl. She was attentively and carefully raised by her schoolteacher mother, who, for some reason, seemed to like me a lot.

But, hell, *nothing* ever works out.

Right?

Bonnie's now dead. Lying right next to her dead husband. Her *second* husband. Leaving behind a daughter and an older adopted daughter.

Earlier this afternoon, I'd roamed rather aimlessly around town, around campus, past Cooper Library, the Horseshoe, Longstreet Theatre, the Tennis Center, the Congaree Riverbank, the stadium, Finlay Park, etc. When I was finished, I banged my damned shoulder getting into a taxicab.

Eventually ending up right here, as intended, as the rainbow slowly dissipated in the forthcoming twilight.

I suppose if it's possible that a cemetery can be prestigious, then Elmwood Cemetery is the most prestigious cemetery in Columbia, with its Confederate dead, with its historic notables, with its lovely grounds. With its labyrinthine winding roads, shaded pathways, impressive mausoleums, and thickly planted trees.

Which all seemed to me, in the late September twilight, perfectly bucolic. As was Bonnie herself. Yeah, she was serious about her future back then, but she was always pleasant, always upbeat, always fun, and always liking everyone, especially me.

I guess I'd say she was kind of perfect.

I checked my watch and pulled out my cell and dialed Colt. After his phone message, I left my own:

"It's Bret. I'd like you to get a hold of two birth certificates: Charleston MacMillan, age 27, which is m-a-c not m-c, and Faulkner MacMillan, age 18. They both live on Palmetto Street in West Columbia, South Carolina. Thanks."

I didn't bother to ask him to keep my brother out of it. I knew he would.

Then I stood up, looked down at the neatly kept grave, and wondered out loud:

"What the hell's going on, Bonnie?"

Chapter 8

Teddy Bear

Friday, September 28

I rang the doorbell for the first time in seventeen years.

It sounded exactly the same.

Charleston was still living in the home she'd grown up in, which was the same home that Bonnie had grown up in.

12 Palmetto Street.

It looked the same. A little two-story dark wood cottage, with pretty white flowers in the flower boxes beneath the windows.

Charleston opened the door. She was still wearing her gray blazer and pink blouse. She looked impeccable, just as she'd looked on the State Capitol steps, but she didn't seem all that happy to see me.

"Come in."

I walked into the living room and sat down on the couch. Even the interior of the house looked exactly the same, homey and perfectly neat, as if Bonnie had left things exactly as they were to honor her mother, as if Charleston had left things exactly as they were to honor Bonnie.

She didn't sit down, and I had the feeling that she planned to get me out the door quickly.

"I want you to read that," she said.

She pointed down at the coffee table in front of me on which there were several fashion catalogues and a single sheet of paper.

It was a copy of an email.

I did as I was told.

> *Dear Bret – Should I intrude again into your life? I know about your terrible tragedy, about your successes, and I think about you more than I should. Am I a bad girl for saying that? For writing out of the blue? Please forgive me for saying hello but remember that it was the rebel girl who first spotted the Yankee boy. Love, Bonnie Jean*

It was dated last year.

Needless to say, I was stunned.

I looked at Charleston.

"What's this?"

"It's pretty obvious what it is. What I want to know is why you never responded."

I looked dead-ahead into her pissed-off brown eyes.

"I never got this email."

She didn't believe me.

"Maybe Bonnie never sent it," I speculated, "but I'm *positive* that I never got this email."

She thought it over.

"How do *you* know about it?" I wondered.

I tried to make it sound like it wasn't an accusation.

"I stumbled onto it after she died, when I was shutting down her computer."

"Is the computer still in the house?"

"Yes."

It wasn't necessary to say, well, why don't you get your accusing-pretty-rebel-ass upstairs and make sure she actually sent the damn thing.

"I'll be right back."

She left the room.

I'd naturally assumed that Charleston was angry at me because I'd supposedly abandoned Bonnie when she was pregnant. Maybe she was. But she was also angry because I'd seemingly rejected Bonnie a second time, just last year, not long before she died.

Frustrated, I stood up and walked over to the bookcase, doing what I always did when I was left alone in people's houses: check out the spines of their books. There was, unsurprisingly, lots of Carolina history, lots of Civil War history, a copy of Vankin and Whalen's great classic *The Sixty Greatest Conspiracies of all Time*, which every serious writer has read cover to cover, and a whole load of other curiosities, like several books about the Rothschilds, something called *The Dahlgren Conspiracy*, and an entire shelf of books about the Knights of the Golden Circle.

When I heard her coming down the stairs, I took my seat again and glanced down at the catalogues: Hugo Boss, Calvin Klein, and Ralph Lauren.

I'd bet anything that gray suit was Calvin Klein.

She re-entered the room and resumed her standing position.

"You're right, she never sent it. It came from her drafts folder. So I was wrong."

She definitely didn't like being wrong.

"But, let's face it," she continued, "you *still* left her pregnant eighteen years ago."

I was starting to get irritated.

"Sit down," I said.

Maybe a bit too firmly.

She never broke her reserve, but she took a seat, just like a polite Southern lady, sitting in an upright chair across the room.

"Like I told you this afternoon," I explained, "I *never* knew that Bonnie was pregnant, and I wrote her a long letter that summer, but she never answered it. So when I got to Scotland, I emailed her another long letter, and she never responded to that one either. I have no idea why she didn't, but I do know that she cut me off back then. Even her phone number was changed. It was hard to take. Very hard. But, eventually, I moved on."

"Could that be the truth?"

"Of course, it's the truth!"

"Why would she do such a thing?"

"I was hoping that you could tell me."

"I have no idea."

"Maybe," I suggested, without much conviction, "she didn't want me to feel trapped. Or maybe she was ashamed for some stupid reason. Or maybe she thought she was protecting me, allowing me to pursue the things that I'd always been planning to pursue."

"I have no idea," she repeated.

"I'll tell you one thing, Charleston, if she *had* responded to that email, I would have left Scotland immediately and come back to South Carolina."

She was trying to believe me.

"Did you love her?"

Which was *really* irritating.

"Of course, I loved her."

She thought it over.

"What did Bonnie say about me," I wondered, "when you were growing up in this house?"

"Nothing bad," she remembered. "Never anything bad. It was always very loving, very good."

We were both silent, confused, worthless.

"I don't get it," I said, repeating myself stupidly.

"Me neither."

Charleston stood up.

"I could use a drink," she said. "You want something?

"Yeah."

"Beer or Chardonnay?"

"Chardonnay."

She left the room again. When she came back with the two glasses of wine, her blazer was gone, and her shoes were gone, and she sat near me on the couch.

"Sorry I've been such a bitch."

"You had your reasons."

We sipped Chardonnay.

"Can we talk about Bonnie?" I asked.

"Of course."

"About Faulkner?"

"Of course."

So we did, for a couple of hours, as I tried to piece together the threads of Bonnie Jean's life.

Beginning with the first husband:

"He was a complete jerk. Some kind of stupid explosions guy."

His name was Rex Kepler, seemingly likeable, a good ole boy, an ex-Army Ranger from somewhere in Alabama, maybe Muscle Shoals, who was working for Controlled Demolition when he first met Bonnie.

"I was twelve at the time, and Faulkner was still a baby, and Bonnie was pretty messed up. She was trying her best to deal with all the pressure."

Then she took a short vacation with some college friends to Myrtle Beach and met Rex Kepler in one of those beachfront clubs. It seems he swept her off her feet.

"He was pretty handsome, I'll give him that, and a real live wire, and she needed some fun in her life. Unfortunately, she made the mistake of marrying the idiot before she really knew that much about him."

Three weeks later, in fact. Which didn't seem like Bonnie at all, who was never really the impulsive type. Yet she'd married Rex Kepler three weeks after Myrtle Beach, and he moved to West Columbia.

"Right into this house!" she remembered.

According to Charleston, who told me to call her "Charlie" like everyone else did, Rex was a controlling braggart, always blabbing about wanting a beach house in Myrtle Beach, always away on the road blowing stuff up.

"And I'm sure," she added, "whoring around as well."

Rex had, apparently, taken no interest in either Charlie or little Faulkner, drank too much, and even snorted occasional lines.

"I was twelve at the time, but I wasn't an idiot."

"Did he hit her?" I asked.

"Yes, a bunch of times, but, fortunately, the bastard was gone most of the time. Finally, Bonnie decided to divorce his silly ass, but he suddenly vanished."

"Vanished?"

"Yeah, he never came back. Even his bosses at the demolition company had no idea where he was."

"Was that the end of him?"

"Yes. We never heard from him again, and I bless the day he went off in that puff of smoke."

"What about the other one?"

Meaning the second husband.

"Oh, he wasn't so bad, just pathetic. A loser kind of guy. A sad sack."

After Rex, Bonnie had apparently settled into a rather comfortable domestic life, raising her two kids while working at the Metropolitan Airport as a flight scheduler, where she met Chase Anderson when she was thirty-one.

"Bonnie was the best mom in the whole world. I know that sounds ridiculously naïve and biased, but she was, and this place was a very happy home. Faulkner would back me up and say the same exact thing. But when I got back from military service, there was some mopey guy hanging around the house."

Anderson was the son of a well-known Charleston politician. After four years at the Air Force Academy in Colorado, he flew recon missions in Iraq, got dumped by his fiancée, and ended up flying for Carolina Air, a small regional flight company out of Columbia.

They met at the local airport.

"He wasn't such a bad guy, just a bit of a depressive, and Bonnie did her best to help him out. She was always a sucker for sorry cases. After all, she adopted me."

"Then they died in a plane crash?"

"Yes."

"Chase was the pilot?"

"Yes."

"What happened?"

"They said it was mechanical failure, but I think his old man got it covered up. I think it was pilot failure."

"You sound like you're still angry about it."

"Of course, I am."

"Are you still angry about a lot of things, Charlie?"

"I guess I am."

"About me?"

"Not so much anymore."

She stared at me with Chardonnay eyes, and for the first time the professional exterior was gone. She looked not just beautiful, but irresistible.

Seductive.

I wondered if she knew it. I wondered if she was letting it happen on purpose.

Uncertain what to do, I changed the subject.

"Can we talk about Faulkner?"

"Of course."

Which we did.

With lots of pictures, lots of memories.

"Would you let me visit her?"

"You don't need my permission."

"I want your permission."

"Of course."

The couch was getting much too comfortable, and Charlie was much too beautiful.

"Could I see her room?"

"Sure."

She took me by the hand, led me upstairs, and we entered the bedroom.

It was Bonnie's old room, and it still had the soft familiar scent of roses. The comforter on the bed was different, but the pillows were still covered with piles of stuffed teddy bears. Eighteen years ago, on many unforgettable evenings, when Mrs. MacMillan was out of the house, Bonnie and I had rolled around in that very bed. Then it suddenly dawned on me, standing there with Charlie beside me, that Faulkner might have been conceived right there on the same bed that later became her own bed.

Charlie stepped over to the pillows and picked up a little brown teddy bear, which I recognized from many years ago.

"This is her favorite. Our mother's favorite, too. But Faulkner forgot to take it with her when she left for Scotland."

"Let me bring it to her."

She thought it over.

"All right."

She handed me the teddy, then she looked into my eyes.

"I miss her something terrible."

Then, as had happened so suddenly this afternoon at the State House, she got far more emotional than she wanted to.

"I'll wait downstairs."

So I stood alone in my daughter's room, looking at her little vanity, the bookcases, the skylight, Bonnie's wooden desk, the framed family pictures, Bonnie's old Hootie posters, Faulkner's Linda Eder posters.

I suppose I was too overwhelmed to get emotional. I stepped over to the bed and touched the white comforter.

Was I thinking of Bonnie?

Was I thinking of the daughter I didn't even know?

I walked over to the little white vanity and looked down at the pink hairbrushes.

When I came downstairs, Charlie was sitting on the couch holding her wine glass.

"I better get going," I said.

She nodded.

She seemed neither pleased nor displeased.

"I've put you through a lot tonight, Charlie," I said. "I'm sorry, but I really appreciate it."

"It's been hard coming back from Bonnie's death. Very hard. And hard for Faulkner, too. We still haven't gone through most of her things. It hurts too much."

I understood.

Charlie stood up and opened the front door.

"Thanks, Charlie."

I didn't know if I should just leave, or nod politely, or shake her hand, but she leaned right into me in a way, whether she meant it or not, that was both evocative and provocative, and she held me gently.

When she stepped back, she said:

"Be good to your daughter, Bret."

"I will."

The door closed, and I was suddenly outside in the cool Columbia night.

Alone.

Pretty damned dumbfounded.

Chapter 9

Quentin Compson

Saturday, September 29

I guess I'm supposed to be Quentin Compson?

Right?

Earlier, I'd boarded American's transatlantic from Charlotte to London at 6:20. It was now past three o'clock in the morning, somewhere over the dark Atlantic. Everyone else was asleep, and I'd just concluded my fourth reading of *Absalom, Absalom!* with poor Quentin trying not to hate his own heritage, his native Mississippi.

Trying not to hate the South:

I don't. I don't! I don't hate it! I don't hate it.

So why had the box-sender (my attempt at a neutral name for the sender of the box) forced me to read the first sentence of *this* particular novel?

12. Now, right now, read the opening of Absalom, Absalom! *up to the dash.*

Part of the reason, of course, was logistical. So I'd be sitting at my desk, perfectly still and absorbed, in the perfect position for a rifle shot. But I suspected that there was more to it than that. The box-sender was obviously familiar with *Writing Fiction*, thus fully aware of my opinions about Faulkner's novel:

Moby-Dick *and* Absalom, Absalom! *are the two greatest American novels. The two greatest novels period. In any language. In any time period.*

So what?

That's my personal opinion.

But maybe the book had more explicit meanings in the present situation?

At the beginning of the novel, 1909, Quentin is summoned by Miss Rosa Coldfield because she wants to relate her own biased version of the story of Thomas Sutpen (the "demon") and the consequent doom that he wrought upon his own children, all of which leads young Quentin into a rather reluctant exploration of the past, specifically the question: Why did Thomas Sutpen's son Henry murder his sister's fiancé, Charles Bon, in 1865?

It's perfectly clear that Miss Rosa wants Quentin, a young man with literary aspirations, to tell her story.

She wants it told.

So Quentin, along with his Canadian roommate at Harvard, 1910, tries to piece together the story from several different and often unreliable narratives, along with their own educated guesses and speculations, in an attempt to get at the truth.

To unravel the past.

Which the box-sender was forcing me to do as well.

As I pointed out in *Writing Fiction*, and which I *always* reminded my students at Southern Cal, Faulkner had once said of his admittedly difficult novel at the University of Virginia:

But the truth, I would like to think comes out.

So what's the truth, if any, that the box-sender wants me to uncover? The truth about Faulkner and her birth? Something else? How is my current situation somehow related to a novel published in 1936? Are there, shall we say, any clues within the text itself?

Absalom, Absalom! is certainly a book with no shortage of themes: revenge, miscegenation, incest, bigamy, slavery, love, compassion, hubris, fate, tragedy, the meaning of history, and the meaning of narrative. Not to mention, the fall of a great house, the Civil War (that "stupid and bloody aberration"), and the fundamental meaning of the South.

Not to mention paternity, of course. Which was certainly at the heart of my own recent (and prompted) discoveries, but which, in no way, resembled the insane complexities of Sutpen's situation.

Of which Faulkner once said:

[He was] a man who wanted sons and got sons who destroyed him.

Maybe the purpose of the book was to provide further guidelines about *how* to tell my own story? In 1834, when Thomas Sutpen, with his dogs and his neighbors, is hunting down the French architect, he talks about his past with Quentin's grandfather late one night, while drinking whiskey, in front of the hunting party's campfire:

> *He was telling a story. He was not bragging about something he had done; he was just telling a story about something a man named Thomas Sutpen had experienced, which would still have been the same story if the man had no name at all, if it had been told about any man or no man over whiskey at night.*

Was I being directed to feign some kind of similar detachment? To tell the presently evolving story as if not I, but some fictional character with my own name, was experiencing exactly what I was experiencing?

I had no idea.

Besides, it wasn't very likely anyway.

I felt another wave of exhaustion, and I knew I should let the soothing hum of the jets and the high-Atlantic darkness lure me into sleep. After all, I was probably just being a fool. The box-sender could have picked any one of the novels that I'd praised in *Writing Fiction*. Or any one of the novels that I'd criticized. Which was quite an impressive list. I've never cared for most of the modernist (including post-modernist) stuff, being fully aware that Faulkner, at least, stylistically, was in the same camp. I'd never, for example, enjoyed Joyce ("too self-conscious, too showoffy in an eggheaded sort of way"), or Woolf ("too dull"), or Hemingway ("too shallow"), etc. Which, of course, got me nailed to the wall by a phalanx of critics/reviewers of my textbook.

As the distinguished literary critic Samuel Maio wrote:

> *This curious "how-to" book is so idiosyncratic in its wrong-minded opinions as to be virtually worthless and unusable.*

I've always loved that quote, and I even tried to get my publisher to put it on the back cover of the book along with the more positive blurbs, but she categorically dismissed the idea as both idiotic and masochistic.

Nevertheless, in spite of Dr. Maio et al., many college professors across the country still found the book useful, using it in their Introduction to Fiction writing classes, probably issuing a caveat, something like this, on the first day of classes:

> *As you can see, this semester we'll be using Buchanan's* Writing Fiction *textbook, in spite of all of its unfounded prejudices and literary quirks.*

Also, to continue in the present negative vein, I've never had much use for metafiction either, the movement/trend/fad of the 1960s. Decades later, when I was studying at Hopkins, I took two fiction classes with John Barth, a self-proclaimed metafictionist, and I actually liked him a lot personally, but I still never bought in to the whole "intrusive narrator" bit. I never cared for *Tom Jones* or *Tristram Shandy* (too distractingly self-conscious), and I never really believed the much-propagated myth that modern metafictions evolved out of Borges, who was never so simple-minded, which, of course, is discussed in the aforementioned "how-to" book. But now, of course, I find myself, oddly enough, being forced to write a book which by its very nature forces me into a kind of authorial intrusion, a kind of unsettling and uncomfortable and undesirable metafiction.

Which might, after all, be the box-sender's point.

A kind of personal insult.

Or maybe, still stretching things a bit, maybe the specter of Faulkner's *Absalom* is related primarily to Judith? Sutpen's willful, dreamy, romantic, heroic, compassionate, stoic, loving, doomed daughter.

Maybe, as a consequence, it was somehow related to *all* the women in my life?

Whom Vinny always says I "push up" on pedestals.

Back when I was writing a screenplay about the legendary screenwriter Frances Marion, he looked at me one day, as if to say, "Yeah, I know what you're doing, Bret."

So I said, "What?"

"I bet you're over-romanticizing as usual?"

"What are you talking about?"

"Let's face it, Bret, you've got a habit of perfectionizing your females. Especially the ones in your own life."

"Why not? I love women."

"Yeah, me too, but they've all got their flaws, pal. Just like us."

So I forgot about Francis Marion and the screenplay and focused on the other three.

(Bonnie, Skye, and Markie.)

"But the truth is, Vinny, the three main women in my screwed-up life were all perfectly amazing."

"No doubt about it, but the first one blew you off, then the second one said, "Go back to Bulgaria." You've always had this fantasy that the three of them just popped into your life, picked you out of a crowd, and that was that. But *you* chose them, too. Just as much as they chose you. When you were down there in Carolina, you were dating lots of Southern belles before you did the steady thing with Bonnie. You also could have dated lots of girls at St. Andrews if you'd wanted to."

"So what? So what if it was mutual? Just as it was with Markie."

"Yeah, but you can't just generically say that they're all 'wonderful,' 'lovely,' 'perfect,' and all the rest of your favorite mushy adjectives."

"But they were, Vin! You met Bonnie. And you knew Markie."

"I met Bonnie for two days of lots of drinking and partying when we were college kids, and, yeah, I thought she was fantastic, but I'm also sure she had her flaws."

"Like what?"

"Like you tell me."

I thought about it.

"Go ahead," he pestered.

"All right, I'd have to admit that sometimes she drank a bit too much. But we were kids back then."

"Keep going."

"I guess she could be a bit hyper sometimes."

"Whoa, she's staring to sound like a human being!"

"She could definitely get a bit jealous sometimes. But I have to admit that I liked it back then, so it's really a non-flaw and shouldn't be added to her flaw list."

"What about the fiddle-playing Scot?"

"There's not much there, Vin. I suppose she was a bit too adventurous sometimes. Which was a hell of a lot of fun back then, but I did wonder sometimes if it would get her into trouble someday."

Uncharacteristically, Vinny said nothing.

Nothing at all.

For obvious and cowardly reasons.

"I guess you don't have the guts to bring up Markie?"

"Well, I have to admit, fully aware that it undermines my argument, that I never noticed *any* issues with Markie Cabrera."

The coward was obviously giving me an out.

I tried anyway.

"She was a neat freak," I admitted.

It was the best I could do.

"So are *you*!"

"Yeah, but she would have driven a slob like you nuts."

"Is that the best you can do?"

"I guess I'd also have to admit that she spent a ton of money on clothes."

Vinny laughed.

"You always used to say that you were the luckiest guy on the planet, and when I finally met Markie, I believed that you probably were. Maybe you really *did* have a charmed life."

"Yeah, well that's all over now."

"Is someone feeling sorry for himself?"

"Of course, I am. It's awfully easy for you to be so cocky about everything, married to the likes of Angie."

"Got that right, pal."

"Maybe you should list *her* flaws?"

"No way, we'd be here all afternoon, but it wouldn't matter anyway, she'd still end up perfect at the end of the day."

"Yeah, that's what nobody understands, that underneath every New Jersey hardass, with the obvious exceptions of our disparate psychopaths, there's a romantic trying not to reveal himself."

"You don't try very hard."

I put the novel away, angled the seat back a tiny bit, and shut my eyes, hearing nothing but the lovely hum of the ever-forward-thrusting jets.

Chapter 10

Fife

Sunday, September 30

T he Bruce stood here.

Right here.

Eight hundred years ago for his consecration. It was 1318, just three years after the great Scot King had crushed the English at Bannockburn.

Kings were crowned here.

Heretics were condemned here.

The relics of St. Andrew, the Galilean fisherman, had once been preserved in the high altar. Then the Reformation happened, and the place was abandoned.

Left to ruin.

All that was left of Scotland's greatest cathedral were various remnants of the nave's south wall, some ruined gables, the west wall of the south transept, and nearby St. Rule's Tower.

I was now sitting in the midst of this desolation, not far from the old tombstones, in the chilling night breezes, listening to the angry high drama of the North Sea crashing itself relentlessly against the coast. It was nearly midnight, and I was still worn out from my flights, but as soon as I'd finished checking my travel bag at Greyfriars, I'd walked out to the old cathedral. Exactly as I'd done when I'd first arrived here, seventeen years ago, at the age of nineteen, for Martinmas semester, eager to begin my junior year at the University of St. Andrews. Back then, I'm certain, I was surely wondering what was "going on" with Bonnie, wondering why she hadn't responded to my long letter and my attempts to call her. But at that point, I wasn't excessively worried about it. I was planning to email her an even longer letter as soon as I was settled on campus.

Back then, I think that I wasn't worried about much of anything. I was exhilarated to finally be in here Fife, to be here in Scotland, to be enrolled at St. Andrews, ready to study Scott and Burns and lots of other stuff. I'd grown up, of course, with Scotland on the brain. The fiddles, the pipes, the tartans, the cèilidhs, the highland dances, the poetry, Robert the Bruce, William Wallace. My mother's side of the family were all Cape Breton Islanders who'd originally been driven out of the Highlands during the Clearances.

Scots never forget.

Never.

Back then, I'm sure that I was also wishing that my mom, someday, could get over here too. And bring along my younger brother, and sit in the ruins of St. Andrews Cathedral, the most important church in the history of Scotland, then plan a trip through the Scottish Highlands.

There's an old cliché that youth is wasted on the young, but I never felt that I was wasting any of it. Or that I lacked an appreciation for what was going on in my life at the time. I was well aware that I was the luckiest guy on the planet: formed in the Bronx, growing-up in New Jersey, living in the deep South, having a perfect Southern Belle girlfriend, and now, ready to matriculate at the best university in Scotland.

But tonight, these many years later, things were different.

Much different.

Even though I was all alone, sitting beneath the North Sea stars, I had the ugly awareness of danger. Of threat. I had the creepy feeling that I was being watched. Or followed. Or stalked. I suppose I was feeling that way because of the sinister photograph of Faulkner, sitting right here within the ruins, with the barrel of a Remington 700 pointing directly at her from the foreground.

I looked around.

I saw nothing but ruins and darkness and the stuff of Scottish romance. I had absolutely no idea what was going on in my life. I was being threatened, bullied, manipulated, forced back into my past, and exposed to life-altering secrets. I had, it seems, a seventeen-year-old daughter who was apparently studying at the same university that I'd once attended, and who'd also visited these very same ruins. Maybe like me, for solace and reflection.

Somewhere, in the back of my mind, I could hear the strains of a fiddle playing somewhere. It was Niel Gow's "Lament for the Death of his Second Wife." His famous, ever-haunted-and-haunting slow air, probably written in 1805. I'd known the tune ever since I was a child, but one night, seventeen years ago, I seemed to hear it playing right here, within the ruins, on my first trip to the cathedral wreckage. It seemed to me, back then, that I was probably just imagining it, as I was now imagining it. Or, more accurately, recalling it. Back then, I looked around to be certain, seeing off in the far shadows of the ruins, a pretty young girl in MacAllister plaids, playing the lament on her fiddle, as unaware of me as I'd been of her.

Her name was Skye MacAllister, and she was from the Island of Skye.

Chapter 11

The Doll's House

Monday, October 1

It was just like the photograph in the box.

She was sitting alone at an outside table, beneath the awning, reading a book, and it crushed my heart to see her for the first time. I can't think of a better, or, at least, more accurate word than "crushed," as I stood there for a moment, watching her from across the square.

This afternoon, Doll's House Café, which I knew quite well from back-in-the-day, wasn't as busy or lively as usual. Maybe it was the middle of classes. Maybe it was the weather. It had rained much of the morning and was still damp and overcast.

Which seemed quite familiar.

And comforting.

"Yes?"

"Is this Faulkner MacMillan?"

"Yes."

"I'm a friend of Charlie's, and she gave me your number. I was in Columbia two days ago, and she gave me something to give you. I'm staying at Greyfriars, and I wonder if we could meet for a moment sometime this afternoon."

Maybe I should have texted or emailed, but I couldn't resist actually hearing her voice. Just in case she put me off for some reason. Last night, on my various plane flights, I'd spent a lot of time writing, memorizing, rewriting, and re-memorizing my opening lines. So much for being a "writer." They all sounded pretty lame, but it was now or never.

"How's Charlie?"

It didn't seem like a test, but I wasn't certain.

"Missing you badly."

That seemed to work.

"I'll be at the Doll's House around 2:30. It's a café on Church Street."

"I'll see you then."

(Beat)

"You didn't mention your name."

"Bret Buchanan."

It didn't seem to register in any way. It seemed as though it could have been any other name.

I wondered if she would immediately email Charlie, to make sure that I was on the up-and-up. I hoped so. I knew nothing at all about being a father, but I still felt protective, hoping that she was always careful in her life.

"See you then."

She sounded like any other American teenage college girl, and I'd taught a lot of them at Southern Cal. She also sounded perfectly normal, remarkably so, and lovely, and she also sounded like her mother, with a much less strong, yet undeniable, Carolina accent.

I walked over to her table.

"I like blueberry scones, too."

She looked up and smiled.

Not knowing what to do, I reached out my hand.

"I'm Bret."

She shook my hand.

"Nice to meet you. Have a seat, and if you'd like to finish off that scone, go right ahead. I've been eating way too many of them."

I sat down, directly across from her, and looked across the small table. I was doing my best to be natural, whatever that means. Trying, at least, not to be too weird about it, trying not to look at her like some pathetic jerk who'd just taken his first look at the daughter he never even knew existed.

She was just as pretty as her mother, and just as stylish as her aunt. She had Bonnie-green eyes with the same killer smile. I always thought that Bonnie looked a bit like the young Anouk Aimée, but blonde, with a rebel accent. Faulkner looked like her too. With high cheekbones, thoughtful cat's eyes, and somewhat pouty lips.

As for her clothes, there was none of that kick-around, look-at-me-I'm-so-casual, college jeans-and-sweats. She was wearing a sharp tweed yellow skirt and blazer, with a red blouse, warm blue/green tartan scarf, and, despite the rain, pretty red Mary Janes. A black trench was lying over the seat next to her, and I could read the label. Burburry.

Charlie would be proud.

"What are you reading?" I asked, even though I could clearly see the cover.

"Henry Esmond. I'm on a Thackeray tear. Is that a bad thing?"

"Who doesn't love Thackeray?" I said, which obviously pleased her.

"So how do you know Charlie?"

"We've only met recently," I explained, "but we have old friends in common."

I sensed that she was sensing my evasiveness, so I reached into the little bag I was carrying, pretending to be fishing around for something, and pulled out the Remington 700 manual and put it on the table in front of her.

"I've got something from Charlie in here," I assured her.

What kind of father tests his own daughter the very first time he meets her? But I felt that I *had* to do it, even though I felt appropriately ashamed, but I had to assume that *anybody* could be involved.

Fishing in the bag, I watched her closely, expecting nothing.

Faulkner looked at the manual closely, with recognition.

"That's odd," she said.

"What?"

"That."

"Why?"

"Because someone sent me one of those in the post last week. I thought nothing of it, and I tossed it out."

Which was clearly a threat, even though she didn't know it, as well as a warning to me.

"That's quite a coincidence," I said.

"It certainly is."

But she seemed unconcerned about it, and I was fully satisfied.

As quickly as I could, as if to assuage my guilt, I pulled the teddy bear out of the bag and held it out to my daughter.

Which pretty much terminated any other lines of thought.

"Professor Bear!"

She took the little brown stuffed thing and cradled it in her arms like a five-year-old. Completely unashamed.

"Thank you so much! I've missed him terribly!"

Professor Bear.

I recalled that ridiculous name from eighteen years ago. Apparently, when Bonnie was a little girl, she thought the thing looked "studious," as well as "ever so cute," so she decided that he was a professor of something. Bearology, I suppose.

None of that mattered right now. I'd made my daughter happy, and I wanted to do it over and over again for the rest of my life.

Of course, within my heart, what I *really* wanted to do was tell her about Bonnie, about everything, but I didn't. Even though it wasn't explicitly prohibited in the guidelines, I still felt that the time wasn't right.

The truth was, I had absolutely no idea what I was doing.

"Are you enjoying yourself at St. Andrews?"

"Marvelously, even more so now that Professor Bear is here. Thank you so much!"

Is this how daughters behave? Is this all it takes? A thirty-year-old stuffed animal?

"What's your major?"

I already knew the answer since Charlie had told me lots of stuff about Faulkner, but I wanted to hear her talk about herself. In truth, I just wanted to hear her talk about anything, just to be within her presence.

"Scottish studies. I've got lots of Scot blood."

So we talked about the Scots, a subject I was very familiar with.

We talked about Bannockburn, and Robby Burns, and Henry Raeburn, and Niel Gow, and *The Wealth of Nations*, and Bonnie Prince Charles (she wasn't a fan), and Culloden, and Glencoe (those damned MacLeods!), and the Clearances and the resulting diaspora, and Mary Queen of Scots, and James VI who became James I, and the Highlands (which she planned to visit next semester), and the Hebrides, and the Orkneys, and the Picts, and the Celts, and the Vikings, and the Gaelic language, and all things Scottish.

Including her current specialty, Patrick Sellar, whom she accurately described as "one of the great villains of the Highland Clearances."

"Why'd you come to St. Andrews? You could have studied Scottish history in a lot of places."

Maybe I was pushing too hard, but it was impossible not to be curious about what she knew, and about what she *didn't* know, about her anonymous father.

"Because it's the best, of course! Besides, my father went to St. Andrews."

Which pretty much kicked me in the stomach, even though I did my Jersey best not to let on. Fortunately, I was rescued by the sudden arrival of her two best pals.

Heather Sinclair, her roommate at Dean's Court, was a tiny shy cute-as-could-be islander in a much-too-big fisherman knit sweater. She came from someplace called Hoy, which she described as "the most forsaken place on the face of the earth, which I totally love." I think it would be fair to say that you couldn't cut Heather's accent with *any* kind of knife, and several times I had trouble understanding her. I've never actually used the word "brogue" before, but I think it applies.

Then Gordon Carlyle bent down and kissed Faulkner on the cheek, and the only reason that it didn't throw me for a loop was that Charlie had passed along her own second-hand info about Faulkner's new college besties. Gordon was definitely a looker, definitely upper-upper class. Charlie had mentioned something about "noble" blood. Or was it "royal" blood? If this was a decade ago, he would have probably been friends with Prince William. But he wore it lightly. He seemed like a smart, likeable, unspoiled kid, who worshipped the ground that Faulkner walked on.

His clothes were what you would expect. A navy tweed suit from Savile Row, a tailored white dress shirt, a burgundy tie, and a Burberry trench. It didn't take much figuring to guess that Gordon had probably bought Faulkner her black trench. Burberrys was pretty expensive for a girl on a scholarship.

Heather and Gordon were both archaeology majors, and little Heather was, already, it seemed, a bit of a recognized expert on Orkney's chambered cairns. It also became clear that Heather was the one who'd introduced Gordon to Faulkner.

After the kiss from Gordon, Faulkner took her trench, placed it across her lap, and the other two kids sat down in the two empty chairs.

Then Faulkner introduced the old American guy in the black wranglers and the black leather jacket.

"What brings you to St. Andrews?" Gordon asked.

Politely.

Over the last two days, I'd been preparing myself for all kinds of questions, including this one.

"I'm knocking off some research for a writing project."

Which piqued their interest more than I'd anticipated.

"Fiction?" Faulkner wondered.

"Actually, more of a memoir."

Before anyone could say, "What's it about?" I added:

"It's actually an assignment that I'm not that excited about, but, at least, it's given me a chance to spend a few days here in Fife."

I knew it wasn't enough. The subject was begging for more specifics, so I did my best to wiggle out of it by changing the subject.

"How about you, Gordon? Where are you from?"

"Inverness, near Culloden."

So I managed to get them taking about themselves again, and the girls particularly liked teasing Gordon who didn't seem to mind a bit.

"He won't admit it," Faulkner mocked gently, "but he's descended from the Bruce!"

"And he's constantly trying to bash his brains out," Heather chimed in.

"He's a waterfall ice climber," Faulkner explained, rolling her eyes. "Have you ever heard of anything so stupid?"

I nodded.

I'd seen pictures of it on the web. It looked absolutely amazing, absolutely moronic.

"Which I'm giving up, by the way, as a sacrifice for the woman I love."

"That's me!" Faulkner clarified.

"But he's still a Krav Maga fighter," Heather insisted.

Good, I thought to myself, then he can protect her.

"And the big shot's just back from New York City," Faulkner pouted, "and he didn't take us along."

"You're much too poor," Gordon said in his defense. "Besides it was just some stupid mock session at the UN, which was dull beyond all believing, but I did manage to get in a couple of plays and some other stuff."

On it went.

Just three good kids enjoying themselves.

As was I, listening in.

Faulkner checked her watch.

"Well, it's time to get to Econ."

"Poor you," Gordon sympathized.

They rounded up all their stuff, and Gordon helped Faulkner into her trench, much like the Duke of Marlboro might have done, and she looked at me directly.

"It was very nice to meet you," she said, "and very nice of you to bring me Professor Bear."

I stood up, and we shook hands.

I really wanted, of course, to hold her in my arms, and tell her who I was, but I didn't.

When the time was right, I managed to convince myself.

Then she took Gordon's arm, as Heather took hold of her other arm, and the three of them walked up Church Street.

Without a care in the world.

Chapter 12

Victoria Café and Bar

Monday, October 1

S he was late.

What else was new?

I was sitting inside the noisy Vic Pub, full of lively students who were sometimes watching the multiple sports screens, mostly soccer, sometimes not, as I was waiting for my fiddle girl.

Remembering that night, seventeen years ago, when I probably shouldn't have bothered her, and risked startling her, but I did anyway, walking across the cathedral ruins beneath the old stone archway. I came up in front of her, making sure that she could see me coming, and she didn't seem either disturbed or alarmed. She stopped playing and rested her bow and her fiddle in her lap.

"I've always wondered whether he also wrote a lament for the first wife," I said, referring to Niel Gow.

She smiled.

"I've wondered that myself."

"Maybe her death was a happy occasion," I suggested.

"Maybe he wrote her a jig."

She lifted her weapon and ripped off a few bars of the fastest jig I'd ever heard. Then she placed her fiddle and its bow back in her lap, looked up at me with her big Celtic eyes, and said:

"By the way, what kind of ridiculous accent is that?"

Meaning Jerseyese.

Which seemed a bit too self-assured coming from a girl with a thicker-than-thick Highland accent.

Within a few weeks, after it was clear that no response was coming from Bonnie MacMillan, she was calling me her boyfriend and I was calling her my girlfriend.

Gladly.

She was Skye Elspeth MacAllister from the Island of Skye, with ridiculously thick copper-red golden hair ("No, I'm *not* Irish, not even the slightest bit, thank God!"), Gaelic brown eyes, and a light Highland complexion. Who wore MacAllister and/or MacDonald plaids pretty much every day of her life, who'd picked up the fiddle when she was four, who'd traveled across the Atlantic to study with the great Buddy MacMaster on Cape Breton Island, who'd also Highland danced in her youth, quadrilled ever since, and fiddled at every and any cèilidh she ever got wind of.

Who was mischievous, fun, a bit of a risk-taker, and easy to love. *Very* easy. Who loved the classic old Hollywood films with Hedy Lemarr, Jennifer Jones, and Joan Fontaine, especially the mysteries, especially the noirs, especially the darkest, like *Out of the Past* and *Double Indemnity*.

Who was pre-med.

Which was why, when I left St. Andrews at the end of my second Candlemas semester, a month after May Dip, we both knew it was over. She was on her "doctor path," and even though we didn't like what that obviously meant, we never questioned that it had to be.

I never saw her again.

When I called her this afternoon after the Doll's House, I got an answering machine for Dr. MacDonald:

"It's Bret. Sorry to pop up like this, but I'm back in St. Andrews, and I'll be at the Vic tonight. If you can make it, I'd love to see you, if not, no problem. (Beat) I hope everything's going right in your life."

A text came an hour later:

"See you tonight, Jersey boy. Around nine."

In the meantime, just as I'd done in Columbia three days ago, I wandered around both the town and the university, which were pretty much inextricable, set as they were between the thick wooded hills of the Fife countryside and the coasts, cliffs, and beaches of the brooding North Sea.

Needless to say, as I wandered around the medieval streets, the narrow cobblestoned alleyways, and the university courtyards, Skye, and my memories of Skye, seemed to be lurking around every corner, and it was, despite all the other stuff going on in my life, very pleasurable.

Very enjoyable.

Did the box-sender intend it?

That I'd actually *enjoy* being forced back into my past, whatever the subsequent ramifications might be? Or was it just an unintended consequence of forcing me to write something that I really didn't want to write?

I had no idea.

So I wandered about town, weaving through the rushing students and the billion bicycles, strolling past the lovely little Scottish houses and the stylish shops and boutiques, passing Sallies Chapel, Barron Theater, and Dean's Court, where Faulkner lived with Heather, where one of the photographs was taken.

Which wasn't so pleasant.

Then I walked over to St. Mary's Courtyard, one of the more marvelous places within the Scottish Oxbridge, and looked at the scraggly old Thorn tree which Mary Queen of Scots had planted over five centuries ago, doing my best to forget that the lovely quadrangle was also the location of yet another one of those damned photographs.

Eventually I wandered away, down to West Sands Beach, where they filmed the famous opening scene of *Chariots of Fire*, and I forgot about the damned cardboard box. Then I strolled up to the Old Course, the world's most famous golf course, where the sport was founded and developed, where even Queen Mary supposedly played a bit of "goff," where every duffer and hacker in the universe eventually visits at least once before they passed on to the final 19th hole.

Like bathing in the Ganges.

I've got nothing against the game, but I never played it much. "Not enough banging around for my boys," my mom would say when we were kids, and maybe she was right. But St. Andrews, although very few non-Brits are aware of the fact, also created and developed another sport, which just might be the most "banging around" sport there is, which I played a bit when I was here at St. Andrews.

Rugby.

By now, the twilight had turned into night, and the North Sea breezes were freezing my painful left shoulder, so I went back into town. Back to the university that took me in when I was nineteen, which had been founded by the Augustinians in 1410 and was, in time, attended by King James II, William Dunbar, John Knox, John Napier, Edward Jenner, Russell Kirk, Prince William and Kate, and a whole slew of Nobelists. Even more important from my pov, were two other graduates: John Witherspoon, the fifth president of Princeton University in New Jersey who educated many of the founding fathers, and James Wilson, a forgotten signer of the Declaration of Independence, who helped create the Constitution, whom Washington later appointed to the first Supreme Court.

Skye walked into the Vic.

Dressed in green scrubs.

Looking great.

Despite the job, the husband, and the eight-year-old boy.

Why not? After all, she was only thirty-five years old, and she'd always taken care of herself.

She weaved through the crowd, kissed me on the mouth like a lover, and said:

"Where's my Grant's?"

Which, as she was obviously aware, was sitting on the table right in front of her.

Waiting.

Skye only drank Scotch that was brewed in Scotland, and she preferred Grant's above all. As someone with a pretty steep Scottish lineage, I was always a bit ashamed that I never really liked the taste of Scotch that much, always preferring the taste of rye, which she called that "Canadian stuff."

Which was true.

After all, I *was* descended from Scot-Canadians.

"Good boy," she said. "It's been a long day."

She took a healthy hit, smiled, and looked me in the eye. It seemed as though nothing had changed. As if it were seventeen years ago.

"It's good to see you again, Yank. You're still looking pretty good."

One thing all the women in my life had in common, including my mother, was the ability to tease me in such a way that felt like affection.

"Well, someone's still the prettiest Highland girl," I said.

"You like a woman in scrubs?"

Then she filled me in on the "woman in scrubs," even though I knew most of the basic stuff from checking her out on the web. Pre-med, St. Andrews; Med degree, Edinburgh; specialty, pathology. Which didn't surprise me a bit. She always liked mysteries. Especially Sherlock Holmes, who was created, of course, by a Scot. So why not medical mysteries? Skye was, by all accounts, a big-time pediatric pathologist and diagnostician, and she also did some forensic pathology and hospital work, but, mostly, it seemed she'd developed a national reputation by unraveling disease-related conundrums.

Nine years ago, she'd married a cardiologist at RIE, the Royal Infirmary of Edinburgh. Then, the year after their little boy was born, she and the family moved the fifty-two miles northeast to St. Andrews.

"It was either St. Andrews or Skye, but Angus still has important connections in Edinburgh, so we came back here."

Angus MacDonald.

The husband.

"So you're finally a MacDonald in name as well as heritage," I said.

She was well aware that there was a long MacDonald line in the Buchanan family tree.

"Aye," she said with a smile, "I guess we're cousins."

We talked about Angus, who sounded like a pleasant enough workaholic, and about her now-dead parents, and about her younger brother, Braden:

"He's off fighting for the English flag."

"I hope they don't send him to the Plains of Abraham."

Then we talked about Lachlan, her eight-year-old:

"A bloody handful!"

Who sounded every bit as mischievous as his mother.

When the Vic seemed to get even noisier, she knocked off her Grant's and said, "Let's get out into the night."

She took me by the hand, and we walked around St. Andrews, and we talked and talked, although mostly *she* talked, and she asked me about Markie, and about the books, and about my plans.

"There aren't any."

"That's ridiculous. There must be something?"

I shrugged.

"I've got a writing project I'm working on.'

"More information, please. What's it about? Explicitly."

"It's about some guy who's forced to write a novel about being forced to write a novel."

She laughed.

"That's not very explicit."

"It's a work-in-progress."

"After that?"

"I've got no idea."

"That doesn't sound like *my* Jersey boy."

We wandered up and down the cobblestone streets, just like seventeen years ago, and I have no idea exactly where we went, but, eventually, we ended back at Greyfriars Hotel.

"Do you miss me, Bret? Tell me the truth."

She was serious.

"Yes, especially tonight."

She looked into my eyes.

"If you want me, I'll leave tonight."

She didn't seem to be kidding.

She seemed serious.

Dead serious.

It was hard to believe.

Looking back, I'm not certain if I was more stunned or amazed.

She had a husband. She had a little boy. And she had a distinguished medical practice.

I kissed her on the mouth, turned, and walked through the entrance of Greyfriars.

I'm really not sure what *that* was all about, but I had more than enough bullshit going on in my life right now.

I didn't need any more.

Chapter 13

MacMaster

Tuesday, October 2

H e looked like Sean Connery, and he sounded like Sean Connery, which, of course, induced nothing but confidence.

He ran a local "Investigatorial Service," and when I'd asked about him around town, everyone seemed to think he was the very best, which is why Colt recommended him in the first place.

I have no idea how Jack Colt knew anything about private detective ratings in a small town in Scotland, especially since everyone knew that Colt almost never left Paterson, New Jersey, or at least, the metro area.

"Call Beaton MacMaster," he'd texted four days ago.

So I did.

"Nothing," MacMaster assured me.

I handed him the photograph of Faulkner at the ruins with the rifle barrel in the foreground.

He looked it over carefully.

Then I handed him the manual.

"It's a Remington 700," I said.

Just as carefully, he looked over the manual. The Remington Instruction Book. Then he flipped to the second page, which listed the "The Ten Commandments of Firearm Safety."

The First Commandment being, "Always keep the muzzle pointed in a safe direction," which had obviously been ignored in the photograph, which had obviously been ignored when I got myself shot in the shoulder eight days ago.

"Does that help?" I wondered.

"Maybe."

I'd called MacMaster from Carolina right after my evening with Charlie, and I hired him to keep an eye on one of the young undergraduates at St. Andrews.

"I believe she's being stalked," I said, "and I believe she's in danger."

But MacMaster and his staff, after several days of surveillance, which was done, apparently, with the utmost discretion, had noticed, as the boss had already summed it up, "Nothing."

"Who is she to you? If you don't mind my asking."

"She's a friend's daughter. A very close friend."

He nodded, just like Sean Connery.

The bill was lying on the desk in front of me. He never acknowledged it or even looked at it, as if it would have been uncouth to do so, so I picked it up and checked it out.

It was, as expected, plenty expensive, but I've got tons of money these days.

"Fine," I said, referring to the billing statement. "I'd like you to continue whatever you're doing."

"As you wish. She seems a bonnie lass, and I hope we can prevent anything unpleasant."

"Good. What about her boyfriend? Anything new?"

"Nothing, he's as upright as he seems. He's got a few half-witted hobbies, but he's from a sound and respected family, and he seems like a good boy with good intentions."

Which was exactly how Gordon had seemed to me. "Good."

I collected the photo and the manual, stood up, as MacMaster stood up as well. We shook hands. Firmly.

"I'll do my best," he assured me, which was extremely reassuring.

When I reached the doorway, I heard him ask, almost apologetically:

"Do you actually know Mr. Colt personally?"

I turned around.

"Yes, I do."

"I've read about some of his exploits."

I waited, with curiosity.

"I'd very much like to make his acquaintance sometime."

"Visit me in the States, and I'll introduce you."

"Excellent."

Europeans visit the US for all kinds of reasons, but I'd never heard that one before.

In the adjacent room, I paid the bill with my Visa card to a very efficient young woman, then I stepped out to Market Street, got in my waiting taxi, and settled in for the hour-long drive to Edinburgh Airport.

About fifteen minutes into the drive, I got a text from speak-of-the-devil Jack Colt.

"It's her. Again."

So I texted back, "OK," and that was that.

Four days ago, before I boarded my short flight from Columbia to Charlotte, I'd FedExed the pink hairbrush I'd stolen from Faulkner's bedroom to New Jersey. To Colt. Maybe I was being overly paranoid, but I had no way of actually knowing if the blonde strands entangled in the first pink brush in the cardboard box were actually Faulkner's. So I took the second brush from her vanity, slipped it into a postal baggie, and mailed it to Colt for a second DNA run.

It seems that the pretty young girl in the yellow tweeds and the red Mary Janes was definitely my daughter.

I was grateful.

Some jerk (the box-sender, the one making me do all this stuff) had blown a hole in my shoulder, threatened me, and bullied me. But the same stupid jerk had given me a gift, the best one I'd ever received, and I was ready to do everything, *exactly* as the guidelines stipulated, to try and protect Faulkner MacMillan.

My lovely daughter.

Chapter 14

El Morro

Wednesday, October 3

I was sitting on the promontory.

Castillo San Felipe del Morro.

Sitting high above old San Juan, staring at what the tour books describe as "the most spectacular view in the Caribbean," yet rather distractedly I was thinking about some crab joint in a strip mall in Baltimore.

Actually, it wasn't even Baltimore, it was next door in Towson.

The Crackpot.

It was my first day in Baltimore, two days before classes started at Hopkins. I'd come back from Scotland, decided that I needed some more Jersey time, then got a Masters in lit, focused on Melville and Hawthorne, at Rutgers. I loved my two years in New Brunswick, made lots of Rutgers buddies, and dated a bunch of pretty Jersey girls. But post-Bonnie, post-Skye, I was taking it easy. I'd failed twice, big time, and I had no expectations that I would ever find the equal of either one of them again, so I focused on *The Whale* and *Twice-Told Tales*.

What to do next?

What does a pre-destined writer do with himself?

Why not write?

I applied to Johns Hopkins, got accepted into the Writing Seminars, then drove my black Chevy Camaro down to Baltimore for department orientations and all the rest of the get-to-know-each-other stuff. Which was pretty much a female festival. They'd accepted twelve poets and twelve fiction writers, and everyone in the fiction group, as I knew before I'd arrived, was a female.

Except, of course, for me.

For several hours, I got stuck on the Delaware Memorial Bridge, so I got there late and was told that most of the fiction crowd had gone over to the Crackpot.

So there I was, sitting in the midst of six of them, eating a cheeseburger, enjoying the get-to-know-you banter, completely disgusted with the whole crab thing. If you've never been to one of those joints, they spread a sheet of thick brown paper over the top of the table, give everyone a wooden hammer, then roll out the steaming, stinking, revolting crabs, as everyone gleefully smashes the little crustaceans wide open and eats the yack that's lurking inside. All washed down with everyone's booze-of-choice.

In general, writers are a lively likeable crowd who appreciate a bit of the drink. These gals were no different. They were fun, interesting, diverse, and quirky, and it all promised a very enjoyable two years ahead, reading each other's scribblings.

Did I neglect to mention that crabs stink something terrible?

The place, surprise, surprise, had a nautical theme, with portholes, traps, lanterns, and stuffed fish of various kinds mounted on the walls. The one above my head was obviously some kind of swordfish. I'm sure that the Crackpot was actually a very nice place, but for a guy who'd smelled way too many open-air fish markets in the Bronx, and who was, as a consequence, on a seafood moratorium for the rest of his life, the place stunk to high hell of hot, steaming, recently boiled-alive, and creepily clawed creatures of the deep.

Earlier, the others were all surprised that the waitress wasn't at all surprised when I ordered my cheeseburger.

"How would you like it?"

"Well done, burning is fine."

I didn't say, as I would have liked to, can you also put it in a barometric pressure chamber, so it won't absorb any of the crab stink.

"She didn't even bat an eye!" one said.

"Yeah, maybe it's like the kid's menu," another one decided. "Or maybe they have to be prepared for people who've wandered into the wrong restaurant."

"Which isn't fair," another one said, "you can't order crabs in a burger joint."

"So what's with you anyway, Bret?" another kidded, "these ugly little monsters are delicious."

I cited the traumatic fish markets of the Bronx.

To no avail.

"That's ridiculous, Jersey," another one said. "Here, try a bite."

On and on.

I could see it would be an entertaining time in our fiction work-shops.

They continued chattering away, banging their mallets, picking their way through the shattered exoskeletons, swigging their beers and their wines. While I buried my burger in ketchup and tried not to breathe through my nose.

She walked into the room.

She was one of the fiction crowd, and she'd also been running late tonight. Some of the others had met her earlier this afternoon, but it was a first for me.

Everyone looked up.

It seemed to me like everyone in the universe looked up.

She was some kind of Latina, and she didn't look like a fiction writer. She looked like a movie star.

Or a model.

But real-er.

Her hair was long, thick, and jet. Her eyes were large, dark, and chocolate. Her lips were a bit pouty, glossed a bright red. She had high cheekbones, high arched eyebrows, and small red topaz earrings. She was tallish, upright, trim, yet still curvaceous, anything but flat, but what was most apparent, most obvious, most unmissable was the naturally indigenous *sultriness*.

Which I need to try and explain.

Generally, it's a "bad girl" word, a loaded description with movie star connotations. Lauren Bacall was sultry, Ava Gardiner was sultry, Dorothy Malone was *very* sultry. So were Dietrich, Kitt, Lake, Lamarr, and Dandridge. Often meaning "seductive," "sensual," and "come-hither." Not to mention "erotic" and "voluptuous." On top of all of that, very often, but not always, a certain kind of demeanor was attached. Above-the-fray, self-wrapped, disengaged, even, on some occasions, smug.

But the word also meant "passionate." A woman who's uniquely radiated, almost without awareness, with a highly charged passionate nature. *Heat.* An overall heat. Not just sexual heat. More like "life" heat. Being as much exotic as erotic, as much charming as seductive.

Which probably doesn't help much at all, but I can assure you that whenever this Latina walked into a room, everyone sensed it.

Oh, yeah, there's *another* problem with the word sultry (sorry to go on about this) because it sometimes conjures a sense of moodiness, of self-absorption, of, maybe even, despondency. But not at the Crackpot that night. There was a very different sense of life-is-good-and-I'm-very-much-enjoying-it sultriness. A tangible upbeatness, a sense that, look, if it's true that I radiate some heat, then I radiate some heat, that's just the way I am.

The way I was made.

You could see it in her eyes, which flecked with seize-the-day sparks, with an avidity for life.

She was wearing a beautiful pinkish/red dress, in a color that was probably unnamable, maybe carnelian, maybe cerise, maybe somewhere in-between, with lace trim, with black pumps.

I would later learn that she *always* wore dresses. Designer dresses. She didn't own a pair of jeans. Or shorts or sweats. At bedtime, it was always flannel nightgowns. All the rest of the time, it was dresses,

dresses, dresses, with a few skirt-and-blouse exceptions for "lounging around."

"Puerto Rican woman *always* dress up," she explained.

"Dress to kill," I suggested.

The carnelian dress, as I would later learn, was a Nolasco, designed by Stella Nolasco, who was one of her friends, who once said that *all* Puerto Rican women love lace.

Marquita agreed.

"We wear it at Baptism, we wear it at funerals, we wear it every-where else in-between."

She liked colorful tropic-print dresses by de la Renta, and lacy white killer gowns from Lisa Cappalli. With lots of Valentino, Versace, Alfara, and some Charlyn Castro-Rojas, who was also a friend.

She walked up to the table and smiled.

"Who's taking me to Poe's grave?"

I put down my cheeseburger.

She had a lovely, not excessively sultry voice, with a Latin tinge.

"I'll take you anywhere."

Which was followed by an appropriate round of good-natured kidding and ball-busting from the other fictionistas.

"Good," she said, "you look a little out of place."

Everyone laughed.

"Look who's talking," I said,

Which the others enjoyed as well.

Her name was Marquita Cabrera. Thirty minutes later we were climbing over the fence, despite her lovely Nolasco, at Westminster

Hall and Burying Ground at 519 West Fayette Street at the corner of North Green.

It was dark, and I'd had a half a burger, four whiskey sours, and I was climbing a fence with the most amazing female on the planet.

What is it about Jersey guys? Why do they assume that *anything* can happen? If a Jersey guy sees a beautiful woman, he thinks, yeah, she's out of my league, yeah, of course, she is, but, hell, pretty women *always* make bad choices, so why shouldn't *I* be her next bad choice?

Marquita knew all about E. A. Poe, and she'd read all his stuff and all the bios, and I told her about the cottage in the Bronx, and then, despite all the sours, I recited, in its entirely, almost flawlessly, from memory, "Annabel Lee":

It was many and many a year ago,
In a kingdom by the sea . . .

Guess who was impressed?

"You really know how to impress a woman."

(Thanks, mom.)

"Just the right kind of woman."

Then she got even righter.

Ever since she'd walked into the Crackpot, she'd been carrying a little tote bag, also carnelian, also laced, which she'd managed to slip through the bars of the graveyard fence before we went over the top. So we stood at the old tombstone, with the little raven carved at the top, and she reached inside her tote bag and pulled out a corkscrew and handed it to me.

Then she pulled out a bottle of Moët & Chandon.

"I hope you like bubbles," she said.

Which I did.

Which she explained later.

"I've *never* been to Baltimore before! And what if something happened? What if I had to rush back to San Juan for some reason? What if I never got back to Baltimore? Well, I'm not about to take the chance. It's off to visit Edgar on the very first night, no discussion, no debate, no hesitation, but none of the fiction girls wanted to go. At least, not on the very first night. So I found some handsome guy with a leather jacket and a black Camaro, and I was able to lead him by the nose."

As mentioned earlier, I'm not really handsome, and I never was, but I wasn't about to argue with the likes of Markie Cabrera about it.

Or about anything else.

Several years later, on the back porch over the Malibu cliffs, her sister, for a laugh, read the obviously rushed email that Markie had sent her, very late, that first night in Baltimore:

> *I've met my boy! It's all over! Who would have guessed?*
> *He's tall, tough, and handsome in a toughish kind of way.*
> *He grew up somewhere in the wastelands of New Jersey, so*
> *maybe that explains it. His name is Bret. More tomorrow!*

We all laughed.

Later, while the sisters were asleep, I went into the bathroom and looked at myself. A man might shave himself every single day of his life, but how often does he *actually* look at himself?

Never.

So I searched for some traces of handsomeness and came away empty. There was just a rather typical Jersey guy staring back at me from the mirror: nice eyes, I suppose, being blackish-brown; high well-placed Scottish cheekbones; blackish-brown hair; reasonable lips, I guess, which liked to do nothing but kiss Marquita's; and all of it quite a bit rough around the edges.

Not that much to write home about.

Not that much to write home to San Juan about.

As for clothes, it was always more of the same: sweats and a Mets cap around the house; a couple of nice Armani suits that Markie bought me for whenever I needed to soup things up; and all the rest of the time: black wranglers, dark buttoned-down Dockers dress shirts, with a black leather in the cold weather, and a windbreaker (Carolina, St. Andrews, Rutgers, or Hopkins) all the rest of the time.

So where did I get off hanging around with the likes of Marquita Cabrera?

Not to mention Bonnie MacMillan?

Not to mention Skye MacAllister?

Now that I'm already underway, I guess I should take a few more moments to try and explain myself.

Even before Markie showed up that night, I knew that I was lucky with women, but I wasn't sure why. Maybe it was just the alignment of the stars. Dumb blind luck. Sure, I was smart, a smart-ass too, and not impossible to look at, and I had some ambitions, but that sounds like lots of guys. Right? That won't even get you in the front door.

"Girls like a guy who's confident," Skye once explained, trying to explain myself to me, speaking much like the oracle at Delphi, "but never arrogant. Which is you, Mr. Springsteen. You've got the self-assurance, and you're good natured as well, and, besides, I've always thought you were kind of funny."

"Mr. Springsteen," of course, was just one of her many cutesy nicknames for her "Yank."

Along with "Mr. Sinatra."

Which, even if it were true, in my opinion, still wouldn't get you through the front door. So I stuck with the alignment of the stars. That I'd met, for some inexplicable reason, within the short space of two years, two perfectly lovely young women, either of whom I could have spent the rest of my life with, both of whom I loved and would have continued to love.

But Marquita Cabrera was something else.

Something even more.

She was something far beyond my meager "writer's imagination." She was something inexplicable, and best left that way. She took one look at me that night, snatched me from a smelly crab joint, and never let me go.

Until she died.

Marquita Cabrera, named in honor of Marquita Rivera, eventually to become Marquita Cabrera Buchanan, was born in old San Juan on Calle Luna, above her father's bakery. Her mother died four years later from pulmonary ramifications from the birth of Markie's younger sister Rosario, named in honor of Willie Rosario. The girls grew up close, sheltered, and very happy, working in the bakery alongside their father, a loving "teller of tales and fables," who was renowned, locally, for his pastries, especially his *quesitos*, which eventually drew in the tourists.

"So what do you want to do with your life, Marquita?" her father had asked her when she was seven years old.

"Help people."

Ten years later, she matriculated pre-med at the University of San Juan, until her father died unexpectedly of a heart attack, still checking the ovens in the bakery, when she was a sophomore.

She switched to creative writing.

"To honor my father."

She wanted to be like Carlos Cabrera, the teller of tales, just as her sister also wanted to be like their father, so she eventually took over the bakery.

In Marquita's senior year at USJ, she wrote a short story called "Guanina," based on the Puerto Rican legend about a Taíno princess who was loved by the Castilian knight and conquistador, Don Cristobal de Sotomayor, which proved to the indigenous Taíno that the Spaniards were actually mortal. Actually human. Just like them. So Guanina's brother, Guaybana, planned to attack the Spaniards and kill Sotomayor. Despite a warning by his Indian lover, Sotomayor was killed, although much admired by Guaybana for his bravery. But Guanina, considered a traitor, was condemned to be sacrificed to the Taíno gods.

The legend was a kind of Puerto Rican Pocahontas meets Romeo and Juliet. When Guanina finally arrives at the dead body of her lover, she tries to revive him with kisses and caresses, but fails, then she dies with her lover in her arms. Buried together, beneath a Ceiba tree, white lilies and red hibiscus soon appeared magically over their graves, and, supposedly, they still come out at night to look at the stars and kiss each other gently, beneath the light of the moon.

The story had all kinds of historical relevance, relating, as it did, to the Taíno uprising of 1511, Ponce de León, and even Christopher Columbus. I'm not, of course, giving Markie's unforgettable version its just due. It was immediately picked up by *Ploughshares*, chosen for *The Pushcart Prize* as well as *Best American Short Stories*, and it was particularly praised for the memorable scene of "the raining frogs," which descend from the treetops in an effort to protect Guanina as she rushes towards her dying lover.

"What's with the frogs, anyway? It's a myth, right?"

"Not really."

I waited for an explanation:

"They're called Coqui Tree Frogs, and they live in the upper branches of the forest, so their predators have to wait for them down below. Whenever the cute little things need to leave the canopy of the forest, they launch themselves outward, gently floating to the ground unharmed. Thus, 'raining' frogs."

"Why don't they crush themselves when they hit the ground?" I asked, as any self-respecting Jersey guy would have asked.

"Because they're so light, silly boy. They're about two inches long and weigh about three ounces."

Which still didn't fully answer my question.

"But I have to admit," she added, "they certainly make a racket."

Which I got to hear firsthand on subsequent trips to the island.

When Marquita finished undergrad at San Juan, she got a Masters in American lit right across the Hudson at NYU, while I was down there in New Brunswick not knowing what I was missing. By the time we both got to Hopkins, she was already the "superstar" of the Writing Seminars.

Which she wore lightly.

Shrugging it off. Just as she shrugged off everything else in her life that couldn't be helped.

My cell vibrated.

It was Colt.

He had the birth certificates.

Both of them.

As expected, Bonnie was listed as Faulkner's mother, and I was listed as her father. Charlie, whose birth name was Charleston Darrow, was the child of Raven Darrow and Kurt Cobain.

"Raven's dead," he said.

"So's Kurt Cobain," I pointed out needlessly.

"Yeah, I'll dig deeper into that one."

"Thanks, Colt."

No one ever called him "Jack."

He ignored my attempt at gratitude. He wasn't much good at being thanked.

"Where the hell *are* you?"

"Sitting in a fortress in Puerto Rico."

He didn't bother to comment. He just hung up. Whatever curiosities Colt might be having about whatever was going on in my life, he didn't show the slightest interest.

It was just the way he was.

I put the phone away, inside my leather jacket, and looked at the darkening Atlantic.

The fortress, first begun in 1539 under Charles V, had six different levels, rising 140 feet above the ocean, with walls that were eighteen-feet thick. It was an incomprehensible labyrinth of turrets, towers, tunnels, ramparts, batteries, barracks, vaults, lookouts, and dungeons. It was the largest Spanish fortress in the New World, and the Spanish crown had always considered Puerto Rico the "Key to the Antilles." On various occasions, it had resisted both the Dutch and the English, including 1598, when Sir Francis Drake not only got driven back to the sea but also got a cannonball blasted through his cabin.

I was sitting in the twilight, at the northwest end of the promontory, next to one of the old stone sentry-turrets known as *garitas*, thinking that the tour books certainly got it right.

The view was spectacular.

This is where she grew up, less than a mile away, on Calle Luna, on the Bay of San Juan, on the Island of Enchantment. But she met the one she inexplicably wanted in a crab joint in Towson, Maryland, and we were pretty much inseparable for the subsequent two years, finishing together at Hopkins, then moving to Malibu, where I saw her cry for the first time.

Which was the first of two.

The two saddest moments of my life.

"I'm in!"

I'd just gotten my acceptance.

"Of course, you're in!"

I think that Markie was even more excited than I was. On a lark, I'd applied for a Chesterfield Screenwriting Fellowship, originally created by Spielberg, then sponsored by Paramount, which picked five young "promising" writers from "anywhere" and brought them to Los Angeles for a year, providing a healthy stipend, an office on the lot, and a billion contacts.

Which all seemed too good to be true.

Markie, by then, was eager to get away, and three thousand miles and a tiny beach house on the Malibu cliffs seemed perfect.

"I'm ready," she said. "Let's hit the road!"

She had a few bucks saved from her half of her father's bakery, which she'd left to her sister, and she was looking forward to a year's worth of writing to work on her first novel, *Cristobal*, which was a prospective expansion on her award-winning short story, "Guanina."

In Puerto Rico, both on the streets and within academe, there was a long-standing belief that the Castilian knight in the tragic love story, whose name was Don Cristobal de Sotomayor, was actually the illegitimate third son of Christopher Columbus, who (Columbus) not only discovered the "New World," but also discovered Puerto Rico on his second voyage to the "Indies." Columbus had two sons, both of whom are well-known to historians, Diego and Fernando, but more than a few historians believed that Cristobal, who'd served as a page in the court of Ferdinand and Isabella, who'd also served under both the Prince of Wales in England and King Philip the Fair in France, and who'd come to the Americas as the right-hand lieutenant of Ponce de León, the eventual governor of Puerto Rico, was also the son of Christopher Columbus.

It was also widely believed, romantically or not, that Cristobal was deeply sympathetic to the plight of the Taíno and that he'd actually tried to prevent the terrible uprising of 1511.

Ending up dead for his efforts.

Markie, thanks to her father, had grown up loving the old Taíno/colonial tales and legends, but she also had the greatest respect for Zeno Gandía's *La Charca*, the first great Puerto Rican novel, which describes, often in harrowing detail, the exploitation of the campesinos who worked the Puerto Rican coffee plantations. The book was first published in 1894, written in the Balzac/Zola mode, harshly realistic, heavy on tragedy, pain, and the despair in the workers' lives.

In Spanish, a *charca* is a stagnant, foul, unsanitary, low-lying pond or pool of water. Which was, of course, heavily symbolic of the plight of the campesinos. Gandía once described his book as one of his "chronicles of a sick world."

Which was a bit too depressing and heavy-handed for the likes of Markie who watched rom-coms, liked rum punch sangria, and danced to La India salsa. What she intended to do was find some kind of compromise. She wanted to write a Puerto Rican novel, rich with history, that would inhabit a fictional world between the two extremes of Zeno Gandía's naturalism and the romantic and fanciful folk tales of her native island.

So we got ourselves engaged and moved to Malibu. I spent my afternoons on the Paramount lot, and Markie got underway on her novel. Then we flew to San Juan, got married, swam in Mosquito Bay, honeymooned on Cape Breton, then returned to Malibu, where I caught her crying one night. It was the end of our first year in LA, and

I'd been working on a screenplay about Frances Marion, the legendary Hollywood screenwriter, and I came home to the cottage one night, and I went out to the patio over the cliffs, over the Pacific, and I saw her sitting at her computer, amidst all kinds of piles of papers and notes, and she was crying.

Which made me sick inside myself.

But Jersey guys, as per some unwritten natural law, are invariably stoic, at least on the exterior, so I walked over, bent down, and kissed her forehead. Then I went into the kitchen and poured two chilled glasses of rum punch sangria.

"It's just not working," she admitted.

Which I already knew, which she already knew that I knew.

After all, what writer, somewhere in the process, doesn't get overwhelmed and frustrated with the deadly despair that it can't be done? Or, even worse, that *even* if it does get done, it won't be any good.

So we talked all night, until dawn, and she said:

"I need to make love to somebody."

So we went to the bedroom, and I left a message at Paramount that I wouldn't be coming to the studio the next day.

But I *did* have a suggestion for my wife.

Which we discussed at length.

"What if you're too close to it, Markie?"

Even though we were presently 4,000 miles away from "it."

Maybe she needed a break from her own life, from her own history, from all the Puerto Rican stuff. Maybe she needed to let it simmer for a while. Why not? She could always go back to it.

"But what would I write about?"

Which was a fair question since she'd been totally immersed, for over a year, in the colonial world of Don Cristobal, not really thinking about anything else.

"Why not take one of mine?" I suggested.

My own writing career, such as it was, had been sidetracked, if not shanghaied, for better or worse, by Hollyweird. Regardless, there was always one thing that I was especially good at. Ideas. Premises. Subjects. This was obvious to everyone at Hopkins, and I gave more than a few of the girls ideas that they eventually followed up on.

Why not my own wife?

"Why not look at it as an exercise?" I suggested.

A writer's "time-out."

A "portfolio piece" to air out your brains.

Something temporary.

"You wouldn't even have to finish it."

She seemed to like the idea.

"Why not? This Puerto Rican thing's dead in the water, and it's killing me."

She admitted that she didn't even have an outline yet.

"If you'd like," I offered, "I can help with that too. With either an old idea, or a new idea."

The truth is, whatever my writerly faults, I was always a holy terror at structure. Back at Hopkins, I'd helped a bunch of the girls and even two of the profs organize their stuff and make it workable, make it doable.

Structure, structure, structure.

Which, back at Johns Hopkins, made me seriously wonder if I were less of a writer and more of a "writing coach." Maybe that was my real talent. Maybe that was my destiny.

So I pulled out my Ideas file, read off about thirty possibilities and curiosities, stopping here and there whenever she wanted to discuss something.

"Think about it, Markie."

"I will."

"I can't stand to see you cry."

"Well, I'd like to see *you* shed a few tears sometime," she kidded.

Her smile was back.

"Don't hold your breath."

The next night I got a text from Vinny.

Hey, Hollywood, there's been an ugly crash in Death Valley.
Yes, DV! Why not come and see me?

Number three on my long list of fictional possibilities was: "An air crash inspector discovers something that he wishes he didn't." Which made perfect sense given that my best friend was a world-class NTSB expert, who'd often let me lurk around on the fringes of crash sites and ask him stupid questions.

I told Markie.

"It's a sign," she decided immediately, "besides it was my favorite on the list anyway, along with the Radium girls."

She was getting excited.

"All right, Miss Markie, grab your pad and let's go to Death Valley."

Which we did.

Then a seagull screeched overhead, snapping me back to the promontory over old San Juan. Then another seagull landed on top of the turret. I got the message. They wanted to be alone.

Amenable, I stood up, looking at the dark Atlantic, which was alluring, deadly, and lovely. For all I knew this might be the last time that I'd ever stand here on top of El Morro.

Thinking of Markie.

Then I turned around, left the fortress, and made my way to El Convento.

Chapter 15

Santa María Magdelena

Thursday, October 4

I was doing it again.

Like six days ago.

Sitting with the dead.

The Santa María Magdelena de Pazzis Cemetery, despite its purpose, is remarkably beautiful. It sits above the Atlantic, just outside the heavy walls of El Morro, being a bright-white spread of bright-white tombs and mausoleums, surrounding a bright-white circular chapel, all of which basks in the bright-white afternoon sun. Most of Puerto Rico's famous are buried here, including Marquita Cabrera Buchanan, the Pulitzer Prize winner who'd died much too young.

Her grave, like so many others, like her father's and her mother's, is a bright-white stone slab, lying on the ground in front of me.

Marquita Cabrera Buchanan
Beloved Wife Daughter Sister
"The Lord is My Shepherd"
Requiescat in Pace

I wondered, self-absorbedly, if she was disappointed in what I'd become.

"Oh, the novels'll come, Brety Boy. Just you wait! When the time is right, the novels will come!"

She had no doubt about it, and yet here I was, a so-called Pulitzer Prize winner in fiction, who'd never written a book of fiction.

Just a handful of short stories that I got published in my early days. The Rutgers and Hopkins days. Namely, "Shroud," about the Shroud of Turin; "Disumbrationism," about the modern art world; "The Plagiarist"; and "Diploma Mill." But I'd never managed to finish "Finding Faulkner" (about some guy who discovers that Faulkner wasn't really Faulkner), "Concordance" (about a guy who believes that Melville's greatest masterpiece was not *The Whale* but its concordance), and "O" (about a single mom who raises her child in a high-oxygen environment to make him intellectually precocious).

Along with a couple of screenplays and a stupid textbook.

Of course, there's also my never-ending-never-going-to-be-completed current projects about cryogenics and the Tylenol murders.

Marquita Cabrera Buchanan

Who was, I'd be willing to wager, the only one in the whole cemetery with a Scottish surname.

Markie would have enjoyed that.

I put down the flowers.

She liked white lilies, and she loved red roses, so I got her a bunch of each.

Five years ago, when Rosie made the arrangements for Markie's burial, I asked her to make sure that there was room for me. Right beside her. Which she did.

I stared down at the empty space.

My destiny.

Which was fine with me.

Chapter 16

Ponce de León

Thursday, October 4

Within this historic place, I'd married the prettiest bride in the history of the human race.

At the high altar of the Cathedral of San Juan Bautista, a few feet away from the tomb of Ponce de León, the sometimes-brutal conquistador, who'd sailed with Columbus when they first discovered the island, who later created the first settlement at Caparra, who later became the first governor, who later crushed the revolt of 1511, who later discovered the Gulf Stream, who later explored the east coast of Florida *not* looking for the fountain of youth.

Looking for gold.

Who was later shot with a poison arrow in a skirmish with Calusa warriors on the coast of Florida, dying an ugly death soon afterwards in Havana.

Puerto Ricans have a hard-to-define relationship with Ponce de León, which I've given up trying to comprehend.

119

"You never will, honey, so why bother?" she kidded.

"Yeah, good idea."

That was that.

I kept out of it, just like I kept out of the whole statehood vs. independence thing. After all, it's up to them, right? And, to tell the truth, they haven't been doing such a great job of figuring it out anyway, so I've minded my own business and focused on *Sports Center* instead.

I was sitting in the first pew, foolishly wondering if getting married here was the happiest day of my life, within this narrow, white, understated, yet always elegant cathedral, being the second oldest in the Americas. Or whether it was that night when I looked up, over my cheeseburger, at the Crackpot.

Markie's wedding gown was some kind of lacy masterpiece from Lisa Cappalli, and my beautiful bride was perfectly happy. My mom and my brother were also perfectly happy, as was Markie's younger sister Rosie and all of our other friends and relatives.

Yet here I am, perversely, sitting in San Juan Bautista, remembering the second time I saw her cry.

Which was worse than the first.

The Chesterfield Fellowship was over, and I was teaching part-time at USC's School of Cinema, teaching a course in introductory screenwriting, while, at the same time, over in the creative writing department, teaching an introductory course in writing fiction, even though my credentials for either class seemed pretty slim to me.

One night when I drove home from the Trojan campus, I found her in the bathroom crying. I was completely baffled. At the time, she'd been rip-roaring along on her novel, which was called *Aircrash*, following the detailed outline that I'd drawn up for her when we got back from Death Valley. She seemed perfectly content.

The door was open, so I stepped into the room. She was standing over the sink with her forehead pressed against the mirror.

Crying.

Sobbing.

Gently.

I was about to ask her what was wrong, but I didn't.

I could see the little pregnancy strip in her hand.

It was white.

It was colorless.

There was no child within her.

There never would be.

Chapter 17

Baineario de Carolina

Thursday, October 4

S he rode up the beach on a black stallion.

Looking exactly like Marquita.

Upright, with an English saddle, English bridal, rider's crop, high black leather boots, tight-white breeches, a white shirt buttoned to the neck, a black four-button riding jacket, without hat, cap, or equestrian helmet.

It's been said that every Puertorriqueña likes to "dress, ride, and dance," and the Cabrera sisters were no exception. Both of them had been riding ever since they were little girls, even competing in local jumping events, Olympic style, even winning a few trophies, but, as they got older, they preferred to ride exclusively for pleasure.

"A horse is a powerful four-legged creature," Markie once pointed out. "Have you ever seen one in New Jersey? Maybe in a zoo? Maybe at the circus?"

I didn't have the heart to tell her that the oldest-running rodeo in the United States was in Pilesgrove, New Jersey.

No one ever believes it anyway.

I was sitting on a white bench, beneath the palm trees, beneath the almond trees, on Baineario de Carolina, the most beautiful beach in the long string of beautiful beaches that make up Isla Verde. Which, if truth be told, looks less like Old San Juan and more like Miami Beach, being lined with upscale luxury hotels, including El San Juan Resort and Casino, where Rosie worked.

I was staring across the bright-white silky warm sand into the blue afternoon sea. Off in the far distance, the blueness of the azured waters blended imperceptively into the eternal blueness of the sky.

Rosie rode up.

She was the younger sister who loved, even hero-worshipped, her older sister, who (Markie), as far as I ever saw, never actually treated Rosie like a younger sister, but more like a twin sister. Who looked a lot like Marquita, but cropped her hair, wore a bit more make-up, and had more than a few racks of business suits in her dress closet. Rosie had become an entrepreneur. A businesswoman. A professional.

As the older sister had chosen to honor her father by becoming a storyteller, the younger sister had chosen to honor her father by maintaining Cabrera's Panadería, then expanding to a second store on Isla Verde. Then she went to culinary school at Universidad Del Este's, the most famous culinary school on the island, rated in the top ten in the US, located in nearby Carolina, named for King Charles II of Spain, the birthplace of Roberto Clemente.

She graduated both summa and Phi Beta Kappa, and despite being only twenty-one at the time was offered the head pastry chef position at Galeria Trattoria in El San Juan Hotel. Now she's the master pastry chef for *all* nine of the hotel's award-winning restaurants, while still running both Carlos Cabrera bakeries, now nationally famous for their *quesitos*, which Rosie was shipping all over the United States to tourists who'd tried them while visiting the island, and who'd decided that they couldn't live without them when they got back home.

"She's amazing," Markie would say.

"Yes."

Especially when her little package arrived in Malibu every Wednesday direct from San Juan, containing three papayas *quesitos* for me and three pineapple *quesitos* for Markie.

Which is an indescribable puffy pastry, drenched with sugary caramelized syrup, stuffed with delicious whipped cheese and fruit preserves.

Three for each of us.

To last the entire week.

"Let's face it, they're body-fat machines," Markie would remind me whenever I suggested that we hint for more.

Not that either of the Cabrera sisters had much concern about their bf, which came in at a fashion-model 12, while I was fluctuating somewhere around 25 or so.

Constantly craving pastries.

I stood as Rosie drew up her stallion beside me.

"Hey, Jersey," she said and smiled.

She was trying to be perfectly natural. Five years ago, we'd both lost the most important person in our lives, and neither one of us had dealt with it very well.

"You look great, Rosie," I tried, "just like the Olympics."

Uncertain how she should respond, Rosie turned a bit on her mount and deftly undid a little white box that was tied to the back of her saddle. Then she turned back to me, handing the box down.

"Welcome back," she said.

I smiled.

"I wonder what *this* could be?"

"Two papayas. Markie once told me never to give you more than two at a time."

"Thanks."

More awkwardness.

"Did you," I asked, "get my message?"

Even though I knew she had.

"Yes, it sounds like fun," she said, trying hard to sound excited.

"Why don't I get a cab," I suggested, "and pick you up around seven?"

"Perfect. I'll be ready."

"See you tonight."

We were done.

Rosie nodded.

Then she rode off, and I watched her go.

Then I sat down on the bench again, opened the little box and ate the both of them, trying not to think about how good she looked.

Chapter 18

The Parrot Club

Thursday, October 4

"I t'll win some stuff, Bret! And so will you!"

Given my current problems, I'd naturally been forced to bail on the premiere of *Aircrash* last weekend in LA, but I still wanted to see the film and so did Rosie.

So we went under the radar, catching a screening at the Metro Cinemas in Santurce barrio, close to the beach. Paramount had done a nice job with the film, and I'd like to think that Markie would have been pleased. Jennifer Lawrence, as always, was excellent, and I can see why both the *Hollywood Reporter* and the *LA Times* were "talking up" Oscar. It was, of course, quite peculiar to sit in a movie theater, maybe even more so in Puerto Rico, and watch Jennifer Lawrence saying the same words that I'd written in Cape Breton when I was adapting the script.

"I thought Benicio was terrific," Rosie added.

Of course she did.

"Which you would have said," I kidded, "if he was terrible."

"An impossibility!"

It was hard to determine which of the Cabrera sisters had the bigger crush on Benicio del Toro, which often made me wonder how Markie could have fallen for the likes of me in the first place.

Rosie and I were sitting at a small table in the Parrot Club, which, tonight, was as bright and jazzed and colorful as always, with its palm tree murals and Caribbean ambience. Women at the Parrot always "dress to impress," and Rosie was no different, wearing a bright de la Renta, a la Markie. She was now working on her third Parrot Passion, which she informed me was some kind of "magical" concoction of rum, triple sec, oranges, and passion fruit. She was also picking at her yummy *ropa vieja* nachos, and I was helping out.

Fortunately, the booze had eliminated much of the awkwardness that was so obvious earlier in the evening, and I was happily working on my fourth Canadian Club sour.

When the next song came on, it was *"La Cuesta de la Fama"* by Willie Rosario.

Rosie smiled, then looked at me, curious to see if I'd "get it," which I did because I'd been well-trained by Markie.

"Your namesake," I said.

"Good boy," she said.

Across the table, she suddenly stood up and gyrated a few lovely salsa moves to the music that, of course, reminded me of Markie.

Rosie had been named after her father's favorite band leader, Willie Rosario.

"Everyone loves Tito," he once explained to his pretty young daughters, "but Willie's my man."

I suppose it might be humanly possible to marry a Puertorriqueña and not learn to salsa, but I was never given the option.

"I don't think I can do that," I told Markie one night in Baltimore when she played a song by Eddie Santiago.

It's even more accurate to say that I'd never wiggled my ass before. Scots, when they dance, keep themselves bolt upright with their hips immobile.

Most Jersey guys don't dance at all.

Unless extremely drunk.

"It's all in the hips, honey."

Which was much easier said than done, but after several years of retraining muscle memory, keeping in mind that there's only three steps to every four beats, I got to the point where I was no longer a totally embarrassing companion to the knockout salsaing centerpiece of each and every dance floor.

Markie loved old-school *salsa dura*, like Willie Rosario, but she also loved *salsa romántica*, especially Santiago, Marc Anthony, and, most especially, her favorite, La India.

When Marquita danced, nothing else mattered. Everyone else stopped and watched.

She was mesmerizing.

So was her little sister.

But Rosie stopped herself, then she took a hit off her Parrot Passion, smiled, and said:

"I need the Ladies."

Then she walked off into the crowd, walking like she was dancing.

I needed to get out of here.

Which I finally did around midnight, dropping Rosie at her condo on Isla Verde, where both of us rather un-deftly avoided the "would you like to come up" problem.

Since it was such a lovely Caribbean night, I decided to walk back to the hotel.

The clubs were still sizzling, still pulsing. As I'm sure the crap tables were as well in the lavish James-Bond-like casinos. As for the wide expanse of the beach, it was dark, deserted, and mysteriously beautiful.

Back in town, I wandered up-then-down the cobblestoned streets beneath the wrought-iron balconies and the lush hanging flowers, especially the purple and red bougainvilleas. Beneath the streetlamps, I walked past the open-air cafes, the shuttered boutiques, the galleries, the monuments, the trees, and the trollies. Past Cabrera's Bakery, stopping to look into the window and imagining the past.

Then I strolled down Calle San Sebastián, past the now-restored two-hundred-year-old colonial mansions, painted in majestic pastels. Blues, oranges, and yellows.

Finally, I arrived at my hotel, El Convento, then sat in the shadowed little park in front of the main entrance. Sitting on yet another bench, thinking of Markie. I'd only been to San Juan a few times in my life, but everywhere I went there was nothing but her. Who'd once been a little girl here, who'd once walked these streets, who'd once worked in her father's bakery, who'd once danced in all the clubs, who'd once decided to become a novelist.

Five years ago, four nights after the car crash, Rosie and I were sitting here in the same little park, completely and equally devastated, equally silent in the aftermath of the morning's funeral, the afternoon's burial, and the evening's reception. It was late that night, just like tonight, and we were trying to say our final goodbyes before I flew back to Malibu and tried to wrap up the perfect California life that Markie and I had created together.

In truth, Rosie and I had spoken very little during the previous two days. With her usual efficiency, she'd made all the arrangements, but she was utterly destroyed inside. As we both were. When I stood up, Rosie stood up as well, then she broke down. She fell into my arms, and I held her gently as she sobbed on my shoulder. I suppose, even a few minutes earlier, I would have believed that *nothing* in this world could have made me feel worse than I already felt. But I was wrong. Seeing Rosie so absolutely helpless and obliterated had made the seemingly impossible possible.

When she got control of herself, she looked up, and I kissed her. On the mouth. Or she kissed me. Or we both kissed each other.

Which really doesn't make any difference.

When it was over, I walked away and went into the hotel, and I've felt nothing but a corrosive guilt ever since.

A sense of having betrayed my wife.

Having betrayed Rosie as well.

Yeah, it was just "a moment of weakness," but it was still an unconscionable betrayal, and, earlier today on the beach and tonight at both the cinema and the Parrot, I could see it in Rosie's eyes as well.

That sense of what we'd done that night. The disbelief. The inability to fathom how we could have done something so terrible, so terrible to each other.

The sense of nothing but guilt.

The sense of self-disgust.

Chapter 19

Newark International Airport

Friday, October 5th

I t was great to be back in Newark.

How often do you hear that?

Kyle was waiting at the baggage claim, chipper as always, and we walked to his black BMW in the parking lot, where he tossed my bag in the trunk and clicked open the doors. As always, whenever one of us picked up the other at the airport, there was a box waiting on the passenger seat.

I lifted the box, sat down in my seat, shut the car door, and opened the box.

Three slices of Vinni's pepperoni pizza.

It was great to be back in New Jersey!

Kyle fired up the engine, and the Boss came on.

As per the past: "Born to Run."

Which we both knew didn't make much sense since it's a song about getting out of little-town New Jersey. Hardly a welcome home song.

Who cares?

Kyle negotiated his BMW through downtown Newark toward Route 21, as I knocked off my first slice.

Come on with me, tramps like us,
Baby, we were born to run.

The Boss was finished, the ritual was over, and Kyle killed the music.

"So what the hell were you doing in San Juan?"

I told him some close-to-the-truth BS about wanting to see how Rosie was doing. About catching Markie's movie in San Juan. Mentioning, of course, nothing about either South Carolina or Scotland.

"It's a great flick, Bret. I think you'll be getting one of those ugly little statues next February."

We talked about the film, the Paterson courthouse, Angie, the kids, and the gory recent double homicide in Prospect Park.

"You taking the lead?"

"I can't resist."

Then he told me about the inner workings of the case, and we talked about all kinds of other stuff, since it seemed that we were the kind of brothers who left nothing unsaid, who had no secrets.

Except, of course, that we did.

A big one.

Twenty-one years ago, after our grandmother died in the Bronx, I was sent into the city to clean out the old apartment, where I found, where I literally stumbled upon, a ratty old gym bag in the back of a never-used storage closet, containing the print-outs of old emails.

Hundreds of them.

Why did the bastard do it?

Why did he cheat on my mother?

Why was he so stupid that he'd saved hard copies of his back-and-forth emails with his surreptitious lover?

Maybe he *wanted* to get caught.

Maybe he didn't care.

I was fifteen at the time, and I sat on my grandmother's old couch, *his* mother's couch, and read every single one of them.

Up to that day, from everything I'd ever heard about our old man, he sounded like a pretty decent guy. He worked hard at the post office, took an interest in his kids, and had a sense of humor. Then he got crushed to death in a loading dock accident when I was six and Kyle was two. My mother, who seemed to love the guy a lot, survived the shock, got on with her life, got herself a job at the post office, and raised her two sons.

With nothing but love.

As good as a mom could do.

But did she know that the bastard was screwing some twenty-year-old postal clerk from Bedford Park? I had no idea. I burned the emails that day in my grandmother's kitchen sink. They were puerile, embarrassing, full of all kinds of sophomoric sexual banter.

I never told my mother.

I also never told Kyle, who'd grown up worshipping the memory of the father he'd never known.

"Uncle Ed says he was a hell of a switch-hitter," Kyle would say.

Because the old man played some semi-pro.

So I was the only one who knew that he was also a rat, and I've been struggling back-and-forth my entire life wondering if I should have told them.

Didn't they have the *right* to know?

Didn't they deserve the truth?

But I couldn't do it.

Not even tonight.

So we drove back to Packanack together, two brothers who were perfectly comfortable with each other, talking about the Giants and the Mets and the Jets, and dad's old semi-pro stats, and everything else under the sun.

Except the truth.

Which I'll have to tell him before this book is printed.

Chapter 20

Sparks Steak House

Saturday, October 6

She's got a "mob" thing.

Who doesn't?

I was sitting at an isolated table waiting for Wendy, reading my own textbook, *Writing Fiction*, and hoping that the maître d' wasn't too irritated that my dinner date was late on a busy Saturday evening. Fortunately, it was still early, just past five o'clock, and the crowds hadn't swarmed the place yet.

It's weird reading your own textbook.

It's even weirder having to use it as the structural foundation for a novel that you're being forced to write at gunpoint.

When I finished rereading the Research section, I went back and looked at the contents.

The book was based on my intro class at USC, in which the kids wrote mostly short stories, as discussed in Section One. At the request of the Creative Writing Department, I also covered novel prep and novel writing in Section Two.

Even though I'd never written a novel!

Introduction:

(Note: Six novels will be regularly referenced throughout the text: Persuasion; Jane Eyre; Moby-Dick; The Great Gatsby; Absalom, Absalom!; *and* The End of the Affair.*)*

I. *The Short Story*

1. *Peculiarity*

2. *It's a* Short *Story*

3. *It's a Short* Story

4. *Reflection*

5. *"The Form of the Sword" (analysis)*

II. *The Novel*

1. *The Premise*

2. *Research*

3. *Settings*

4. *Plot: Short Outline*

5. *Characters*

6. *Chronology*

7. *Plot: Detailed Outline*

8. *Opening*

9. *Style*

I noticed Wendy snooping around outside the restaurant, beneath the awning. I knew exactly what she was doing. She was trying to figure out, trying to imagine in her head, precisely where the hits took place.

Sparks might be the best steakhouse in the city, one of the best in the entire country, but it was also notoriously famous for the 1985 rubout of Gambino crime boss Paul Castellano and his underboss Thomas Bilotti. The two of them had driven to Sparks for some prime sirloin, but they never got inside the door. John Carneglia, the apparent triggerman, popped them both as they got out of their car. Then, as their blood was flowing into the streets, another car drove slowly past to inspect the quality of the work.

John Gotti, who'd ordered the hit, was in the second car. Two weeks later, a secret capos meeting in Manhattan approved John Gotti as the new Gambino mob boss. Seven years later, with the help of Sammy the Bull, Gotti was convicted of the murder along with a long list of racketeering charges, then ten years later he died in a federal prison.

The date of the hit was December 16, 1985, as everyone in the Metro area knows by heart, or at least everyone who's ever watched *Godfather I* and *Godfather II* ten times or more, which is pretty much everyone in the Metro area.

Eventually, Wendy came inside and sat down. She looked lovely, as always, dressed in a navy pencil dress, with matching navy blazer with bright gold buttons, which made me feel even more guilty about our ill-advised relationship.

Not to mention, my sloppy break-it-off.

It seems that over the past ten days, I've had nothing but awkward encounters with attractive women.

This one was a smart and pretty Irish-Italian girl from Staten Island who'd gone to Columbia for English, then Emerson for publishing, before working as an associate agent at Writer's House, before, finally, starting her own agency with three similarly young female agents, before stumbling onto Markie Buchanan.

She lived on 83rd.

She did Boxaerobics at Flanagan's Gym Annex, dressed a bit preppy, which was always nice to look at, and liked to listen to Adele and Celine Dion, even though she never liked to admit it to anyone. Any guy in Manhattan, or New Jersey, or anywhere else, would have killed to get a date with the likes of Wendy Parks, but I was still more than a bit messed up.

Ever since Markie's death five years ago, I'd only kissed two girls, Rosie and Wendy, and both were serious mistakes.

The first one being catastrophic.

But Wendy was a trooper. She tried to keep things from getting "too weird," and she did her best to be up-and-up.

"You scrape any blood off the street?" I asked.

"Ha ha, wiseguy."

I stood up and helped her take her seat

"Where have *you* been?" she wondered.

I sat back down.

"Getting ready to write a novel."

She seemed amazed, as if momentarily stunned.

"Was it the bullet?"

Meaning, I assumed, did getting shot with a rifle make you realize that you need to do something worthwhile with your life?

"Yes."

It certainly had.

We had an excellent meal together, and no one in the old-fashioned comfortable restaurant, except for the two of us, would have ever guessed that we were busted-up lovers just a few weeks ago, which Wendy never brought up, even though we were both thinking about it over bites of steak fromage.

Eventually, finally, we got down to business.

The box-sender had listed the necessary guidelines, and I needed Wendy to set everything up, especially the quick turnaround date for the book publishing.

9. Arrange to have the novel published on February 24.

"How come?" she wondered.

Reasonably.

"It's part of the deal, Wendy. There's absolutely no wiggle room."

She looked sad, as if I'd broken up with her again.

I did my best to reassure her:

"Look, Wendy, I'll explain everything in a few months. Just trust me. Please. I need your help."

Wendy had always helped Markie, and she liked helping everyone, and she was ready to do the same for me.

She smiled.

"All right," she said. "I can make this happen."

"It means a lot."

Which meant a lot to her.

"But it's a good thing you won that Pulitzer," she laughed.

Meaning "that's my leverage to pull this off."

Later, after chocolate mousse cake for me and New York cheesecake for Wendy, I drove back to New Jersey and started writing the damned thing.

This thing.

III.

SETTINGS

Always have interesting settings. Take your readers to Bangkok, Waikiki, or Times Square. Don't take them to Dullsville, USA, unless there's an earthquake, a séance, or a quadruple murder.

Chapter 21

The Bronx

The northernmost of the five boroughs.

Named for Jonas Bronck, the first settler in the northern regions of New Netherland, 1639.

The "greenest" of the five boroughs, being 24% parkland.

Home of the Bronx Zoo, the world's greatest zoo.

Home of the Yankees and Yankee Stadium.

Home of the New York Botanical Gardens.

Home of Fordham University; Poe Cottage, where Edgar Allan Poe lived with his wife Virginia; Van Courtlandt House, where Washington stayed twice during the Revolution; the American Hall of Fame; Orchard Beach, the "Riviera of New York City"; Woodlawn Cemetery; and St. Nicholas of Tolentine, "the Cathedral of the Bronx."

Where salsa was born, where hip hop was born.

Where the Capitol Dome, the statue in the Lincoln Monument, and the New York Public Library lions were made.

Where JFK lived as a child, attending Riverdale Country Day School.

Which would be, if it were its own city, the ninth largest city in the United States.

***

Where Bret and Kyle Buchanan were born, where their father died, where their mother worked in the post office, where Bret injured his shoulder in a fire escape accident, where Bret discovered that his father was an adulterer.

Chapter 22

Packanack Lake

Twenty miles from Times Square.

The first of the lakes in the famous Lake Region of Northern New Jersey.

Named for indigenous Pacquanacs.

Founded 1928.

Each resident being a member of the PLTC, the Packanack Lake Country Club.

Being a rather exclusive lake community, set in a small valley, with two sand beaches, eleven tennis courts, an award-winning golf course, a lakefront Clubhouse for meetings and social events, churches, grammar schools, a firehouse, and multiple ballfields.

Where one can swim, boat, fish, and play sports.

Residents have included Cecil B. DeMille, Tom Cruise, and Kim Alexis.

***

Where the Buchanans moved when Bret was eight years old, moving into the "Jack Burke" house, a small brick house at 4 Laurel Drive in the Gulch section of Packanack, near Rotman's Creek, across from the tennis courts, where Bret learned that he was related to Jack Burke, where Bret grew up until he went off to college, where Kyle still lives with his wife Angie and their two sons, where Bret, two years ago, eventually returned to, buying a small log cabin on Osborne Terrace.

Chapter 23

Columbia, South Carolina

T he Capital of South Carolina.

    Named for Christopher Columbus.

Where the State Secession Convention voted in 1860 to secede from the Union, initiating the Civil War.

An early center of the textile industry.

Known as "The Capital of Southern Hospitality."

Home to the University of South Carolina.

The Gamecocks.

Designated by *Kiplinger* as one of the "Ten Great US Cities to Live In."

***

Where Bonnie was born, where Faulkner was born, where Bret attended the University of South Carolina for his first two years of college, where he met Bonnie, where Bonnie would later adopt Charleston Darrow, where Bonnie would marry.

Twice.

Chapter 24

St. Andrews

The ancient ecclesiastical center of Scotland.

Named for the fisherman apostle, the brother of Peter.

Home of St. Andrews University, founded 1410, the third oldest English-language university in the world, after Oxbridge.

The birthplace of Golf.

The home of the Old Course, created 1552; the home of the Royal and Ancient Golf Club, founded 1754; the home of the Open Championship (aka the British Open), initiated 1860.

The site of the ruins of St. Andrews Cathedral (begun 1158) and the ruins of St. Andrews Castle (c. 1200).

***

Where Bret attended the university for two years after transferring from South Carolina, where he met Skye MacAllister, where Skye now lives with her husband and her eight-year-old son.

Chapter 25

San Juan

Capital of Puerto Rico.

(Which Faulkner calls "Porto Rico" on pages 372 and 373 of *Absalom, Absalom!*).

Established 1509, named for St. John the Baptist.

The gateway city to the Caribbean.

The gateway city to *La Isla del Encanto*.

Encompassing "old world" Old San Juan, El Morro, Castillo San Cristóbal, La Fortaleza, luxurious beaches, first-class resorts, and the best nightlife in the Caribbean.

Born in San Juan: José Ferrer, Tito Rodríguez, Wilfredo Gómez, Raúl Juliá, Gigi Fernández, Ricky Martin, Jorge Rafael Posada, etc., etc.

La más bella.

***

Where Marquita was born, where Rosario was born, where Marquita attended the University of Puerto Rico, where Bret and Markie were married in the Cathedral of San Juan Bautista, where Markie is buried, where Bret kissed Rosie.

Where she kissed him back.

Chapter 26

Malibu

Discovered in 1542 by Portuguese explorer Juan Rodríguez Cabrillo.

An affluent, upscale, luxurious beach town, with over twenty-one miles of the Pacific coast, high cliffs, countless canyons, set beneath the Santa Monica Mountains.

Home of movie stars.

Haven for surfers.

Zuma Beach, Surfrider Beach, Malibu Beach, Topanga Beach, Point Dume Beach, etc.

Home of the Getty Villa, Pepperdine University, Malibu Bluffs Park, the Malibu Pier, the Malibu International Film Festival, and Tony Stark's Iron Man residence (fictional) on the Point Dume cliffs.

Paradise.

With occasional coastal storms, wildfires, mudslides in the canyons, and intermittent San Andreas tremors.

***

Where Bret and Markie moved after Johns Hopkins, after getting engaged, where Bret was enrolled in the Chesterfield Fellowship Program at Paramount, where Bret took a part-time teaching position at USC, where Markie wrote *Aircrash*, where Markie almost completed *Radium Eyes*, where Markie, five years ago, died in a car crash on the Pacific Coast Highway near Topanga Beach, hit by a drunken middle-aged male.

Chapter 27

Cape Breton Island

The rugged rocky jewel of the Canadian Maritimes.

The prize of Nova Scotia (New Scotland).

An enchanted island set in the high Atlantic comprising the northernmost part of Nova Scotia.

Home to indigenous Mi'kmaq.

Home to Arcadian French, especially at Chéticamp and Isle Madame.

Home of Scot Highlanders who began arriving around 1802, having been forced out of Scotland by the Clearances.

Isolated from mainland Canada until the construction of the Causeway in 1955.

Home of the Gaelic College at St. Ann's, Alexander Graham Bell's home in Baddeck, beautiful Bras d'Or Lake, the scenic Cabot Trail, the Celtic Colours International Music Festival, and Fiddler's Row on Route 19.

With bald eagles, moose, black bears, whales, etc.

The bastion of traditional Scottish Celtic Culture, dancing, pipes, kilts, tartans, whiskey, the Gaelic language, and, most important, the fiddle.

The most famous being master-fiddler Buddy MacMaster, his niece Natalie MacMaster, Howie MacDonald, Jerry Holland, Bill Lamey, Rodney MacDonald, Kinnon Beaton, Ashley MacIsaac, and countless others.

***

Where Bret goes after the death of Marquita, living in the family's "brown cottage," where he writes *Writing Fiction*, completes and edits *Radium Eyes*, and writes the screenplay for *Aircrash*.

IV.

PLOT: SHORT OUTLINE

Plot is *everything*. (Assuming that you've already got a kickass premise.) Repeat: Plot is *everything*. The best writing, the most fascinating characters, and the most exotic locations will never be able to salvage a poorly constructed story. Aristotle placed it first, at the "apex" of writing. So should you.

Chapter 28

Short Outline (so far)

I. *The Premise*

The box

Shot at his desk

Hospital

Hires Colt

Air Crash Site

The premise

II. *Research*

Re-reading *Absalom*

The obituaries

DNA results

South Carolina State Capitol – Charleston

Bonnie's grave

Charlie's home – teddy bear

St. Andrews Ruins

Café – Faulkner

Skye

Scottish private investigator

San Juan – Rosario

Sees *Aircrash*

Return to New Jersey – Kyle

Meets Agent – reading *Writing Fiction*

III. *Settings*

The Bronx

Packanack

South Carolina

St. Andrews

San Juan

Malibu

Cape Breton

IV. *Plot: Short Outline*

Brief rough outline (so far), with possible resolution

V. *Characters*

Characters list

Character bios

VI. *Chronology*

Chronology

Suspect list

VII. *Plot: Detailed Outline*
Writing progress
Further developments
Detailed outline
Revelations list
Themes

VIII. *Opening*
Opening

IX. *Style*
Style
Millarisms

X. *Dialogue*
Dialogue

XI. *Place Diagrams*
The Log Cabin

X. *Ending* (to be ascertained)
Drops off manuscript
Publication of the novel
Confrontation with the perpetrator (?)
Arrest (?)
Resolution
Ending

V.

CHARACTERS

Creating interesting characters is relatively easy. Not to mention fun. Give them interesting professions, quirks, obsessions, hobbies, issues, problems, ambitions, beliefs, etc. Avoid all naturally boring characters like writers, teachers, students, and hookers.

Chapter 29

Characters List (so far)

Bret Buchanan (36) – reputed novelist

Marquita (Markie) Cabrera Buchanan (deceased) – wife

Rosario (Rosie) Cabrera (30) – sister-in-law

Kyle Buchanan (32) – brother, prosecutor (wife Angie)

Jack Colt (32) – private investigator

Vinny Erickson (36) – best friend, NTSB air crash investigator

Wendy Parks (29) – agent, recent girlfriend

Melanie Thomson (36) – Paramount executive

Irene Davis (32) – Air crash survivor

Bonnie Jean MacMillan (deceased) – South Carolina girlfriend

Faulkner MacMillan (18) – Bonnie's daughter

Charleston (Charlie) Darrow MacMillan (27) – Faulkner's "aunt"

Rex Kepler (missing) – Bonnie's first husband, demolitionist

Chase Anderson (deceased) – Bonnie's second husband, commercial
   pilot

Skye Elspeth MacAllister (35) – St. Andrews girlfriend (husband Angus MacDonald, son Lachlan)

Gordon Carlyle (19) – Faulkner's boyfriend

Heather Sinclair (19) – Faulkner's roommate

Beaton MacMaster (56) – St. Andrews PI

Chapter 30

Characters Bios (so far)

For one's own reference, keep them tight.

(Includes much repetition from the text, please skip if so inclined.)

Bret Buchanan (36): Born in the Bronx, Scot maternal, Irish/German paternal, 6'1", dark hair, dark brown eyes, fair skin, reasonably attractive but not classically handsome, trim, athletic, initially home schooled by his mother, reads Poe, visits Poe Cottage (age 5), decides to become a writer, his father (Edward) working for the post office is crushed to death in a loading dock accident (age 6), his mother (Mary) gets a job in the post office, they move to Packanack Lake in Wayne, New Jersey (age 8), Bret goes to parochial schools, plays shortstop on DePaul's baseball team but injures his left arm in a fire-escape accident in the Bronx (age 14), leading to nerve damage, roots for the Mets, the Giants, and the Jets, attends the University of South Carolina, the University of St. Andrews,

Rutgers, and Johns Hopkins, participates in the Chesterfield Fellowship Program, collects MLB Hall of Fame bobbleheads, runs around the lake to keep in shape.

Marquita (Markie) Cabrera (deceased, would be 34): Strikingly attractive, naturally seductive, wears loud designer dresses with a Caribbean flair, tall, carries herself like a model, salsa dancer, skilled horsewoman, extremely personable and unassuming, loves raspberry ice cream, romantic comedies, Rum Punch Sangria, José Feliciano, La India, Eddie Santiago, Willie Rosario, and Marc Anthony, born in old San Juan, named after Marquita Rivera, her mother dies when she's a child, she works in her father's bakery, very close to her younger sister, very close to her father (a storyteller), spends a month each summer in the south Bronx with her aunt Mariana and her younger cousins, attends the University of San Juan as a pre-med student, when her father dies unexpectedly of a heart attack, she decides to become a writer, after graduation she attends NYU for an English master's degree and publishes an award-winning short story set in Puerto Rico, she then attends The Johns Hopkins Writing Seminars, meets Bret (me), when he gets a Chesterfield Fellowship, they move to Malibu together where she attempts to write an historical novel set in Puerto Rico but encounters difficulties, when Bret suggests trying something new, they visit a Death Valley plane crash and Bret helps her write the novel, Wendy Parks becomes her agent and close friend and the book is highly successful, Markie almost completes her second novel, but, five years ago, she dies in a car crash (age 29).

Rosario (Rosie) Cabrera (30): Very attractive like her sister, with shorter hair and more of a professional businesswoman's appearance, loves the kitchen, the beach, horseback riding, even did some surfing at Rincón, similarly born in old San Juan, named after Willie Rosario, four years younger than Marquita, she idolizes her older sister, works in the bakery, decides to go to culinary school at the Universidad del Este, ends up the head pastry chef at the five-star El San Juan Hotel, visits Markie and Bret in California, is devastated by her sister's death.

Bonnie Jean MacMillan Anderson (deceased, would be 34): Pretty Southern belle with marked Carolina accent, thick blonde hair, green eyes, tallish, athletic, upbeat and fun, yet serious about her future, grows up in West Columbia, her father was an ex-marine who married late and died when she was young, her mother was a grammar school teacher, Bonnie attends the University of South Carolina, enrolls in ROTC, majors in political affairs, plays on the tennis team, meets Bret in her second semester during SC/Clemson week, loves horror films, George Strait, Reba, and Lonestar, after Faulkner is born (age 18), she adopts Charleston Darrow, a year later she marries (age 19) Rex Kepler, an abusive husband who abandons her the following year, she then works part-time at the Columbia airport where she eventually meets and marries Chase Anderson, a commercial pilot with depression issues, a year ago (age 33) they die together in a plane crash at Lake Moultrie.

Charleston (Charlie) MacMillan (26): Born in Charleston, South Carolina, the illegitimate child of a pretty "white trash" trailer-park girl named Raven Darrow, who dies of an overdose, Charlie (age 10) is then adopted and raised as a daughter/sister by Bonnie MacMillan, whom she worships, Charlie is strikingly beautiful, with cropped dark hair, brown eyes, tall, graceful, and clothes conscious, she's also a loner, a rabid Southern rebel, fascinated with historical conspiracies, disliking Lincoln, disliking *all* Yankees, she joins the army after high school (age 18), does a six-year hitch, serves in Afghanistan as a non-combat communications specialist, then returns to West Columbia (age 24) where Bonnie had recently married Chase Anderson, Charlie enrolls at South Carolina, studies politics, and secures an internship at the State House, she's always been very close to Faulkner, who considers Charlie her "aunt," and they're both equally devastated by Bonnie's death in the airplane crash.

Faulkner MacMillan (17): Like her mother, blonde, green eyes, a bit taller and more stately but less athletic, like her aunt, she's much more fashion conscious than her mother, fun-loving yet academically-minded, born in West Columbia, South Carolina, she's the illegitimate daughter of Bonnie and Bret (me), raised by her single mom with the help of her "Aunt Charlie," who's really her adopted older sister, she grows up unaware of the identity of her birth-father, after her mother's death, despite her close relationship with her aunt, Faulkner decides to study abroad at St. Andrews, where, given a lifetime fascination with her Scot heritage, she decides to major in Scottish history, during her second month at university, her roommate Heather Sinclair introduces her to Gordon Carlyle.

Skye MacAllister MacDonald (35): Attractive, charming, with thick honey-reddish hair and brown eyes, a Highlander from the Island of Skye with a heavy accent, a highland dancer in her youth who's still a first-rate fiddle player who often wears MacAllister and Mac-Donald plaids and plays at local cèilidhs, she studied the fiddle with the great Buddy MacMaster on Cape Breton Island, she's very clever, adventurous, deductive, and a bit of a risk-taker, when she meets Bret at St. Andrews she's in the pre-med program, which is why their relationship ends when he returns to New Jersey, her hero is Arthur Conan Doyle, she reads lots of mysteries, after Bret leaves, she completes her medical training at the University of Edinburgh and becomes a highly-respected pathologist, marries (age 24) Angus MacDonald, a cardiologist, and eventually they move back to Fife, where they now live with their eight-year-old son Lachlan.

Wendy Parks (29): Personable, appealing, attractive, hard-working, preppy-dressing, Irish-Italian girl with cropped black hair from Staten Island, who went to Columbia for English and Emerson for publishing, eclectic tastes with a literary bent, interns at Writers House, then creates the Parks Literary Agency with three other young female agents, discovers and develops a deep bond with Marquita, lives in Manhattan, exercises at Flanagan's Annex, listens to Adele and Celine Dion, the Markie/Bret books are clearly her biggest successes, after Markie's death, she encourages Bret to continue writing, then, almost by accident, they fall into a relationship, which Bret found too uncomfortable so he broke things off about two weeks ago, although Wendy wasn't very happy about it.

Kyle Buchanan (32): Likeable and smart like his older brother, but more outgoing, engaged, and articulate, a very good husband and father, four years younger than Bret, looking a lot like him, dark hair, brown eyes, athletic, basketball, and tennis, after DePaul Diocesan High School, he goes to Rutgers for a BA in political philosophy, then a doctorate in constitutional law at Columbia, then Seton Hall for his law degree, a friend of Jack Colt, he's now the Head Prosecutor in Passaic County at the Paterson Courthouse, appointed by the governor on Colt's recommendation, married to his high school sweetheart (Angie), they have two mischievous twins (one of each), age three, he's renowned as both fair and honest, the best criminal lawyer in north Jersey.

Jack Colt (32): Legendary Paterson private detective, rescued the governor's kidnapped daughter two years ago, then unraveled the "Little Girl Killings," etc., 6'2", intimidating, taciturn, a New Jersey hard-ass, wise guy, tough guy, who wears his hair greased back, dresses like the mob, always wearing shades and a dark suit, went to DePaul Diocesan like the Buchanan brothers, played middle linebacker, went to Rutgers, then Seton Hall Law School in Newark, like Kyle, he's a former homicide prosecutor in Passaic County, a nocturnal, he likes Tasers, loves his Colt Python, drives a black Cadillac XTS, likes White Castle, Jersey diners, and Broadway Pizza.

Vincent (Vinny) Erickson (36): Elite NTSB air crash inspector, Bret's best friend from both grammar and high school, Irish/Italian, likeable, a bit overweight, thinning red hair, loses his parents in a plane crash (age 12), helps to raise his younger sister Rita, plays first base at DePaul, goes to Rensselaer Polytechnic for engineering, becomes a pilot, marries his high school prom date (Jenny), goes to flight school at Embry-Riddle, gets a PhD at MIT, travels to numerous crash sites, still living in Packanack with Jenny and their two sons.

Gordon Carlyle (19): A likeable archaeology major from the Highlands near Culloden, royal blood, supposedly descended from the Bruce, fearless, into martial arts combat and waterfall ice climbing, promises to give up the latter for Faulkner MacMillan.

Heather Sinclair (19): Faulkner's quirky cuteish college roommate, small, quiet, self-contented, from Hoy, an archaeology major who introduced Gordon to Faulkner, already somewhat of an expert on the Orkney ruins.

Chase Anderson (deceased, would be 34): Born the son of Mayor Virgil Anderson of Charleston, he enrolled at the Air Force Academy in Colorado (age 19), became a pilot despite depression issues, flew recon missions in Iraq, after being dumped by his Charleston fiancée, he completed his military service, began working for Delta Air Lines out of Atlanta until he was fired, takes a job with Carolina Air, a small regional company out of Columbia, South Carolina, where he meets Bonnie MacMillan, they decide to get married (age 31), despite Bonnie's efforts, his depressions accelerate, they die together in a plane crash a year ago near Lake Moultrie (age 33).

Irene Davis (32): Adulteress who miraculously survived a private plane crash in New Mexico and believes that the novel *Aircrash* is about her own personal experiences, an estate lawyer, she grew up and still lives in Delaware, after the novel's publication, she files multiple repeated lawsuits against Markie, then against Bret, each of which is thrown out of court, then she begins stalking Bret and hacking his computer, after Bret procures a restraining order, she seems to be leaving him alone.

VI.

CHRONOLOGY

Work out both your narrative and your backstories very carefully. Arthur Miller once said, "Begin at the end." Know where your narrative is going, and, of course, where it's already been. Also, it's a good time to begin creating useful and pertinent lists: realizations, revelations, suspects, detections, etc.

(Of course, I have *no* idea where I'm going!)

Chapter 31

Chronology/Backstory (Bret's POV)

The Chronology/Backstory

0   Born in the Bronx

4   Brother Kyle born

5   Reads Poe, visits Poe Cottage, reads Scott, etc.

6   Father dies, mother begins working for the US Post Office

8   Moves to Packanack Lake, into the "Jack Burke" house"

13-17   DePaul Diocesan High School

14   Injures left arm in the Bronx

15   Paternal grandmother dies in the Bronx, learns his father's secret

17-19   The University of South Carolina, meets Bonnie, who ends up pregnant and doesn't tell him

19-21   University of St. Andrews, Lit degree, dating Skye

21-23   Rutgers, MA Lit, publishes some short stories

23-25   Johns Hopkins, the Writing Seminars, meets Markie, publishes more short stories

25-26   Chesterfield Fellowship, lives in Malibu with Markie, they marry in San Juan, honeymoon on Cape Breton

26-31   University of Southern California, teaches part-time in the Filmic Writing Program, also teaches introductory fiction writing and helps Markie write *Aircrash*

31   Markie dies, *Aircrash* is published, very successful, Bret's mom dies in Packanack, he sells the film rights to *Aircrash*

32   Cape Breton Island, "to get away from everything," writes *Writing Fiction*, completes and edits Markie's *Radium Eyes*

33   *Radium Eyes* published under both of their names, writes the screenplay for *Aircrash*

34   Returns to Packanack Lake, lives anonymously in a small log cabin, *Radium Eyes* wins the Pulitzer Prize, he then writes the screenplay for *Radium Eyes*

35   Planning his own novels, but unmotivated, taking his time

36   The box arrives, he's shot in the shoulder, he involves Jack Colt, travels to South Carolina, then Scotland, then San Juan, where he attends the film version of *Aircrash* with Rosie, then he returns to New Jersey to write the book, *this* book, *now*

Chapter 32

Suspect List (so far, with commentary)

Faulkner: *It's hard to contemplate, but why not? She seemed perfectly lovely, perfectly stable, when we were sitting under the awning at Doll's House Café, but maybe, somewhere along the line, she figured out who I was and felt impelled to force some kind of "involvement" on my part, on the part of her totally uninvolved and seemingly anonymous father? In the moments after I was shot at my desk, while I was still bleeding from the wound and waiting for the Wayne police and the EMTs to arrive, I considered the possibility that maybe the bullet wasn't supposed to actually hit me. Maybe it was supposed to be a warning, a threat, a motivator, and that maybe the shooter shot me by accident. Whatever the case, I was still fully obligated to take the threat to my daughter seriously, and I'm fully aware that including anyone on this list, especially such a charming and seemingly innocent young woman like Faulkner, who is, after all, Bonnie's daughter and my own flesh and blood, is undeniably un-*

conscionable. Nevertheless I have to keep an open mind, both as the sap at the center of this ugly mess, and as the assigned chronicler of this ugly mess. I have to consider absolutely everyone, no matter how much I detest myself for doing so, especially because, in doing so, it implies that one of them, at best, is unstable, most likely deranged, even though no one on this list would ever seem, in any way possible, to fit that description. Excepting maybe Irene.

Charlie: *She's a bit quirky, right? Conspiracy theories and a pretty rough background. Ten years in a tin trailer with a junkie mom. After all, Charlie clearly believed that I'd abandoned the pregnant woman who eventually raised her, and that I'd also rejected Bonnie a second time, as recently as last year. Maybe she wants to punish me?*

Wendy: *An agent's biggest client refuses to write any more books, then he sleeps with her, then he rejects her.*

Skye: *Who knows what she's been thinking about for the past fifteen years? She was always fearless, always risk-craving, always a lover of mysteries, who now solves medical mysteries for a living as a distinguished pathologist. Maybe, like her fellow Scot Arthur Conan Doyle, she's decided to create a mystery and bring me back into her life. Of course, how could Skye have known about Faulkner when I didn't even know about her? I have no idea.*

Rosie: *Yes, even Rosie, which breaks my heart. Which is why I had to go to San Juan, in spite of all the awkwardness, to look into her lovely eyes and see if I could see anything besides the guilt of having betrayed her sister. For which maybe she blames me? Why not? I was more at fault anyway. I was her sister's husband, supposedly grieving. Like her. But grief, sorrow, and guilt can motivate pretty much anything, although, like Skye and most of the others on this list, I have no idea how she could have known about Faulkner. Which also makes me wonder if Markie somehow knew that I had a daughter. Which is a terrifying speculation. Utterly disturbing.*

Gordon: *Guys descended from the Bruce who climb up ice-covered water-falls don't mess around. The kid's clearly gone blotto over Faulkner, so maybe he's also gone nuts on me? With a sense of royal prerogative? Besides, it sounds like he was visiting NYC when I got myself shot.*

Kyle: *Totally ridiculous. Right?*

Irene: *She's been hounding me for years, even stalking me at one point, and she's also a lawyer and more than clever enough. She's also clearly nuts, but she's got, as far as I can tell, no apparent connection to South Carolina (my "daughter"), St. Andrews ("Scotland"), or San Juan ("Medical School"), all of which were referenced in the box-sender's note.*

Others: *Why not stretch things a bit more? Not that the preceding list isn't already perfectly preposterous. What about a past student? Or maybe a deranged reader of* Writing Fiction, *who's got nothing better to do than shoot the non-novel-writing author of a self-assured book about writing novels? Or what about some jackass Faulkner lover. After all, I got plugged, as instructed, while reading* Absalom. *Maybe he/she knew about the proposed "Faulkner wasn't really Faulkner" short story (although only a few of my old Hoppy classmates knew about that one). Or maybe he/she learned that I'd named my daughter Faulkner (which I hadn't), and he/she took offense. Or how about one of the Radium Girls' descendants whom Markie interviewed for the novel? Millie Rogers seemed to have a lot of personal issues and pent-up anger. Or maybe some cryogenics relative who read that I was planning to write a novel on the subject and didn't like the sound of it.*

The "Calais Coach" solution: *All of the above. Or several working in concert. Which is really as paranoid as I can get right now, even speculatively. Except for the final grouping down below.*

The dead: *Maybe Bonnie isn't dead. Maybe she survived the crash, swam to the far side of Lake Moultrie, and began plotting to make me write this stupid novel. Or maybe, (God forgive me) it wasn't Marquita that we buried in San Juan. Or maybe (God forgive me) it's all been perpetrated by Mary "Mollie" Buchanan, my own wonderful mother, who'd always encouraged my writerly aspirations. Maybe she faked her death, even though I saw her lying dead in her coffin, waited five years in hiding, then initiated a crackpot scheme to introduce me to my "I-never-even-knew-she-existed" daughter and force me to write a bloody novel.*

I'm completely crapped out.

(Ignore all the above.)

VII.

PLOT: DETAILED OUTLINE

Human beings are the story-telling animals. The "story-loving" animals. Remember: Plot is *everything*. Also, once you've ascertained your pov, make your life easier and write the first line of every chapter.

Chapter 33

The Novel-In-Progress

Thursday, October 25

Writer's block is a load of crap.

As made perfectly clear in *Writing Fiction*.

I also don't believe in farmer's block, fisherman's block, or plumber's block.

"Hey, honey, call the office today and tell them I won't be coming in."

"What should I tell them, hon?"

"Just tell them I'm blocked. They'll understand."

Anyone, of course, can have periods of physical, mental, or emotional debilitation in their lives, but generally speaking, writers write, farmers farm, fisherman fish, and plumbers plumb.

A death in the family, physical trauma/illness, a debilitating break up, etc., can knock anyone out of action for a while, which is perfectly understandable, but that's *not* "writer's block," which is, as Webster defines it:

> *The problem of not being able to think of something to write about or not being able to finish writing a story, poem, etc.*

If you can't think of something to write about, then you're not a *real* writer anyway, and if you can't finish writing something you've started, then you're not a *real* writer either.

Which, of course, is what everyone assumed about me.

"That poor sap hasn't written anything since *Radium Eyes* three years ago [which I didn't write anyway]. I guess he's got writer's block."

Which wasn't true.

I remember one particularly ugly piece in the *Huffington Post* entitled something like, "What's Bret Buchanan Up To? Nothing!" claiming that I was essentially a fraud who was living off the royalties of my wife's two novels, which was true, and that I was "apparently incapable of sitting down at a keyboard and typing out a single sentence," which wasn't true at all.

During the past four years, I'd written a textbook and two screenplays, and I've had loads of novel ideas. Any day of any week, I could have sat down at my computer and written whatever I wanted to write. But I didn't *want* to.

It's that simple.

Yeah, I did some planning, some organizing, for both the cryogenics novel-idea and the Tylenol novel-idea, but I much preferred to read and/or reread stuff like Homer, the Brontës, the Russians, Camões, the guy from Stratford, Dickens, Macdonald, Borges, Faulkner, and, of course, most recently, Dante.

> *[Note to the Box-Sender: If you're doing this just to get me to write my own novel, it's not really necessary. I can write anytime I want, and the novels would have come in time.]*

For the past nineteen days, I've been writing the mandated novel. The first nine days, as per *Writing Fiction*, were spent organizing my notes, doing research, conjuring up a short temporary outline, prepping the settings, then writing the character list, the character bios, the chronology/backstory, and the suspects list. As of today, sitting at my computer desk, right next to my reading-and-writing desk (where I was shot a month ago), I've completed 194 pages in Word, averaging approximately fifteen pages a day.

I suppose that might seem like a lot of pages to some people, but I've been writing in one way or another ever since I was five years old, and, once I'm organized, I move very quickly. As instructed by the box-sender, I'm doing *everything* in accord with the Novel section of *Writing Fiction*. It's impossible to know exactly what I'm supposed to include (reprint) from the book (if anything), so I've decided to give short little summaries, based on the original text, of each major topic, except for the first. "Premise." Since the book, of necessity, begins with "Premise," and since it's not *my* premise, I felt that it was too awkward to give a little summary from the textbook on the very first page.

So here it is.

Belatedly:

The premise is everything! If you don't have a uniquely interesting premise, don't bother to write a single word, scrap the whole project, and eat some pizza. As W. D. Snodgrass once said, "Why should anyone read my poems if they're not interesting? They can go watch a movie instead, or make love, or have a delicious meal."

That would *still* be my advice to any would-be aspiring writer, but since *I* didn't pick the premise of this ridiculous book, I wasn't convinced that it was a good one:

A man is forced to write a novel about writing a novel about being forced to write a novel.

Hell, I don't think I would *ever* write a book about something like that!

Nevertheless, I've got no choice, so I'm doing it anyway.

As best I can.

Right now.

Which leads to another question: what exactly *am* I writing? It's not really a novel, right? It's some kind of non-fiction, which, when you think about it, seems to defeat the box-sender's overriding objective, to get me to write a novel.

Which leads to another obvious problem: naming the characters. Normally, I very much enjoy conjuring the names for my fictional characters, and I keep long lists of my favorite names: first, last, male, female, Italian, Hispanic, Irish, Scot, Portuguese, Polish, Jewish, Japanese, etc. But what am I supposed to do with the names in *this* book? Make up bogus names for the characters, who are, after all, real people? Or simply use their real names?

Which risks, in some cases, as with Irene Davis, future lawsuits?

Regardless, I've decided, at least for now, to use the real names. I don't think most of them would mind if they knew the awkward and threatening circumstances under which this book is being written.

Maybe I'm naïve.

Which leads to yet another problem: revealing real stuff about real people. For example, when the book is published, everyone will know that my father was an adulterer, that I got a young girl pregnant eighteen years ago and didn't know about it, that Irene Davis is a certified lunatic (maybe, from a legal point-of-view, I should rephrase that?), that Rex Kepler was an abusive husband, that Rosie Cabrera kissed her messed-up brother-in-law on the same day as her sister's burial, etc.

Screw it.

Screw everything.

There's a rifle barrel pointing at my daughter in one of the photos.

Everything else can be damned.

[Note to the Box-Sender: Did you consider any of this stuff? More instructions would have been helpful.]

Now, regarding "modus operandi," which it seems the box-sender wants delineated as well:

I'm nocturnal.

I wake up every day at noon, walk over to my large window, and gratefully look outside. Looking at beautiful Packanack Lake (although not the lake itself), which is lovely in every possible kind of weather, seeing a few neighboring houses, but mostly trees and leaves, which are now turning to yellows, reds, and burnt oranges before my eyes. Along with some striking patches of the dark blue sky.

I'm dressed in my everyday work outfit: navy Everlast t-shirt, navy Russell sweatshorts, white cotton socks, and an old beat-up ten-year-old max-comfort pair of Rockports. Since it's now late October, I'll soon be substituting my navy Champion sweatpants and my black "USCinema-Television" sweatshirt.

Then I flip on the computer and prep my breakfast: oatmeal with bran, which initiates every single day of my life, even when I'm traveling, along with a huge glass of Crystal Light, combining Lemon, Peach Tea, and Grape flavors.

Next, while enjoying my breakfast, I check my emails, Google ESPN, and check several of the news sites to make sure I'm not missing anything important.

After cleaning my cereal bowl, I read over my outline for the upcoming chapter, check relevant notes, and start typing. Since I'm convinced that one's creative output is directly dependent on one's sodium intake, I keep a forty-ounce bag of Chex nearby, for occasional reanimating handfuls, and since I also believe that every human being should be rewarded for work accomplished, I place a single York peppermint patty, one of the smaller ones from the family-size bag, at the edge of my desk, motivating me forward.

Nearby, on my non-computer desk, my "shot-in-the-shoulder" desk, Willie Mays, Edgar Allan Poe, and Roberto Clemente bobbleheads keep a close eye on things.

It was two years ago, when I finally realized that it was a bit embarrassing, (although, apparently, "cool" in other ways), that a thirty-four-year-old man should have a collection of two hundred silly baseball bobbleheads, all MLB Hall of Famers. My first bobble, bought in the Bronx when I was four years old, on the advice of my ever-wise mother, was Willie Mays. I still keep the other one (Roberto) because he reminds me of Markie, who like everyone else in Puerto Rico, reveres the memory of the great right fielder. Most probably the second best of all time, after Babe Ruth, and certainly in the top three with Hank Aaron.

Nevertheless, as mentioned, it was getting a bit embarrassing, so when Kyle and Angie had the twins, who would obviously grow up to be sports fanatics, I gave them my entire collection, minus two, and minus my EAP outlier.

I'm not sure that Angie was pleased.

"They can go down in the basement with your brother," she said.

Meaning they were all relegated to the basement, where Kyle kept his office and his fifty-five-inch sports screen, where we often watched the Mets and the Giants together, while the twins toddled around trying to reach up to the shelves so they could smash, dismember, and decapitate the various Hall of Famers, who'd been valued at over $30,000.

"Maybe we could sell them to some other man-child," Angie once suggested, "and buy someone's wife a new car."

Normally, on a typical writing day, I'll go right through the allotted pages. Maybe thirteen or so. Then I'll go back over them very carefully, expanding a bit, until I've ended up with about fifteen or so. Then I check the clock and it's usually somewhere between 5:00 and 7:00, so I eat my York, put on my New Balance sneaks, and jog around the lake, listening to one of my several hundred pre-prepared tapes.

The Stones, Springsteen, La India, Jones, Sinatra, etc.

Yeah, I still use a Walkman.

Deal with it.

Running around (or walking around) the lake is a way of life at Packanack. When the weather's good, hundreds of Packanackers, of all ages, circumnavigate the lake, enjoying the views, getting some exercise, and waving to friends. When the weather's excessively nasty, I go over to LA Fitness in Preakness and do some elliptical.

From where I call for pick-up.

In California, Markie used to cook some yummy stuff sometimes, and I did as well on rare occasions. Mostly soups and Italian. But ever since her death, both up in Canada and down here in Packanack, I haven't bothered to cook for just me.

Besides, New Jersey is a culinary paradise. So I'll call up Positano's for some baked ziti, or Zorba's for a gyro, or Vinni's for a pepperoni pie, or maybe stop at Five Guys (like tonight) for a burger, or Firehouse Subs for a smokehouse beef & cheddar brisket, or maybe even a Macs, or a BK, or a Subway, or Jersey Mike's, or any of the other gastronomical ecstasies readily available in the Garden State.

Then I'll sit down in the main room of the cabin, surrounded with its old log walls, facing my Samsung twenty-five-inch TV screen which sits right in front of the stone fireplace, and watch my already DVR'd *PTI* (*Pardon the Interruption*) while eating my supper. When I'm finished, even though I know I shouldn't, I'll have two Entenmann's devil's food frosted donuts (chocolate inside-and-out), or two black-and-whites from the Packanack Bakery, or two packs of Tastykake butterscotch cream-filled krimpets.

Then I'll get back to work.

Carefully re-editing the day's fifteen or so pages, and then reading over my notes for the next day's session. Then it's time to anesthetize my brains with DVR'd TV shows, movies, or sporting events, like my five favorite football teams or the World Series or NASCAR.

Back in the halcyon days before the box arrived, I would spend several evenings a week at Kyle's, or Vinny's, or hanging out with my Wayne or Rutgers buddies, or heading into the city to meet with Wendy and/or my multifarious writer friends, or going to concerts at the Garden, NJPAC, the Newton, or MPAC. Like Mariza, Clare Bowen, Linda Eder, Toby Keith, Roger McGuinn, or John Fogerty. But that's all over now. At least, it's in abeyance.

Nothing, of course, will keep me from finishing this novel and handing it to Wendy on December 12th.

As of today, I'm ahead of schedule.

Feeling good.

Chapter 34

The Peninsula Bridges

Friday, October 26

"**I**t's a matter of intent."

He spoke a bit wearily, having said it more than a few times before.

I'd just run around the lake, still sweating, and was now sitting next to the billion-year-old priest who'd been my mother's confident and confessor. Even though I don't believe she ever had anything to actually confess. Alistair Ferguson, Priestly Fraternity of St. Peter, who'd looked a billion when I first met him in the Bronx when I was around five years old, probably *really was* a billion years old by now.

We were sitting at the north end of the lake on a white wooden bench, with the two peninsula bridges behind us, facing the blueness of the lake beneath a late afternoon's bluish-gray October sky.

A few disoriented ducks were wandering around, doing whatever ducks do. Creating ambience, I suppose.

"We've been over this a million times before, Bret."

Actually, we'd been over it three times before. When I was fifteen and discovered my old man's adultery, when I got married and wondered if it was time to come clean about it, and right after my mother died.

"Detraction," he reiterated, "is an offence against the truth, which, as the catechism makes perfectly clear, is a matter of intent."

When I was fifteen, I'd memorized Fr. Hardon's dictionary definition, and I still remembered it:

> *Revealing something about another that is true but harmful to that person's reputation.*

Well, let's face it, it was perfectly obvious that the old man was dead, but he still maintained a reputation of sorts.

Father F. opened his catechism. I guess he already knew what I wanted when I called him in the Bronx, so he must have grabbed his book before he drove out to New Jersey. Then he read out loud, what I'd already read many times before:

> *A person is guilty of detraction if he, without objectively valid reason, discloses another's faults and failings to persons who did not know them.*

"Yeah," I said, "so is *knowing* the truth a valid enough reason? Maybe detraction's a technical violation of the truth, not to mention justice, but don't some people have the *right* to know the truth?"

Even as I was saying it, it sounded flimsy, unsubstantial.

Not to mention self-important.

Look, all I really wanted to know was whether I should tell my brother that his father was a scumbag. As a corollary, I also wanted to know if I'd violated my own mother's trust by, in essence, deceiving her for the last twenty-one years of her life.

By burning my old man's disgusting emails and keeping the whole ugly mess to myself.

Maybe some people wouldn't think that detraction is anywhere as serious as calumny, defamation, libel, slander, or even premature judgement. But not the old guy sitting next to me on the wooden bench with the catechism in his hands. And I, of course, fully respected his opinion. Detraction's serious stuff, always considered a mortal violation. Look, even though I'm hardly some kind of holy-roller (actually what I *really* am is much-too-long-lapsed), I still wanted to do whatever was right, especially regarding Kyle. Especially since it was too late for my mother.

If I'm obligated to continue to keep my mouth shut, fine. I can always go back and edit the old man's adultery out of this stupid book (out of this stupid chapter as well), but I needed some kind of guidance.

I needed to decide.

Time was running out.

"All right, Father," I tried, "let me hit you with another quote from Fr. Hardon."

Whom I knew he respected.

Implicitly.

Which I then recited from memory:

No one is bound to reveal the truth to someone who does not have the right to know it.

"Well," I said, "does Kyle have 'the right to know it,' or doesn't he?"

Then he said exactly what I knew he'd say.

"You know I can't tell you that, Bret. It's a vague-ary. A matter of conscience. And it's *your* conscience, not mine."

I laughed.

"Vague-ary? Is that a word?"

He laughed too.

"You're a great help," I said, frustratedly, which was something less than a compliment.

"And you're a perfect pain in the ass, Bret. Maybe if you went to Mass every once in a while, you'd know what the hell you're doing with your life."

"You're right, I have no idea what I'm doing with my life. Besides, I'm re-reading Dante."

Which I said as though it explained everything.

"Reading the Florentine can be a good thing."

I waited for his "or."

"Or a bad thing."

"That sounds like a vague-ary to me."

He laughed again.

The truth is, I loved the old guy. I loved what he'd done for my mother, I loved his unqualified admiration for Markie, and I loved his better-than-Jesuit intellectual acumen, but he was never one for taking his charges by the hand.

"You're a smart boy, Bret," he'd said the last time we talked about it. "*You* figure it out."

Which was no help at all.

Which was exactly his point.

"Two weeks ago," I explained, "I was standing in the antechamber of hell, looking at Celestine, and thinking that maybe I should be down there with the Sicilian since I'm also a coward and an equivocator."

I was, of course, exaggerating a bit, but, first, the old priest wanted to clear up some historical wrangling.

"If saintly Celestine's in hell, then we're all headed to a very hot place," he pointed out. "The reason that he vacated the papacy in 1294 – *il gran rifiuto* – was to return to the ascetic life, and the reason, as you well know, smartypants, that Dante seems to have placed him where he placed him in the antechamber of hell is because Celestine's so-called "refusal," his retiring from the papacy, led directly to the disastrous papacy of Boniface VIII, whom Dante, as a loyal Florentine, fully detested."

"Yeah," I agreed.

Since I was getting nowhere fast, I tried again.

"Then, the next day, I was standing within the eighth circle, in the sixth bolgia, staring at Caiaphas, crucified and staked to the ground, *crucifisso in terra con tre pali*, and I was thinking, hell, (no pun intended), who *isn't* a hypocrite?"

"That's a bit over-dramatic, Bret, even for you."

"Well, everyone seems to think I'm some kind of Pulitzer Prize winner, even though I didn't write the damn thing, and everyone seems to think I'm some kind of reasonably decent guy, but I just sit on my ass in my log cabin all day and read about Jane Eyre, and Vasco da Gama, and the good king Macbeth."

"Where should I start?" he started, clearly frustrated.

But I cut him off.

"Look, I look at my own brother, and I see a guy who runs the entire Passaic County court system, treats his wife like the Queen of Sheba, plays on the front lawn with his little kids, runs something called the North Jersey Twins Club, sits on the board of all kinds of do-gooder stuff, including the American Cancer Society, and even has time every Sunday to play tennis with two mentally-diminished twin girls who can't even keep score."

"It sounds like someone is feeling sorry for himself."

"Is that what it sounds like? I don't think so. To me, it sounds like the truth."

He sat up straight.

Fr. Ferguson was smallish, thinish, virtually indestructible, with an inexplicable shock of wavy white hair above his craggy old face. Whenever Fr. F. sat-up-straight, it meant that he was ready to set someone else straight.

Meaning me, of course.

"First of all, you *did* write your fair share of that book. Both of them in fact. Marquita told me *all* about it, rather explicitly, that you gave her the ideas for both of the books, that you drew up a long and detailed outline for each of them, and that you assiduously edited the first book, or, as Marquita put it, you 'edited the daylights out of it.' Then, as we both well know, you actually finished the second book and edited the daylights out of that one, too. Markie, of course, had wanted co-authorship on the plane crash book, and when you wouldn't agree, we both know what she wrote in the dedication."

Dedicated to Bret Buchanan, the love of my life, who wrote most of this book.

"We also know that she gave you no choice on the second book, arranging with both her agent and her publisher to have the book published with *both of you* listed as co-authors. So maybe you should just honor your wife's wishes and get over yourself."

No vague-aries there.

"Which I'm trying to do," I tried rather weakly. "But there's no denying that Markie wrote the book. She wrote both of the books, in fact."

He ignored me, as if I was the least significant of the meandering ducks.

I responded in kind, by ignoring the fact that he was ignoring me.

"Second?" I insisted, knowing that Fr. F. never had a "first of all" without, at least, having a "second."

"Second of all," he continued, "I happen to know that you donate almost all of the royalties to charity."

"How could you possibly know that?"

I was astonished, even slightly irritated, but he just looked at me like I was an idiot.

Of course, Kyle had probably told him.

Even though I'd told him not to tell *anyone.*

"Well," I qualified, "it's a lazy man's charity anyway. It's not exactly like I'm working in a soup kitchen. I pass along money that I don't deserve, with negligible effort."

"Not to the family in Bolivia that's getting food to eat."

I had no smartass answer for that one.

So we sat in the silence for a moment, but he was never silent for long.

"Are you always," he wondered, "so hard on yourself? Or is it just when you're with me."

"I save the best for you."

He laughed, and I explained:

"You're the only one I can complain to. New Jersey guys aren't allowed to complain. Except about taxes and traffic."

He shrugged.

"You've managed to wear out an eighty-three-year-old man," he said with a smile. "Are you proud of yourself?"

"Is that all you are? Just eighty-three?"

He laughed again.

He had a great laugh.

"There's something else, Father."

"Fine," he shrugged, "here we go again."

I turned on the bench and looked directly into his ancient blue eyes.

"I have a daughter."

Chapter 35

"Amada Amante"

Saturday, October 27

I was on a two-day "Markie break."

(With the exception of my bench-talk with Fr. F.)

I felt I deserved it. The so-called novel was moving along nicely, even though I had no idea where it was going, and I had every confidence that it would be finished in time.

So why not remember?

Why not relive?

If only within my mind.

Back in our Malibu days, every couple of months, Markie would suddenly decide:

"Let's have a Puerto Rican film festival this weekend!"

Adding:

"And let's have a Puerto Rican *music* festival, too!"

I suppose she was feeling lonely for the island.

So we'd set two days aside, prep the Miramelinda Rum Punch Sangria, which was apparently invented at Casa Lola, a restaurant in the Condado district of San Juan, consisting of a secret combination of sangria, Bacardi's Big Apple, and fresh fruit juices. Of course, Rosie was old pals with the head chef at Casa Lola, and she'd finagled to get the secret formula for Markie. Then we'd buy two gallons of raspberry ice cream, Markie's favorite, order Domino's pizza, pepperoni, black olives, with green peppers, then sit in our huge bed, propped with pillows, watching:

The Road to Rio, 1947, the fifth of the seven Crosby-Hope-Lamour road pictures, to catch the brief, uncredited, almost momentary, non-speaking appearance of Marquita Rivera, the "Queen of Latin Rhythm," born in Fajardo. The "Latin Hurricane." Who was Markie's namesake, who was the first Puerto Rican to sign a Hollywood contract, who caused a sensation at the 1939 New York World's Fair performing for King George VI. Later, she did Carnegie, the Paramount, the Roxy, the Apollo, and Radio City Music Hall, sharing stages with the likes of Sinatra, Ella, Ann Miller, Kathryn Grayson, and Betty Hutton.

Cyrano de Bergerac, 1950, staring the great Ferrer, born in San Juan, the first Puerto Rican Oscar winner.

West Side Story, 1957, featuring a Greek-American as a very convincing cool-as-humanly-possible Bernardo, the leader of the Nuyorican Sharks, with the lovely Russian-American Natalie Wood as Maria, with, most important of all, the "real deal" and always marvelous Rita Moreno, born in Humacao, Puerto Rico, as Anita, for which she won an Oscar.

Traffic, 2000, the hard-hitting badass drug film, seemingly a bit out of Markie's usual wheelhouse, except for the fact that it featured her favorite actor, Benicio del Toro, born in San Juan, who also won an Oscar.

Maid in Manhattan, 2002, Markie's favorite movie of all-time, featuring Jaylo, born in the Bronx, as Marisa, a modern-day Cinderella, who arrives alone at an upscale reception at the Met, looking far-beyond-stunning in a pearl-pink, strapless, floor-length chiffon gown, designed by Albert Wolsky, with her hair up, perfect earrings, and a Harry Winston wreath necklace.

> *MARISA*
> *(to the soon-to-be-senator)*
> *I only came to tell you that "this" – you and me –*
> *can't go anywhere beyond this evening. It just can't.*

> *CHRISTOPHER*
> *Then you should have worn a different dress.*

"The best dress in the history of the universe," Markie would whisper, as if to avoid disturbing the movie she'd already seen over twenty-five times.

I couldn't disagree, as we watched the hotel maid slow dance with the famous politician to a moody Glenn Lewis version of "Fall Again."

As Markie would hold me tight.

Which was fine with me.

Later, when Jaylo cried on the swings in the Bronx, Markie would hold me even tighter. Later, when Ty, Marisa's young son, comes up behind his mother in their kitchen, while she's preparing supper at the stove, gently putting his arms around his mother's waist to comfort her, Markie would pretty much cut off my circulation.

Almost crying.

Not quite.

Misty-eyed.

One time she said:

"You know what I think about sometimes?"

Which, of course, was one of those not-to-be-answered questions, so I waited, and she told me:

"I think about the four of us, when we were younger, all living in the Bronx at the same time, during those summers when I'd visit Aunt Mariana."

"Four?"

"Of course, silly boy, you, me, and the two Boricuas."

I waited for clarification.

"Jaylo and La India!"

I'd never thought about it before, and I wasn't sure if the dates worked out, but who cares?

"Of course."

In between movie screenings, there was lots of music. La India, naturally. And Eddie Santiago, "Livin' la Vida Loca," Feliciano, etc. One time, in the midst of one of those weekends, we got to talking about music, and I decided to put her on the spot:

"All right, pal, list me the very best singers in the world."

Meaning the *best*, not just her personal favorites.

"Alive?"

"Yeah."

She didn't hesitate. Not a second.

"La India, Mariza, Ana Gabriel, and Soledad."

Which seemed rather prejudicial.

"Yeah," I said, "that's not biased at all. Nothing but females, all of whom are either Hispanic or Portuguese."

She thought it over for a mini-moment, then amended her list.

"Feliciano."

Well, at least the other gender finally made the cut.

"What about dead ones?" I asked, given that she'd already raised the "dead or alive" issue.

For this one, which was apparently exceedingly difficult, she lay back into the pillows and covered her eyes with her hands. As if to think better. As if her life depended on it.

Then she finally sat up in bed with her final answer:

"Amália Rodrigues, Clara Nunes, Piaf, and Judy Garland."

Well, it was nice to see an American getting on board, but once again it seemed more than a bit gender-biased.

"There's not a guy in sight!"

"Boys get muscles; girls get pretty voices."

Which settled it.

When *Maid in Manhattan* had reached its Cinderella conclusion/denouement, she stood up immediately and blasted "*No Me Ames*," the lovely-mushy *salsa monga* sung by Marc Anthony and Jaylo back when they were falling in love. It was one of Markie's favorite songs, and I liked it too, even though I had no idea what the lyrics were about, even though I'd read several English translations.

When it was over, like clockwork, she'd play "*Amada Amante*," Marc Anthony's beautiful cover of the already-beautiful Roberto Carlos song.

"Dance with me, Jersey."

As always, I obeyed her command and held her close, not fully understanding what those lyrics meant either, except for the title/refrain, which was more than enough: "*Amada Amante, Amada Amante*."

"Beloved lover, beloved lover."

"Can I be your Senator?" I kidded.

"If I can be your hotel maid and wear that amazing chiffon dress."

Later, closer to bedtime, she put on La India's seductive "*Sedúceme*," dancing in place in front of me, moving her hips almost imperceptively, saying:

"Let's make some babies."

So I hung around my cabin for two full days, watched the same exact movies, listened to the same exact songs, and broke my stupid heart over and over again.

Which I suppose (these memories) all sound a bit too good to be true.

Maybe they are.

Maybe they're the pathetically glossed-up memories of a lonely still-youngish widower, but I don't think so.

We were young back then. We were in love, and we were living in a small cottage on the Malibu Cliffs. Yes, maybe Marquita seems too good to be true, but that's *exactly* what I was thinking back then, and what I'm *still* thinking right now, five years after her senseless death. If it seems in some way unlikely or contrived, or some kind of "romance novel" crap, I couldn't care less.

Markie was perfectly remarkable. She might have looked like the highest maintenance female on the planet, but she was, in reality, *always* easy, *always* loving, entirely maintenance-free.

What we had back then is something that I'd wish for everyone. (Even the damned box-sender.) It's also something that I'll never get back again, something that I'll never come close to experiencing again.

My cell buzzed.

"What the hell happened over there!"

It was Charlie, angry as hell, as I re-entered the real world.

Four weeks ago, when I returned to New Jersey from San Juan, I called up Charlie and told her about my meeting with Faulkner at the Doll's House. About how lovely Faulkner was. About giving her the teddy bear. About how much she was missing her aunt. About the fact that I'd decided that it wasn't the right time to tell her the truth.

That I was her father.

All of which Charlie had all been fine with.

"What's wrong?"

"She's missing."

"What? What do you mean 'she's missing'?"

"I haven't heard from her in two days, and she's not responding to my texts or my emails or my phone messages."

I tried to sound unconcerned.

"She's probably off with some of her friends."

Actually, I was *extremely* concerned. After all, this was a young girl living, completely unaware, under a death threat, and I was actually in possession of a photograph with a rifle barrel pointing at her face.

We talked a bit, and I managed to get Charlie to calm down.

She'd been trying to contact Faulkner's roommate with no response, and she'd also called their Dean's Court residence a number of times, but no one seemed to know where Faulkner was. She'd also tried, unsuccessfully, to locate a phone number for Heather's parents in the Orkneys.

Eventually, I managed to convince Charlie that I'd done nothing wrong in Scotland, nothing that could have caused a problem, but she was still terrified.

So was I.

"Look, I'll go back over there," I said.

She seemed astonished. Both astonished that I'd offered, and astonished that I'd just get-up-and-go.

But, let's face it, I was a sometimes writer, with no real job, with far more money than I needed.

"Would you do that, Bret?"

"Of course."

She seemed reassured, and she thanked me.

I hung up, called MacMaster, and left him a message:

"This is Bret Buchanan. Faulkner seems to be missing. I'll be there tomorrow afternoon."

Then I called Delta.

Chapter 36

The Kirkwall Hotel

Sunday, October 28

E veryone was twentyish, drunk, and having a good time.

I was none of those things.

It's called the Fusion Nightclub, but it seemed more like a large-and-loud kids' bar, located somewhere in Kirkwall, the capital of the Orkneys in the high North Sea. Which, according to my hotel's travel brochure, was founded by Norse invaders over a thousand years ago, then gifted, along with the entire Orkney archipelago, over seventy islands, to the Scots in 1469 as part of the dowry of Princess Margaret of Denmark when she married King James II of Scotland.

Not a bad wedding gift.

The Orkneys were also, as I remembered from reading the novel when I was a kid, the place where "cursed" Victor Frankenstein came to create a mate for his monster, before thinking better of the idea.

A few hours ago, in the early evening, I got off a Delta flight in Edinburgh and called up MacMaster.

"We think she's with Heather, the roommate," he said. "Up in the Orkneys somewhere. Maybe at Heather's place."

"Any idea what's going on?"

"Not really. We've talked to several of the students who live at Dean's Court, and they have no idea. Maybe it's something to do with all the archaeological sites in Orkney. Maybe it's a classroom assignment of some kind."

"Is Gordon with them?"

"I believe he is."

"Why wouldn't they respond to texts? Or emails?"

I could sense his shrug over the phone.

"Let's just say that Wi-Fi's a bit iffy in some parts of the islands. Even the cell service isn't very good. But I'm thinking that it might not be that complicated. Maybe they're just being kids and getting away from everything for a few days."

"I hope so."

"We do, as well."

I flew to Kirkwall in an excessively vibrating prop, settled into my little room at the Kirkwall Hotel, and watched the fishing ships returning to the harbor in the twilight. Then I roamed around the town, showing everyone Faulkner's photo without any luck.

I finished my drink, a third whiskey sour, trying to ignore the flashing lights, the much-too-loud rock music, which I could neither identify nor distinguish. But the kids seemed to be having fun, although it was getting closer and closer to getting rowdy, and I felt certain that more than a few fights had erupted on the Fusion's overcrowded dance floor.

As if conjured from the non-thinking part of my jet-lagged brain, I wondered if I should call Skye, assuming, of course, that everything was all right with Faulkner. It would be nice to see her again, if "nice" is the operative word.

Even if it might be inappropriate.

For far too long, I thought about her smile, her scent, her silly green scrubs. Then I stood up and went back to my hotel room to sleep it off.

Chapter 37

Rackwick Bay

Monday, October 29

T his time I was sitting in Bothy Bar, which was much more my speed, after a long and somewhat promising day. Then unexpectedly, amazingly, Charlie MacMillan walked through the front door of the pub.

Everyone stopped.

Everyone looked.

With good reason. She looked incredible. She looked like the kind of woman you *had* to look at.

Earlier that day, I'd taken the ferry across the sound to the Island of Hoy, heading for the home of Heather Sinclair. MacMaster texted me the names of her parents, Kathleen and Graham, and I'd decided to show up unannounced.

Hoy, which apparently means "high island," is extremely remote, sparsely inhabited, bleak, desolate, and windy, with endless rolling moors and darkish bogs and high rugged cliffs over the ocean.

It was also the site of the "never-ending battle" from the great Norse saga between King Hogni and Prince Heoden, who'd kidnapped the King's daughter Hildr. After a brutally bloody battle, Hildr managed to somehow incant all of the dead back to life, so that they could, naturally, start slaughtering each other all over again, which continues, over and over, forever and ever, until Ragnarök.

All of which was explained to me in gory detail by Thor, the young kid with the extremely impressive first name whom I'd hired at the dock to drive me around Hoy in his father's muddy Land Rover.

On today's overcast afternoon, there were no Norse armies roaming around Hoy. As a matter of fact, ever since we'd left the harbor, I'd seen exactly *no one*, just tons of whirling seabirds over the coast, as we headed to Rackwick Bay.

"You know the Sinclairs?" I asked.

"Aye, a bit."

"Do you know if Heather's at home?"

"Not that I've seen."

We drove through the gray afternoon, beneath the dark gray sky, above the darker gray sea. It was like a postcard from the Orkneys. Beautiful, atmospheric, stark, and ever-so-lonely.

We talked about the island, the Picts, the Danes, the Vikings, and the Celts, but mostly about young Thor, who was only fourteen years old, but driving anyway, keeping his ever-alert eyes focused on the narrow roadways of Hoy.

When we came over a rise, both the valley and the bay, with dramatic high cliffs, lay before us. Accompanied by the sound of pounding waves. Eventually, Thor pulled over his Rover, alongside a low stone wall that led to a completely isolated stone house with, what looked like to me, being a guy from New Jersey, a thatched roof.

What's called a croft house.

"Here it be."

I got out of the Rover and walked to the front door, feeling rather exposed, feeling as if this might be a good place to get shot a second time.

Kathleen Sinclair came to the door.

No, Heather wasn't home today, but she'd been here yesterday. With two of her friends.

She was kind, extremely welcoming, and I agreed to come inside for tea.

"Do you know what they're doing?" I asked. "Faulkner's aunt is *very* concerned."

Which concerned Kathleen.

"Oh, they're just taking a break, visiting the Quoyness Cairn at Sanday. It's a special interest of Heather's."

Finally, I was able to relax a bit.

It seemed that everything was all right, but after traveling over 3,000 miles, on what now seemed to have been a fool's errand, I wasn't about to go back to New Jersey without actually seeing and talking to Faulkner.

Over tea, Kathleen and I talked about the kids, not that I knew very much, about Hoy, "You *have* to stop at St. John's Head," and about Sanday Island, the cairns, and the brochs. In the meantime, I ate two indescribable blueberry scones.

Then I left for the Rover.

"My Graham'll be sorry he's missed you," she said at the door.

"I'm sorry as well."

Apparently, he was off hunting something somewhere, which he'd done on several previous occasions with Gordon, whom both parents liked quite a bit.

Who knows? Maybe they wished that he was interested in Heather?

But I never sensed any kind of antipathy towards Faulkner. On the contrary, Kathleen had called her "lovely," "special," "wonderful," and a "blessing."

Which made me feel proud, even though I'd done absolutely *nothing* to contribute to the young girl's life or her upbringing or what she'd become. Regardless, it was still nice to hear such things, and equally nice to know that Faulkner's best friend had such a nice mother.

I waved goodbye and wondered if they had many visitors out here.

Probably not.

Certainly not from New Jersey.

Thor wheeled me up the coast to get a close look at the cliffs at St. John's Head, being the highest vertical ocean-cliffs in Great Britain, being, as Thor explained, "exactly 350 meters high," meaning well over a thousand feet, and every bit as impressive as it sounds.

Then he drove me down to see the Man of Hoy, a very peculiar, one-of-a–kind vertical rock formation that loomed above the western coast, above the ocean, which was, apparently, the main tourist attraction on the island, even though I never saw any tourists.

"Climbers come here to climb it sometimes," Thor pointed out, and I wondered if Gordon had climbed to the top.

When we got back to the harbor, I slipped Thor a ridiculous tip, and he gave me a ton of thank yous. Then I caught the ferry back to the main island, where I immediately made arrangements for my trip tomorrow to Sanday Island.

Then I came to Bothy Bar.

Where I was relaxing in their comfortable pub, with its fired-up fireplace, handsome wooden bar, multiple rye-and-gingers, and excellent North Ronaldsay lamb stew. The place had an old-time/old-world atmosphere, with lots of black-and-white photos of hard-working locals on the walls, and a very quiet and likeable clientele, entirely local. Needless to say, I was feeling pretty good, much relieved after talking to Kathleen Sinclair, and, if everything went well tomorrow, I could expect to be back at my writing desk within two days.

Besides, I was way ahead of schedule anyway.

Then the Carolina girl walked into Bothy Bar. As if from another planet. Wearing a classic, vintage, though, I'm certain, designer "1940's" navy skirt with a button-up mustard-yellow knit-sweater and a double-breasted red trenchcoat, walking over to my table as casually as if we were meeting for a pre-planned dinner date.

"Did you find her?"

Chapter 38

Sanday Island

Tuesday, October 30

"**W**hat's *that*?"

I crawled out of the narrow, thirty-foot-long, hyper-claustrophobic passageway of Quoyness Cairn, and saw Charlie, wearing her bright-red trench, sitting on top of a pile of Neolithic stones.

Apparently, the Orkneys are flush with stone-age cairns, brochs, and standing stones, and the Quoyness Cairn is one of the most famous. It's about 3,000 years old, older than Maeshowe, once serving as some kind of Neolithic funereal tomb. Its narrow dark passageway leads into a main chamber, which is thirteen-feet high and connected to six smaller chambers. Whatever its significance, be it sacred, ritualistic, or the house of the spirits of the dead, the cairn has always been treated with fear and superstition, and it's generally avoided by the locals. Archaeologists, of course, have no such qualms, even after the skeletal remains of ten adults and five children were discovered inside the cairn in the Nineteenth Century.

As for me, I'm with the locals.

The place is creepy.

I looked up.

Charlie was pointing towards the ocean, at what was obviously a lighthouse

"Yeah, let's check it out," I agreed.

We walked over to Start Point Lighthouse, close to the end of Elsness peninsula, surrounded by the North Sea, and *there* they were. The three of them. Just sitting on the front steps of the lighthouse, looking exactly like young twenty-somethings, drinking wine coolers.

Faulkner was visibly shocked to see us, especially her aunt, and she seemed instantly aware of what she'd done.

"Oh, my goodness!" she said, sounding very much like her mother.

She immediately stood up and ran over to Charlie and held her close.

"I'm so sorry, Charlie. I should have told you."

All was forgiven.

Instantly.

Kathleen Sinclair had been exactly right. Heather needed to check something at the cairn, something related to her studies, and the other kids had come along on a lark.

"It was my idea to go webless and phoneless," Gordon admitted, although later admitting that he'd warned his own parents and figured that Faulkner had similarly alerted Charlie.

"I'm such a silly girl!" Faulkner admitted to her aunt, who couldn't have cared less.

We all sat down for a while. Charlie and I each had a cooler, which was a sorry shade of pink and tasted disgusting, and we talked about all kinds of stuff with the kids. Even ever-shy, ever-reluctant Heather talked about her research, which had something to do with possible Viking graffiti close to the cairn.

I have absolutely no idea what the three kids thought of me. Or of my being there. Probably they were thinking that I was Charlie's boyfriend.

What else would I be doing there?

Last night, at the Bothy Bar, Charlie had said:

"Why not tell her?"

So I stood up and said to Faulkner:

"Could we take a walk?"

Which didn't seem as odd at the lighthouse as it reads on paper. Maybe the kids figured I wanted to talk to Faulkner about my assumed relationship with her aunt, and that, naturally, I wanted some privacy. Maybe they even wondered, "Who knows, maybe this guy's engaged to Charlie? And maybe he's about to tell Faulkner?"

So I walked away with my daughter up the sandy Sanday beach.

It was graying towards sunset. The waves were surging nearby, and there was a light breeze in Faulkner's hair.

"Heather says that a really big ship, the *H.M.S. Goldfinch* or something like that, shipwrecked off the coast back in 1915. Right out there."

She pointed at the sea.

She was remarkably relaxed and comfortable walking the white deserted beaches on rugged Sanday, which she told me meant "sandy island," just as she told me lots of other interesting stuff that Heather had told her about the island.

Then she spotted an otter basking in the dead-cold waters.

"Look!"

Faulkner was at that marvelous place in her life when everything seemed like an adventure, where life seemed both good and promising. She seemed very much like her mother at that age.

Eventually, we stopped at the end of Start Point, surrounded with ocean.

I was telling her about my visit to Hoy yesterday afternoon and about my meeting with Kathleen Sinclair.

"Heather's such a lucky girl," Faulkner decided, "to have a mother like that, and a father like that."

Which made me wonder if I should do what I was planning to do, but I decided to press ahead anyway.

"Do you know who I am, Faulkner?"

She seemed intrigued.

"You're Charlie's friend, right? Unless you're something *more* than just her friend."

"It's not that, Faulkner," I said stupidly.

She waited.

"I'm your father."

She seemed amazed.

With an amazed curiosity.

"Your mom and I," I tried to explain, "knew each other when we were students at the University of South Carolina, but I never knew she got pregnant until about a month ago."

"Which is why you came to see me with my teddy bear?"

"Yes."

Taking it all in, she sat down on a large coastal stone and looked at me closely. As if looking at me for the first time, and I felt rather naked. Rather exposed. But, at least, she didn't seem angry.

"Is it good to hear such a thing?" I tried.

"Yes."

I couldn't imagine what she was going through.

Within herself.

"Are you disappointed?"

"No."

But of course she didn't know a thing about me.

"I'm sorry I was never there. I really am."

"I understand."

"Do you believe me that I didn't know?"

"Yes, my mother once told me that she'd never told you."

"Did she tell you who I was?"

"No."

"Do you know *why* she never told me?"

"No. She never explained it, at least not in so many words. But I think she felt that it was *her* problem, and that it wasn't fair to mess up your life."

"Neither you nor Bonnie could have *ever* messed up my life."

She stood up, put her arms around my neck, and held me close. It's hard to describe how I felt, but the primary (primordial) things were love and protection. I didn't even know she'd existed a month ago, and now I was ready to break anyone in half who'd ever do anything to make her feel sad, or concerned, or threatened.

Including the box-sender.

We talked for a while, and she told me that Bonnie had revealed a few things over the years: that I was a "good guy," that we'd loved each other, that I was a "would-be writer," that I didn't live in Carolina, and that, someday, maybe, I'd be back in their lives.

Is *this* what everything was all about? I wondered.

Is this what the box-sender intended? Is this the reason I got shot? If so, I felt nothing but gratitude, as odd as that might sound.

Eventually, we strolled back to the lighthouse and watched, along with the others, the magnificent setting of the Orkney sun. Then Charlie and I took another rickety little plane back to Kirkwall, had a pleasant dinner together at the Bothy, along with a few too many drinks, then returned to our separate rooms at the Kirkwall Hotel.

The previous night, Charlie had given me a manila folder and told me to open it before I went to bed. Which I did. The folder contained the original copy of my handwritten letter to Bonnie from seventeen years ago, and a Xerox copy of the emails that I'd sent her from St. Andrews. It was obvious that Charlie had recently found them somewhere in Bonnie's papers, and that she wanted to let me know that she now believed what I'd told her a month ago at her home in West Columbia.

Both letters seemed as though they were written by someone else. Which they were. By a sincere young boy who was missing his girl-friend:

"Hey, Bon, what's up with my girl?"
"How come I haven't heard a word?"
"Did you really change your phone number?"
"What's going on, Bonnie?"
"Look, just let me know if you're OK."
"I'm missing you, Bonnie."
"A lot."
Etc.

I read them over a few times, without much emotion, beyond an overall sense of loss, with a sense of gratitude to Charlie. I placed them down on the little desk in my hotel room, where they were still lying tonight.

About an hour after we'd returned to the hotel, around midnight, Charlie knocked on my door. She was wearing a soft flannel nightgown. She came inside, and we fell into each other's arms easily, without a word, making easy lovely love together.

Later, within the harbor nightlights, within the traces of moonlight that were seeping through the curtains, I saw the smallish stars-and-bars flag that was tattooed between her breasts, and I touched it gently.

"It was just a stage," she explained. "Maybe my little bit of rebellion against Bonnie, who was always so perfect, who never had a problem with Yankees, who'd even loved one of them."

So we talked about Charlie's "rebel" period, which was also her "conspiracy" period, and she remembered that Bonnie believed that enlisting in the army was a good idea.

"You'll make some Yankee friends."

"Did you?"

"Yes."

She also made it clear that she never gave Bonnie "too much" of a hard time, and that, in fact, she loved and worshipped her mother. But Charlie had been abandoned as a newborn by an anonymous father and forced to live in a crappy druggy trailer park with a disinterested junkie mother until she was ten years old. Naturally, she had some anger issues, which she'd foolishly vented on "Yankees," even though she'd never met any until bootcamp.

Then she asked me, tactfully, about my own life, so I told her about Skye, and I told her about Markie.

Honestly.

"What about you, Charlie?"

"I had some guy in the army," she explained without detail, "but I got rid of him. I'm pretty fussy, just like Bonnie used to be when she was a girl."

Which seemed to be a kind of compliment.

So we talked some more about Bonnie, and, eventually, about her death.

"For a while, I thought Bonnie did it," she explained, guiltily. "Even though it wasn't at all like her. But her life had been going nowhere, Chase was depressed all the time, and Faulkner and I were growing up. As I told you in Carolina, I believed that you'd rejected her a few weeks before the crash."

"What do you think *now*?"

She didn't hesitate.

"I think Chase did it."

"Another conspiracy theory?" I kidded.

She didn't mind. She just shrugged her naked shoulders in the darkness.

"Maybe."

"Or maybe it was just an accident," I suggested. "Maybe some kind of mechanical failure?"

"That's what the cops said. Exactly. Explicitly. 'Some kind of mechanical failure.' But I don't think so, Bret. Chase was a basketcase back then, and he was ashamed of himself, and he knew that he'd failed Bonnie in all kinds of ways, and I think he finally decided to put an end to it. To everything."

"That's pretty harsh, Charlie."

It was a question.

"I guess it is," she admitted. "Chase wasn't the worst kind of guy, but he was a first-rate pilot, and I've always been suspicious of the whole thing. Right from the beginning."

She paused, then continued.

"Maybe I've just had trouble accepting it."

"I'm sure it hasn't been easy."

She looked at me in the moonlight and smiled.

"Is it wrong for me to like it when you kiss me?"

Which seemed a further invitation, so I kissed her again.

Early the next morning, in order to catch my flight, I was up-and-out early. Charlie was still asleep, naked, warm, and content within the bed, looking far too lovely to leave behind, so I kissed her on the forehead, as she murmured something pleasant, and I left the room.

Wondering what the hell was the matter with me.

Chapter 39

Rackham, Douglass, & Clark

Wednesday, October 31

My brother hates law firms.

He says they're repositories for overpaid clerks who've never been in a courtroom. Which, I'm sure, is an exaggeration, although it looked rather dead-on this afternoon at Rackham, Douglass, & Clark.

Since I was completely lagged from the flight to Amsterdam, then the flight to Dulles, I'd hired a driver to drive me 120 miles to Dover, Delaware. I was feeling way too worn out to rent a car and drive it myself, especially after being up most of the night with Charlie.

What was *that* all about anyway?

In the five years since Markie's death, as already mentioned, I'd kissed exactly two women, Rosie and Wendy. The brief moment with Rosie was disgraceful and unforgivable, and I was trying each and every day to forget about it. As for my few-weeks-thing with Wendy, it felt nothing but awkward, inappropriate, and wrong, so I put an end to it as graciously as I could.

As for the rest of the five years, I'd been assiduously avoiding women. Avoiding involvement.

Now there was *this*.

Whatever *this* was.

I'd just slept with someone I barely knew, who was Bonnie's daughter, who was my own daughter's sister/aunt. What would Fr. F. have to say about that? Actually, I knew *exactly* what he'd say. As for me, I had no idea what should happen next. Or how I should feel about it. Or how I should handle it. Should I send Charlie a text? Should I call her? If I did, what would I possibly say?

Maybe I should just wait a bit and see if Charlie contacts me?

Since I had absolutely no idea of the appropriate answers to any of those questions, I tried to push the whole bloody mess from my weary mind, even though I kept remembering, almost inadvertently, her loveliness, her scent, and how much I'd enjoyed being with her.

Earlier, when I arrived at Dulles, there were all kinds of vampires, Spider-Mans, little-kid zombies, and Princess Elsas, etc., roaming around the airport, hoping to get home as quickly as possible to get some candy.

Who could blame them?

Even the law firm, RD&C, was in the Halloween spirit, and the receptionist looked like a pretty convincing Katniss, with a crossbow lying across her desk. On my way upstairs to the third floor, to Wills and Estates, I ran into a flapper, a pirate, an overweight Batman, a greaser girl, and two mob guys, who were all mixed in with various normals dressed in their everyday business suits. I suppose they believed that their clients, at least most of them, would enjoy the dressing-up, although I'm sure some could have done without.

I liked it.

The third-floor receptionist, uncostumed and friendly, led me to a comfortable private waiting room, with a nice view of downtown Dover, where I waited alone, trying to think about nothing much.

As with Rosie in San Juan, I needed to look into this one's eyes and see whatever I could see.

Two nights ago, alone in my room at the Kirkwall Hotel, I did some more web snooping. I'd already decided not to write any more of the novel during my trip to Scotland since my main focus had to be on Faulkner, which it was. As a result, having nothing to do at the hotel that night, I re-Googled everyone, for the millionth time: Skye, her husband, Gordon, Bonnie, Charlie, Faulkner, etc.

Learning nothing new.

Then Irene.

My stalker.

This time I uncovered a more detailed resume on the state's website for the Delaware bar. I learned, for the first time, that she'd actually started college at Clemson, before transferring to the University of Delaware.

It was a long shot of course. *Very* long. But Clemson's about 135 miles from Columbia, and it wasn't totally impossible that she might have met Bonnie back then. That she might have learned something about Bonnie's life.

Mine as well.

Sure, it was probably a ridiculous idea, but what *hasn't* been ridiculous in my life these days?

She entered the room.

Snow White.

With her bobbed dark hair parted in the middle, her pale ivory skin, wearing, of course, the classic dress, with its dark blue bodice and high white collar, with its short puffy light blue sleeves, with what Markie had once described as "red Tudor slashing," with light brown pumps with little yellow bows on each shoe.

With a red hairband and red bow in her hair.

It definitely wasn't what I was expecting from my deranged, court-restrained, stalker-hacker.

She looked, I'd have to admit, perfectly charming.

Quite naturally, she was astonished to see me.

"Is it really you?"

I stood up.

She was much prettier than I'd expected from the pictures on the law firm's website. Maybe a bit too thin, maybe a trace of offness in her hazel eyes, maybe a sense of the kind of wariness that, as I knew better than anyone, could easily migrate into paranoia.

Oddly, she seemed happy to see me. I didn't know if I should shake her hand, but I did, and she was pleased.

"Should you be here?" she wondered, referring to the restraining order. "Can we meet like this?"

"I really don't know, but we need to talk. Can we sit?"

"Of course."

We sat.

"I'd just like to talk," I repeated.

What I *really* wanted to do was to find out whether she'd put a bullet hole in my shoulder and was forcing me to write a novel that I didn't want to write. I even wondered, although I suppose it's a sign of my own recent paranoia, whether she *knew* that I was coming here today, and that she'd intentionally worn the costume of Markie's favorite cartoon character.

Which was absurd.

"I just want you to know," she assured me, "that I'm over everything now. I'm truly sorry. I *really* am. Especially about what happened to your wife."

I listened, and I watched her closely as she told me about the tempestuous affair that she'd had with her married boss twelve years ago, about their reckless trip to Cabo, about the crash in New Mexico near Carlsbad, about her survival, about her injuries, about her boss's death, about the subsequent exposure of their adultery, about the termination from her job, about her subsequent bulimia, anorexia, depression, and suicidal impulses.

Then she read the book.

Aircrash.

"I know it seems foolish now, but I was completely transfixed. It seemed to be *all* about me, and it seemed to be exposing me to further public humiliation. I was an unemployed lawyer with time on my hands, so I started with the lawsuits. Then it accelerated."

"The book had nothing to do with you," I assured her.

"I know that now. I've been getting help. I've managed to get this new job, and I'm doing well."

Then she told me the rest.

About living with her parents, about the failed therapies, about the more useful ones, about the kindness of her uncle, Edward Clark, who'd taken a risk and brought her into his law firm.

"I'm happy here, Bret. It's wills and estates, and I'm actually helping people."

Which, I think, was also a way of saying, "I hope you're not here to expose me."

"Don't worry, Irene, I'm not here to cause any trouble."

It seemed odd to call her by her first name.

To hear her call me "Bret."

Suddenly, there were tears in Snow White's eyes, and they seemed sincere.

"I don't deserve your kindness."

I asked her about Clemson and her two years in South Carolina.

"I was a complete mess back then. I was homesick, and I was missing my boyfriend back here in Dover."

"Did you ever meet Bonnie MacMillan?"

"No."

She seemed confused.

As I'm sure is perfectly obvious by now, I'm not much of a detective, but I searched her face and her eyes and all her movements and gestures, and I saw nothing but a screwed-up young woman who was trying her best to straighten out her messy life.

Telling me the truth.

"Did you ever go to Columbia?"

"Once. For a football game. And a few in-and-outs at the airport."

I was finished.

I stood up, and Irene stood up as well.

She looked into my eyes, with a rather unsettling desperation, something that she'd, apparently, had to deal with throughout most of her life.

"Can you forgive me?"

It wasn't easy.

Not because I cared about her pain-in-the-ass harassments of me, but let's face it, she'd filed frivolous lawsuit-after-lawsuit against Markie. Markie, of course, had taken it, like almost everything else in her life, in stride. When she was a little girl worrying about the pastries in the bakery oven, her father would reassure her, "Don't worry, Marquita, if they get burnt a bit, they get burnt a bit. We'll give them to the poor. It's not as if it's the end of the world." So she learned to think like her father.

She also believed what they told us at Hopkins about occupational hazards. That writers often get accused of "stuff like this," and she actually felt sorry for the "poor girl."

Whom she'd never met.

"Of course," I said.

Irene leaned into me and hugged me, taking me by surprise. She held me around the shoulders and rested her face against my neck, and I could feel her trembling.

Saying, softly, "Thank you."

I left, uncertain about what had just happened, just wishing to get back to peaceful uncomplicated New Jersey, into my log cabin, crashed into my bed for some much-needed rest, what Van Morrison called in one of his songs, "heavy rest."

Chapter 40

Detailed Outline

[Note to the Box-Sender et al.: in accordance with the guidelines, the next section of Writing Fiction *is a discussion of how to create a simple but extremely useful outline. Uncertain how to proceed, and, in an effort to avoid irritating redundancies, I've given (below) a brief sample of my own as-yet-unfinished outline, specifically the first four chapters, each chapter including the first line.]*

I. THE PREMISE

1. (9/25, Tuesday) The Box: "I was reading, actually rereading, the initial thirty-five words of *Absalom, Absalom!* when I heard the crack at the picture window, felt the burn in my left shoulder, and realized I'd been shot." – shot at his desk, slides his chair back, stares at the box, the contents within, he *doesn't* have a daughter, calls 911, calls Colt.

2. (9/26, Wednesday) Puerto Mosquito: "Her clothes were off."
   – wakes in the hospital from a dream of Puerto Mosquito,
   the pain, the nerve damage, Wendy's asleep, Kyle's gone, Colt
   arrives, what if I knew what kind of rifle it was?, Colt leaves,
   gets an air crash text from Vinny.

3. (9/26, Wednesday) The Poconos: "I was sitting on a ridge in
   the Poconos, in the Appalachians, high above Cherry Valley,
   not far from the Sorrenti Vineyards, seven miles southwest of
   the Delaware Water Gap." – above the crash site, recalls Death
   Valley, hypoxia, Markie's contentment, her note-taking, on
   Vinny, Dante's Peak, "I can do this."

4. The Premise: A man is forced to write a novel about writing
   a novel about being forced to write a novel.

II. RESEARCH

5. (9/27, Thursday) *Absalom, Absalom!*: "So I read it
again:" – etc.

Chapter 41

Revelations/Realizations List

[Selected, so far.]

Bret's a father.

Bonnie is dead.

Faulkner's in Scotland.

Bonnie considered contacting Bret last year.

Skye is still in love with Bret.

Gordon hunts with Graham Sinclair.

Irene went to Clemson.

Irene's in therapy.

Chapter 42

Themes

[I have no idea. After all, it wasn't my idea to write this stupid book. What I've listed below is the best that I can conjure up for now, which seems rather lame.]

Paternity

Detraction

Omission

"The right to know."

VIII.

OPENING

Don't fiddle around. We're not Thackerays anymore.
(Even though we all love Thackeray. Right?) Get to it.
Immediately. A crisis. A problem. A dilemma.

Chapter 43

Opening

[One more time with feeling:]

I was reading, actually rereading, the initial thirty-five words of *Absalom, Absalom!* when I heard the crack at the picture window, felt the burn in my left shoulder, and realized I'd been shot.

IX.

STYLE

Overrated. Don't sweat it. Just write a lot and your style will develop in time. When you're young, imitate the best (Austen, Poe, Melville, Faulkner), then bag it and write, write, write. Don't worry about it, if you're supposed to be a writer, it'll come.

Chapter 44

Style

As per instructions, see Chapter 45.

Chapter 45

Millarisms

A *s mentioned in* Writing Fiction, *I collect what I call "Millarisms." Stuff that Ross Macdonald (real name Kenneth Millar) wrote in his Archer novels (and stories) that I wish I'd written myself. Here's a short sample from several hundred excerpts that I've memorized over the years, each of which is cited in* Writing Fiction *as an inspirational instructional.*

> "There was nothing wrong with Southern California that a rise in the ocean level wouldn't cure." —— *The Drowning Pool*

> "She was trouble looking for somebody to happen to." —— *The Wycherly Woman*

"It was a Friday night. I was tooling home from the Mexican border in a light blue convertible and a dark blue mood." —— "Gone Girl"

"There are certain families whose members should all live in different towns – different states, if possible – and write each other letters once a year." —— *The Blue Hammer*

"When there's trouble in a family, it tends to show up in the weakest member. And all the other members of the family know that. They make allowances for the one in trouble ... because they know they're implicated themselves." —— *Sleeping Beauty*

"As a man gets older, if he knows what is good for him, the women he likes are getting older too. The trouble is that most of them are married." —— *The Zebra-Striped Hearse*

"It was some time since I had gone to sleep in the same room with a girl. Of course, the room was large and reasonably well-lighted, and the girl had other things than me on her mind." —— *The Blue Hammer*

"I like a little danger. Tame danger, controlled by me. It gives me a sense of power, I guess, to take my life in my hands and know damn well I'm not going to lose it." —— *The Moving Target*

"The past was filling the room like a tide of whispers." —— *The Instant Enemy*

"He hadn't wanted to be helped the way I wanted to help him, the way that helped me." —— *The Doomsters*

"... a thin woman about fifty with a face like a silver hatchet." —— *The Wycherly Woman*

"Night streets were my territory, and would be till I rolled in the last gutter." —— *The Drowning Pool*

"No more guns for you." —— The Chill

"Some men spend their lives looking for ways to punish themselves for having been born." —— *The Chill*

"In wine was truth, perhaps, but in whisky, the way Hoffman sluiced it down, was an army of imaginary rats climbing your legs." —— *The Chill*

"She smiled, and I caught a glimpse of her life's meaning. She cared for other people. Nobody cared for her." —— *The Far Side of the Dollar*

"His wife's face hung like a dead moon over her drink." —— *The Far Side of the Dollar*

"She probably had a lot of practice slamming doors." —— *The Far Side of the Dollar*

"Girls leave home all the time. It tears the hearts out of their mothers, but they don't know it. They don't find out till their own kids grow up and do it to them. —— *The Way Some People Die*

"Parking spaces in downtown Hollywood were as scarce as the cardinal virtues." —— *The Way Some People Die*

"The walls were lined with books, many of them in foreign languages, like insulation against the immediate present." —— *The Underground Man*

"She had the kind of beauty that made you want to explore its history." —— *The Goodbye Look*

"He was saying and doing all the wrong things. I knew, because I'd said and done them in my time." —— *The Goodbye Look*

"She looked me up and down, like a woman practicing to be a divorcee." —— *The Goodbye Look*

"I caught the glint of larceny in his eyes, and something worse." —— *The Galton Case*

"She was an ordinary-looking woman, decently dressed, who would never see forty again." —— *The Galton Case*

"Flowers bloomed competitively in their yards." —— *The Galton Case*

"Put away the violin. It doesn't go with a knifing rap." —— *The Galton Case*

"Her brushed hair shone like gold in the sunlight. Fool's gold." —— *The Galton Case*

"When you talk about old trouble sometimes you can talk it back to life." —— *The Goodbye Look*

"She lived on the Montevista shore in a rectilinear cliff-top house made of steel and glass and money." —— *The Goodbye Look*

X.

DIALOGUE

Tight, appropriate, and always clear who's speaking. Don't bother dialoguing the small stuff.

Chapter 46

Conversation

Sample 1:

"You set quite a pace. Slow down."

"Are you telling me what to do?" he said distinctly and unpleasantly.

"I'm willing to listen to your story. I want you to be able to tell it."

"You think I'm an alcoholic or something?"

"I think you're a bundle of nerves. Pour alcohol on a bundle of nerves and it generally turns into a can of worms. While I'm making suggestions you might as well get rid of those chips you're wearing on both shoulders. Somebody's liable to knock them off and take a piece of you with them."

[*The Chill*, Ross Macdonald]

Sample 2:

And you are–?
Henry Sutpen.
And you have been here–?
Four years.
And you came home–?
To die. Yes.
To die?
Yes, to die.

[*Absalom, Absalom!*, William Faulkner]

XI.

PLACE DIAGRAMS

Sketch out key locations so you (and your reader) don't get lost logistically.

Chapter 47

The Log Cabin

Rough sketch of my work area:

[If I could draw, I'd include a sketch of the desk, chair, bobbleheads, and picture window.]

XII.

ENDING

The most important advice ever given to writers was written twenty-three centuries ago by Aristotle (naturally): "The ending should be unexpected, but not unbelievable." Which is much easier said than done. (P. S. The only people who don't like surprise endings are lousy writers and so-called "literary critics." Everyone else who's ever lived on planet Earth enjoys them immensely.)

Chapter 48

The Parks Literary Agency

Wednesday, December 12

I drove the mile to Route 23, went south to 46, merged into Route 3, hitting the tunnel at 12:46.

I crossed Manhattan, parked on Park, and met Wendy in the lobby.

2. Give the completed manuscript to your agent on December 12.

It was good to be finished. I'd done the best I could, finishing on time.

Wendy, as always, looked lovely.

"I wish I knew what was going on."

I felt like saying, "Me, too," but I didn't.

"You look lovely."

Chapter 49

Christmas Eve

Monday, December 24

I wasn't alone.

I was hanging with Dante again.

Rereading Canto V, as Paolo and Francesca, still lusting after each other, are whirling around in Circle Two, unable to touch.

Pleasant reading.

Maybe it wasn't the most normal way to spend Christmas Eve, but tomorrow morning I'll be in the midst of a pile of toys with Kyle, Angie, and the twins.

Besides, I was also packing for Cape Breton tonight.

The you-know-what was about to hit the fan, and I was getting out of Dodge. Two clichés for the price of one.

Chapter 50

Cape Breton Island

Wednesday, December 26

*I*t was time to do some figuring.

As planned, I flew to Halifax, picked up a rental, drove 145 miles to the Canso Causeway, crossed the straits into Cape Breton, took Route 19 north to Troy, parked in front of the little brown cottage, went inside, put on some fiddle music by Howie MacDonald, sat down on the old couch in the darkness, and planned to stay there until I'd figured everything out.

Later that night, Colt called:

"He's at Camp Pendleton."

Which was another surprise.

Chapter 51

The Red Shoe

Friday, January 18

I was now listening to the real thing live.

Donna DeWolfe was fiddling away, a few feet from my table, and I was tapping my foot and thinking about the Oscars. As expected, I'd been nominated for Best Adapted Screenplay, and Melanie had called from Paramount insisting that I show up.

"You *have* to come, Bret."

Why not?

I knew exactly who to ask.

Chapter 52

Musso & Frank's

Sunday, February 24

"*Is this where he used to sit?*"

Meaning Faulkner.

Sixteen years ago, I gave her a copy of *Absalom, Absalom!*, but I'm not sure if she ever actually read it.

"Not exactly," I explained, "but Marilyn did, and so did George Clooney."

Which she found more impressive anyway.

I'd picked her up early this morning at LAX, then we went directly to Rodeo Drive.

Where the stores were open on Oscar Sunday.

To get an Oscar dress.

Which cost a ton.

Which I insisted on paying, but she absolutely squashed the idea.

"No way, Jersey, you're already paying for everything else. Besides, I make a bunch of money."

"I hope so. Have you seen the price tag?"

"Who cares? There'll never be another night like this one!"

It was nice to see her so excited, enjoying her trip to Los Angeles. Her "escape." Two weeks ago, I'd invited both Skye and her husband to come to the Oscars, but she said that he couldn't make it.

"Who cares?" she shrugged over the phone. "He's a drag anyway."

As for the dress, it was a Valentino that the saleslady described as a "fuchsia tulle floor-length, with lace-appliqué and a bateau neckline," whatever the hell that meant, costing a measly $12,995, and when Skye came out of the dressing room, she looked like a Scottish queen.

Better.

I dropped her off at the Pink Palace, and we met here for early dinner at 4:00. She showed up gownless, wearing her casuals, a sea-green skirt, dark green MacDonald blouse, and a dark green trench.

"You look great, by the way."

"I hoped you say that."

We settled into our red leather booth, beneath the high ceiling and the dark paneled walls, close to the mahogany bar. She ordered roast lamb, I ordered the braised ribs, and I answered all her questions and told her what I remembered about the famous "back room."

Explaining that back in the day, when the Screen Writers Guild was right across the street, many of the writers would walk across Hollywood Boulevard and hang out at Musso & Frank's. Chandler was a regular, so was Fitzgerald, and of course, so was Faulkner, drinking too many mint juleps. Whenever they were in town, Dorothy Parker, Steinbeck, and O'Hara would also stop by.

Of course, the movie stars came here as well, which was much more interesting to Skye than the writers, who perked up at the legendary names of Pickford, Chaplin, Garbo, Welles, Bogart, Monroe, and, more recently, Clooney, Pitt, and Depp, right here in the "new room."

"I'm confused," she said, enjoying her Grant's on the rocks.

"The back room was closed in 1955, and this room, known as the 'big room,' was opened a year later."

"What happened to the 'back room'?"

"It's no longer owned by the management. The last I heard, it was a rather low-rent bar calling itself The Writer's Room."

"What a shame."

"Nothing lasts forever, right?"

She reached across the table and took my hand.

"Maybe not *everything*."

She looked into my eyes, with her pretty Highland brown eyes beneath a magnificent tumble of honey-red hair.

I used to tell her that she looked like the young Maureen O'Hara, which she found both flattering, and not flattering.

Flattering because O'Hara was so beautiful. Not-flattering because O'Hara was Irish.

"Are you excited about tomorrow night?" she wondered.

"If *you* are."

She liked my answer.

"Of course," I warned her, "you know that I don't have a chance. Peter Morgan's a lock."

"Maybe."

Chapter 53

The Academy Awards

Sunday, February 24

*A*nd *the Oscar goes to . . .* "

It was, as they say, "like it wasn't really real":

The limo drop-off in front of the Dolby.

The security.

The jacked-up crowds pressing to see the stars.

Some stupid reporter calling out questions about the novel, which had been published earlier this afternoon in New York City, oddly on a Sunday, as required in the guidelines.

"Is *she* the Scot?"

We ignored him.

Walking the red carpet.

Surrounded by cameras.

Flashing everywhere.

Walking the grand staircase.

Until, finally, we were sitting in our seats.

When I heard my name announced, I kissed Skye on the cheek, stood up, and somehow made my way to the famous stage of the Dolby Theatre.

Stunned.

Speechless.

Without a speech.

Chapter 54

San Ysidro Boulevard

Monday, February 25

*W*hen she finished chatting with Jennifer Lawrence, who was charming as always, I strolled over with our drinks.

A whisky sour and a glass of white champagne.

Which had happened last night.

Late last night.

At Paramount's after-party at Hotel Bel-Air.

Skye was looking nothing-short-of-amazing in her pink Oscar gown. Everyone was completely charmed by her just-happy-to-be-here good spirits and her cut-it-with-a-knife Scottish accent.

She was also a bit of a celebrity, given her role in the new novel, which no one, fortunately, had actually read yet, although "a Scottish ex-girlfriend" had been mentioned in the advertisements. There was, however, one persistent reporter from one of the networks who seemed to know more than the rest. Fortunately, Bel-Air security had done an excellent job of keeping him away from the party.

Earlier, when we'd first arrived at the hotel, he tried to ask questions about Skye and her role in the book, but she paid no attention, as I called out to the guy, "Look, pal, it's just fiction. Just like the film."

So we ignored the guy.

But it was impossible to ignore the belle of the ball.

She sipped white champagne, smiling, admitting:

"It'll be awfully hard to go back to scrubs."

"You look cute in your scrubs."

She smiled again.

"I need a favor," I said.

"Anything."

"I need your brother for something tomorrow."

Which was clearly the last thing she expected to hear.

She was definitely confused.

A bit taken aback.

"Braden?"

(We both knew that she only had *one* brother.)

"Yeah."

"How do you know about Braden?"

"I know lots of stuff."

The next day (today), we were sitting in the bright sunny parking lot of a Jack in the Box on San Ysidro Boulevard, a block from the US Port of Entry at the Mexican border.

Earlier, we'd picked up Braden at Camp Pendleton, in San Diego County, the home of the 1st Marine Expeditionary Force, a few miles from the ocean, which was also the home of the 1st Intelligence Battalion, where Braden was "on loan" from British SIS.

"Some kind of intelligence crap," Colt explained, with as few words as possible. "Training of some kind."

Apparently, Braden, who was a little kid the last time I saw him sixteen years ago on the Island of Skye, was now an in-training operative for SIS, and the MI6 home office at Vaux Hall in London had sent him to California to learn a few things from the Americans.

Which, of course, Braden, now twenty-six, couldn't talk about, so I didn't attempt to discuss it. Today was Monday, and he was officially off-duty, and he was surprised, to say the least, to see his big sister inexplicably popping up in San Diego. But he was "more than glad" to help out his sister's Yankee novelist, whom Skye described as an old family friend.

Even though he didn't seem to remember me.

Braden was a good-looking Highland kid, who'd spent some time in the weight room. He wore jeans and a polo, and he hopped in my rental, a black Escalade, and we drove south to the border.

"What's this about?"

I was doing the driving, with Braden up front. When I didn't answer, Skye responded from the back seat.

"I've got no idea. It's a mystery, I guess."

They both looked at the driver.

Me.

"It's better if you don't know," I said.

It was best to keep the mystery a mystery.

Besides, Skye had always loved mysteries.

When I pulled into the parking lot, the Jack in the Box, as always, was jammed with customers, so I pulled around the back where things were more deserted.

Then I saw her.

Standing alone, checking her watch.

She was wearing navy sweat-shorts and a zipped-up navy hoodie, carrying a navy gym bag.

I turned and looked at Skye.

"You stay here."

Then Braden and I got out of the car.

I didn't need to tell him to come along, and he followed me across the lot towards Irene.

"Irene."

She was startled to see me. She looked confused and irritated.

"What are *you* doing here?" she said, angrily.

"We need to talk," I said.

She was in no mood for talking.

"Screw yourself, Buchanan, go back to wherever you came from."

"Not until you answer some questions."

"Beat it, I don't have time for this, and take that kid with you."

I stepped closer.

"I mean it," she said.

"So do I."

She pulled a gun.

Which Braden later identified as a Ruger 9mm.

"They're light and good for concealed carry," he explained.

"Don't mess with me, Bret," she threatened. "I'm going over the border, and that's the end of it."

Feeling cornered, she lifted her weapon and pointed it at my face.

Immediately, Braden, who'd come unarmed, stepped in front of me, into the line of fire.

"Get lost, kid," she said.

But Braden stayed right where he was, protecting me.

"I'm not going anywhere."

"But I am," she said, as she backed away and started moving toward the sidewalk, the boulevard, the port of entry.

"By the way," she called out, "congratulations."

I couldn't help but admire her sarcasm.

"What do we do now?" Braden wondered.

"Nothing."

We stood there together and watched her as she backed away. Down San Ysidro Boulevard. Then she dropped her Ruger into a trashcan and vanished into the migrating crowds.

She was gone.

"What the hell was that?"

"It's between me and her."

He didn't press it.

"Do you want me to retrieve the weapon?"

"No."

We both looked back at the Escalade, where Skye was watching everything.

Horrified.

"Come on, kid, let's get out of here."

Which we did.

Chapter 55

The Beverly Hills Hotel

Monday, February 25

I *poured two glasses of Krug 2000.*

Two *additional* glasses.

I was standing in the spacious bedroom of her bungalow at the Beverly.

Just as she'd decided a few weeks ago:

"If I'm going to Hollywood, I might as well stay at the Beverly. In one of the bungalows."

"Which one?"

We knew that #10 was Marlene Dietrich's favorite, #4 was Elizabeth Taylor's favorite, and #7 was Marilyn's favorite.

"7."

I wasn't surprised. She always loved *Bus Stop* and *The Misfits*.

"I'll see if I can get it," I said, "but it might not be available."

She knew.

"I'm paying," she also decided.

I ignored her, called Melanie at Paramount, who called somebody at the Beverly, and they made it work.

After all, where else would a movie buff like Skye want to stay in LA? The Pink Palace, of course. Where she could meander through Hotel California, the Polo Lounge, the Coterie, the pool, and the gardens, surrounded by the ghosts of Hollywood's past.

Sinatra, Grace Kelly, John Wayne, Fred Astaire, Kate Hepburn, Sidney Poitier, Richard Burton, Carole Lombard, Joan Crawford, Gregory Peck, etc. Not to mention the Duke and Duchess of Windsor, Howard Hughes, and the Beatles.

Not to mention that the bungalows were supposed to be haunted, which made them even more fun.

At the moment, she was lying on her huge bed, amid the peachy pinks and greens, the apricots and yellows, propped on a half-dozen pillows, wearing nothing but a loose, *very loose*, bright white, Beverly Hills Hotel terrycloth robe, looking as lovely as the movie stars themselves, looking a bit starry on the bubbles.

I handed her one of the glasses and sat next to her on the bed. She held my hand and clinked my glass, as we sipped together.

"Will you need some help taking off your clothes?" she asked, with the same mischievous smile I'd seen that first night in the St. Andrews ruins. "I could call for room service?"

There was a knock on the door.

"That was fast," she said with a smile, slightly confused, "but I didn't ring for anything. As a matter of fact, I told them to leave us alone."

"It's open," I called out.

We waited.

Angus, her husband, walked into the room.

Angus MacDonald, MD, was a good-looking, rather tallish man, with graying hair. He was nicely dressed in a tweed suit, but he looked a bit worn out. Maybe worn out from work. Maybe worn out from the trip. Maybe worn out from the nearly naked woman lying on Marilyn's bed.

"What are you doing here?" she said.

Oddly enough, she didn't seem embarrassed. Not a bit. She also didn't seem concerned. Just disappointed. Terribly disappointed. As if this was all an unfortunate inevitability.

Angus walked over to the edge of the bed.

"Cover yourself up."

She closed up the front of her robe.

He looked at me.

"What am I supposed to do?"

"Sit down."

He did.

Then he waited.

Our obvious collusion and our obvious conspiracy didn't seem to surprise Skye at all, so she sipped again at her expensive champagne, direct from the Clos du Mesnil vineyard, and she did exactly what her husband was doing.

Wait.

I sat down on the edge of the bed again and looked into her eyes.

"I know what you did, Skye."

She didn't respond. As a matter of fact, she was altogether unre-active, as if everything was already pre-ordained, as if inexorable.

"I know that Braden shot me."

"What!" Angus said.

He was dumbfounded.

Utterly.

Skye ignored him.

"But he didn't mean to," she said softly, a bit defensively.

"I assumed that."

Obviously, she'd assumed that I would have already assumed it.

She looked over at her husband, but she spoke to me.

"You better fill him in."

Which I did.

I told him that his wife, for some as yet inexplicable reason got her brother to shoot me with a rifle, threatened to shoot my daughter, and forced me to write a novel about the whole experience.

Angus, for his part, just sat there, bewildered, dismayed, occasion-ally glancing over at his wife.

When he did ask a few questions, I did my best to clarify as honestly as I could.

When I was done, he turned to his wife and asked the same exact question I wanted to ask.

"Why?"

"Yeah," I agreed. "Exactly. Good question."

Which was why we were here.

She thought it over as we stared, like two mesmerized adolescents, at her beautiful face.

"More champagne," she said. "It's £85 a glass and I don't want to waste a single drop."

I stood up, poured her another glass, returned to the bed, and handed her another Grand Cuvée.

Satisfied, she told us "why."

To her totally clueless husband.

To her semi-clueless one-time boyfriend.

"I think I'll start off with the excuses, even though I know they're not in any way excusable."

Then she went down the list:

She'd lost their second child, at seven months.

Their marriage had flatlined.

I could feel Angus squirm.

A close childhood friend from the Island of Skye had died of some bacterial issue that she'd never been able to diagnose. For which, she felt entirely responsible.

"I was a mess, so I started thinking about us."

She looked at the old boyfriend, not the husband.

"I started Googling."

"First you, then your wife, then your South Carolina girlfriend.

"As I was stumbling around the web, I discovered a short rather nasty article on *The Huffington Post* that said you were 'blocked,' that you were wasting your talents, that you'd never live up to your potential, that you were just living off your wife's accomplishments. It was pretty ugly, and I didn't believe most of it, but on the other hand, it was pretty obvious that you weren't doing much of anything except adapting your wife's novels and writing a textbook.

"A book which I immediately ordered online, which seemed rather peculiar, being a how-to book by a guy who'd never really how-to'd a novel himself, and who didn't seem capable of any future how-to-ing.

"In the meantime, I was astonished to discover that Bonnie MacMillan had died in a plane crash, and that she'd had a daughter named Faulkner, who was, according to somebody's Facebook page, enrolled at St. Andrews.

"Who *must* have been your child, Bret.

"Which you didn't even seem to know about.

"Given the date of her birth, given her unusual name, given the fact that you and Bonnie were exclusive, and given the kind of girl that I believed Bonnie to be.

"Because you'd told me *all* about her, years ago, when I asked you about your Carolina girl, when I was jealous of your previous girlfriend, when we first met at St. Andrews.

"So I started thinking that you should definitely know your own daughter.

"I also started thinking that you definitely needed to get going on some kind of writing project.

"I also started thinking about how much I wanted to see you again.

"So I did it."

She shrugged.

The two men in the room were silent.

"Did I mention," she reminded us, "that I was disturbed at the time?"

"That's not true," Angus insisted.

"It *is* true, Angus," she insisted. "I kept it from you at the time. From everybody. Besides, you were crazy busy at the hospital, and I didn't want you to know."

He had nothing more to say.

"Obviously," she added.

Then she remembered:

"So I made a point, during the first week of classes, to give a talk at the School of Medicine, so I could go out afterwards with some of the students, with the intention of trying to catch a glimpse of Faulkner MacMillan. Which I did. From a distance. She was *so* lovely, Bret, so I went ahead with everything."

"Which was pretty dangerous, pretty damned convoluted," I pointed out.

She smiled.

She seemed pleased with herself.

"I was reading a lot of Ross Macdonald at the time, along with the wacko mysteries of Agatha Christie and W. E. B. Besides, I was out of my mind."

No one bothered to argue.

"The hairbrush?" I wondered.

"Braden got it for me. Just before he shipped out to the States, he slipped into her room at Dean's Court one afternoon while she and her roommate were off in class. He told me it was a piece-of-cake."

"Then he shot me in the shoulder."

"Because he slipped on the roof. The bullet was supposed to miss. It was intended to scare you a bit. To make you come to me. To come to Scotland."

She thought of her brother.

"Poor Braden, he's felt terribly guilty about it."

She sipped at her Krug.

"Good," I said.

"You were testing him yesterday. Correct?"

"Yes."

"Who was that woman?"

"Someone who owed me something."

Who did what she did because of her *own* guilts, spurred by my promise to drop the restraining order and change her name in the book.

"It was a set-up, right?"

"Right. Did you know it at the time?"

"Not really. I had no idea *what* was going on."

"Well, you can tell your brother that her Ruger was empty."

"I will."

She thought about it some more.

"Can you forgive him?"

"It's hard to forgive such a dangerous stupidity. Even if he did try to protect me at the border."

"He did it for me, Bret! He'll do *anything* for me, even risk his commission, and I took advantage of him."

"Yeah," I agreed.

"So what about me, Bret? Can you forgive me?"

It sounded rather desperate.

"Were you really out of your mind?"

"I was suicidal much of the time."

"Why didn't you tell me?" Angus said, sounding a bit desperate himself.

She shrugged again. It wasn't a shrug of dismissal; it was more a shrug of complete bewilderment.

"I don't know."

"Will you get some kind of help?" I asked, trying not to sound like a touchy-feely marriage counselor.

"Yes."

"Then, of course, I will. I forgive you, Skye."

Angus spoke again.

This time to me.

"Is that it, Bret? No police?"

"No police."

He was greatly relieved, but Skye seemed as if she didn't care in the least.

"But," I reminded Angus, "it's still in the book."

Which he hadn't read yet.

"*All* of it?"

"Yes, all of it."

"She'll lose her position."

"I don't care," she insisted. "I'll do some therapy, I'll get myself cleared, and I'll get a second chance somewhere else. I'm still a hell of a pathologist."

He didn't disagree.

Angus stood up and asked the hardest question of them all.

"Did you love him that much?"

Of course, I happened to be the "him" in the room.

"Yes," she admitted, "in my mind, at least."

It wasn't exactly what a husband wants to hear.

"But it's all over now," she added.

Which seemed to flash a flash of hopefulness into their flatlined relationship.

It was definitely time for me to get the hell out of there.

I stood up and looked at the both of them.

Warning:

"The book is out, and people are starting to read it, and they're starting to ask a lot of questions."

Neither of them responded.

So I left them alone with their busted marriage in Marilyn's bungalow.

Chapter 56

Rockefeller Center

Tuesday, February 26

I^t *was nearly midnight.*

I was alone in my brother's office at the Paterson Courthouse watching the video that Wendy had sent me of this afternoon's press conference at Simon & Schuster, 1230 Avenue of the Americas, Rockefeller Center.

It was about all the "problems" and the "questions" relating to the novel entitled *Novel*.

Anticipating the coming storm, I'd flown back from LAX early Monday morning, got what I needed from the cabin, then moved into Vinny's basement.

Out of sight.

At least, until I could meet alone with Wendy.

Now I was sitting in my brother's office, watching Wendy's recording of everything, which she recorded through her cell phone, which I was watching on *my* cell phone.

I could see that the conference room was packed with literary dorks, pencil-neck geeks, and a mess of reporters, as Camilla, S&S's Acquisitions Editor, was doing her best to answer their aggressive questions, as Wendy was doing her best to let Camilla deal with the whole bloody mess.

"The book's full of *real* people!"

The tone was accusatory, as were all the subsequent questions.

Even though I couldn't actually see Camilla, I could sometimes catch a glimpse of her from behind. Wendy, I assumed, was sitting at a table on the small stage of the conference room behind Camilla, with her cell facing the audience, recording away.

"That's correct. Which is not that unusual in fiction."

"It certainly is when *every* single name in the book seems to be a real person!" someone else yelled out.

When Camilla didn't respond, a young woman stood up, a reporter of some kind, and said self-importantly:

"I've contacted over fifteen people mentioned in the book, and they all say that they have absolutely no idea what's going on. It's hard to believe that this isn't some kind of hoax. Some kind of fraud."

Those two interesting words, "hoax" and "fraud," seemed to be the currency of the day, and they'd been bouncing around the literary websites for the past two days, even the imperial *Times* had decided that "something's clearly amiss."

"Yeah, you've got no idea!" I thought to myself when I first read the quote.

"Well," Camilla tried, "I think it's important to remember that we're talking about fiction, and that . . . "

Somebody I couldn't see in the frame cut her off:

"Or *is* it? Is it possible that this preposterous story is actually real? Or just purporting to be real?"

Then the reporter was back:

"I've been able to verify that the author, Bret Buchanan, who's also the main character, was treated for a gunshot wound on September 25th at a New Jersey hospital, just as it's described in the book. I've also verified all kinds of other real-life details cited within the book."

There was a flurry of dissatisfied murmurs and grumblings. It was starting to look like the agitated crowd that chased down the Frankenstein monster. All they needed were flaming torches.

Poor Camilla made another feeble attempt.

"We have to remember that all kinds of things can happen in a novel. Even, sometimes, the truth."

"But if it's non-fiction," someone else called out, "then why has it been promoted and sold as a novel? Why is it heading up the fiction bestseller list? And, by the way, where the hell's the author anyway? You said he was going to be here."

It was torch time, and I was the monster.

Hiding in New Jersey.

"I apologize for that," Camilla said, "but his agent told me that he'd be here today."

All eyes shifted to Wendy and her cell phone, as if they were seeing right through her phone and right into my brother's office.

"He was delayed in Los Angeles."

It was definitely Wendy's voice, but it sounded uncharacteristically weak and disembodied. She wasn't much of a liar, and I'd always admired her for that.

A bearded professor-type yelled out:

"Wasn't that the Scot woman with him at the Oscars the other night? Has she been arrested? And what about her brother Braden?"

This time, Wendy said nothing. I felt certain that she was sitting there, looking lovely, hoping that the vengeful eyes of the mob would eventually shift back to Camilla.

They did.

"I don't know."

It was pretty obvious that Camilla didn't know much of anything.

"That's another thing," some scrawny guy in a Columbia wind-breaker squeaked out, "it makes you wonder if his Oscar was on the up-and-up. And what about the novel he supposedly wrote with his wife Marquita?"

The video ended.

Abruptly.

Maybe Wendy did it on purpose since Markie's name had surfaced.

The video had popped up in my cell a few hours ago, attached to a text:

You don't make things easy, Bret.

I appreciated her understatement, and I felt terrible about every-thing. I needed to meet with her soon, but I didn't know what I could possibly say tonight, so I emailed back:

NOVEL

I'm sorry.

Chapter 57

The Algonquin

Wednesday, February 27

"*How much of it is real?*"

We were sitting at the end of the Blue Bar, in yet another writer's hangout.

This one on 59th Street.

I had no problem with Edna Ferber, a late addition to the Roundtable at the Algonquin, but most of the rest of the so-called Vicious Circle – Adams, Hale, Grant, Connelly, Broun, etc. – didn't mean that much to me. But Wendy loved Dorothy Parker, and we *never* met at the Algonquin without her quoting some lines.

"I *love* DP!"

"Who doesn't love a New Jersey wiseass?" I agreed.

Authors and actors and artists and such
Never know nothing, and never know much.

"Can you give me a little more time, Wendy? A few more months to process everything. Then I'll take you to Newark, we'll stand in Dutch Shultz's bloodstain, and I'll answer every single question you have."

"You *never* make things easy."

"You say that a lot."

"It's true."

"I know it's true. I'm sorry."

She took a hit off her Manhattan, which was a drink she actually liked and which I'd never understood since they taste absolutely horrible.

It was her third one tonight, and she had the lovely daze of an almost high on her lovely face.

Her eyes were especially alluring.

"What's next, Bret?"

"I think I'll vanish for a while. Maybe go somewhere I've never been before, live alone, and avoid all the members of that peculiar sex of which you are a member, initiating a kind of sabbatical of sorts from each and every female on the face of the earth. Then I'll write another book."

"So this whole mess did you some good?"

"I suppose it did. I'm not sure why, but I feel the urge to write some *real* fiction.

"About what?"

"Maybe the Tylenol idea."

"I've always liked that one."

"You always say that, Wendy, because you're the best agent in the world. And the best friend."

She seemed pleased.

"Kiss me before you go."

I did.

The marvelous taste of Wendy and her moist mouth obliterated the untasted ugliness of her three Manhattans.

Chapter 58

The New York Times

Sunday, March 3

*W*hoa!

THIS WEEK	HARDCOVER FICTION	LAST WEEK
1	*NOVEL* Bret Buchanan (Simon & Schuster.) A threatened novelist is forced to write a novel.	1
2	*CITY OF NIGHMARES* Michael Connelly. (Little, Brown.) Harry Bosch attends the funeral of someone he knows is alive.	5

Chapter 59

Ending

Monday, March 4

*F*ive days later, on a Vieux Carre balcony in the French Quarter, I
started working on my first novel.

APPENDIX

Re-resolution.

Chapter 60

The Parks Literary Agency

Wednesday, December 12

I drove the mile to Route 23, went south to 46, merged into Route 3, hitting the tunnel at 12:46. After a little congestion at 34th, I took 9th down to 23rd, crossed the island, then parked in a lot near Gramercy Theatre.

After walking back to Park Avenue South, I entered the large glassy lobby and waited for Wendy.

2. Give the completed manuscript to your agent on December 12.

Maybe I could have emailed it, but I was sticking as tight to the rules as possible. Besides, it was a nice brisk December day, and I'd been hermitizing myself in the log cab for the past six weeks, and my brother had started referring to me as the Unabomber, even though he respected my privacy and encouraged me to do whatever the hell I was doing.

It felt good to have the book completed, and, oddly enough, I'd enjoyed the writing and the discipline of writing. Maybe that was because, for the most part, I'd managed to push all the rest of it out of my mind. But now, as I was driving into the city, then waiting in the lobby, it was all rushing back. The rifle shot, the threat to Faulkner, and everything else.

[Note to the Box-Sender: It's done. Written to the best of my abilities. Honor your commitment.]

When the middle elevator doors opened, Wendy stepped into the lobby. She was wearing black pants, a white shirt, and a light tan (camel?) colored double-breasted blazer. She looked like she always looked, preppy-business-casual-impeccable and lovely.

She looked like a girl that only an idiot would break up with.

When she saw me, she walked over and kissed me on the cheek

Then she looked at the manuscript.

"What's it about?"

"It's about a guy who's forced to write a novel about being forced to write a novel."

"I like it."

She sat down on a padded bench.

I didn't, so she looked up.

"Is it about us?"

"No."

"Maybe it should be."

"Maybe the next one."

Which I hoped didn't sound as sarcastic as it sounded, but she didn't seem to mind.

"Tell me more."

I hesitated.

"I'm taking it upstairs to read it anyway," she pointed out.

"It's about a thirty-six-year-old guy who learns he has a daughter."

She had a look on her face that I'd never seen before.

A kind of astonishment.

"Sit down, Bret."

Why not?

The book was done, and I certainly didn't want to be rude, so I sat down next to her on the padded bench.

"*You're* thirty-six, Bret."

"Exactly."

"Is it about you?"

"All my books are about me."

She laughed. After all, it was my first book.

"Tell me what's going on."

"I can't."

She was, of course, intrigued, and I knew she'd feel even more so later in the afternoon when she'd finished reading the manuscript. So I decided to deal with it now, rather than wait for her phone call.

Or a surprise visit to New Jersey.

"Why not?" she asked.

"Remember what we talked about last September, Wendy? You need to trust me. I need your help with this."

"All right."

That was it.

"No more questions?" I checked.

"No more questions."

She was, as always, being the good soldier, and I knew that I owed her a lot, especially for making everything happen as per the twelve ridiculous demanding guidelines.

Which she'd be reading within the next half-an-hour or so, a few pages deep into the manuscript.

"I'll tell you everything," I promised, "by the end of the year."

"Promise?"

"Promise."

"But you don't always keep your promises."

I was surprised to hear her say that, so I waited for her explanation.

"You once told me that you'd take me to the place in Newark where Dutch Shultz was gunned down in 1935."

I smiled.

In spite of myself.

"That was when we were together, Wendy."

"So what? When someone breaks things off with someone, does that efface all previous promises?"

I wasn't sure.

I thought it over.

She wasn't really feeling sorry for herself, and I liked the word "efface."

"You're right, Wendy, it shouldn't. We'll go to Newark on the same day that I tell you about the book."

She was satisfied.

She stood up.

"You know, you're much more peculiar than I'd realized."

I had no idea if that was a good thing or a bad thing.

She kissed me on the forehead, walked to the elevator, and vanished.

Chapter 61

Christmas Eve

Monday, December 24

I should have been watching *It's a Wonderful Life.*

Or listening to Markie's Johnny Mathis Christmas CD.

Instead, I was re-reading Zeno Gandía's *La Charca*, which was hardly upbeat Christmas fare.

At least, it was taking my mind off "the other business." Besides, I knew that I'd have a great Christmas tomorrow with Kyle, Angie, and the twins.

I was slogging my way through ZG's tragically harrowing tale of abused coffee campesinos, as they struggled to survive in the coastal mountains of Puerto Rico in the late 1800's.

The novel's convoluted plot is quite peculiar, especially given the fact that its two main characters never actually meet. *Never.* Sometimes, the novel (just like this one), is frustratingly repetitive, and its lush romantic descriptions of the natural environment are often overdone. Especially within such a grim Zolaesque kind of story. But what affected me the most in the novel was not the brutal tribulations of the beautiful young Silvina (as horrible as they were), but rather the uncompromising portrayal of the relentless self-recriminations of Juan del Salto, the wealthy and cultured plantation owner.

During a telling dinner and post-dinner discussion between del Salto, Padre Esteban, and the materialist Dr. Pintado, the latter dismisses the current generation as hopelessly lost:

> *Es menester escribir en su frente lo que leyó el Dante sobre*
> *la puerta de su célebre infiernoe.* "Lasciate ogni . . . ."

Which, despite my embarrassing Spanish, might be rendered as something like this:

> *We might as well inscribe on their foreheads what Dante*
> *read above the entrance of his famous inferno.* "Abandon
> . . . ."

Meaning "Abandon all hope ye who enter here."

Nevertheless, each of the "intellectuals" offers a simplistic solution for future progress.

Dr. Pintado: economic reform.

Padre Esteban: faith and morality.

Juan del Salto: physical (health) improvement.

In truth, only the priest is actively trying to improve the lives of the peasants, and del Salto, as he admits, always takes the easy way out, does nothing, remains "*silencio*," and wastes his time "theorizing" and "intellectualizing."

Which both he and the author Zeno Gandía know is reprehensible.

The deadly sin of omission.

Which leaves the poor campesinos stranded in their miserable *charca*, in their foul stagnant pond, so that, at the novel's end:

En el misterio de la noche, Dios sollozaba.

[*In the mystery of the night, God wept.*]

I shut the book.

What a way to spend Christmas Eve!

No wonder Markie had trouble writing *Cristobal*.

There was a knock at my door.

It reminded me of the knock at my door on the day the mysterious box arrived. I got up immediately, went down the stairs, and opened the door.

She was standing in the snowscape holding her travel bag in one hand and a rifle with a mounted scope in the other.

"Merry Christmas!"

With a happy Carolina accent.

I glanced around the neighborhood. No one was lurking. There were two trails of indecipherable footprints in the light snow-dust.

"I hope you don't mind the surprise," Faulkner said, probably finding my non-welcome a bit unwelcoming.

"Of course not! I'm delighted."

I kissed her on the forehead, beneath her red wool-knit cap, then I stepped back and looked down at the rifle.

"It was lying here," she explained, looking down at its fading imprint in the snow next to the doorway.

I took the rifle in one hand and her bag in the other, and we walked back upstairs into the cabin.

She liked it.

"It's so cute!"

Which isn't exactly what a Jersey guy wants to hear about his man cave, but I was happy that *she* was happy.

I put her bag on the bed in my little guest room and looked, once again, at the Remington.

So did Faulkner.

"Is it a Yankee tradition to leave weapons outside one's house on the night before Christmas?"

I laughed.

It was good to see her comfortable and kidding around. I also took an undeserved fatherly pride in her wiseassishness.

Maybe it was genetic.

"Let me put it away somewhere," I said, not really explaining anything.

I took the rifle into my bedroom and laid it down on top of my red comforter. I had no doubt that it was the rifle that had blown a hole through my shoulder, and I also had no doubt that it would be fingerprint free and serial number free. Even Faulkner's prints would be missing since she was wearing red knit gloves that matched her cap as well as her scarf.

What did it mean?

It clearly contradicted the guidelines.

11. When all the conditions are met, and only then, the rifle will be forwarded to you and the threat will terminate.

But *all* the conditions hadn't been met. The book hadn't even been published yet. Was it a sign that the box-sender was satisfied with my progress? Was it some kind of bizarre Christmas gift? Was it an indication that something had changed? That maybe the box-sender was pleased? Or not pleased? Or was it some kind of veiled threat? Or most important of all, was Faulkner in some kind of danger just by being here in New Jersey where all this started with a box and a rifle shot three months ago?

I had no idea.

I also had no time to think about it. My daughter was standing in the living room of my log cabin, reading the spines on the books in my bookshelves.

Like father, like daughter.

She looked perfectly lovely.

Being the best Christmas present I've ever had.

Just like her mother, she was full of fun and mischief, and we listened to Christmas music, ate Christmas pizza, drank Christmas plum wine, and had a wonderful time doing nothing much of anything, just sitting around the living room and talking.

About *her* life.

And then, whenever she wanted, about mine.

Much of the time she reminded me of me, but most of the time, she reminded me of Bonnie, with a little bit of Charlie thrown in.

"Oh, Charlie's fine with the idea," Faulkner explained, explaining that she'd called her aunt last week with the idea of laying over in Newark for a night before flying down to Columbia for Christmas with Charlie.

So she could surprise her father.

I was, of course, very grateful that Charlie had approved.

After what had happened in the Orkneys, things seemed to have resolved themselves rather smoothly, without any awkward complications.

Or weirdness.

The night after our night in Kirkwall, Charlie had sent me an email:

> *Thanks for doing what you did, Bret. I think you'll be a good father and a good friend to Faulkner. To me as well, who enjoyed our night together. – C.*

Whatever her idiosyncratic syntactical choices, Charlie wasn't one to beat around the bush, and she'd made things easy for the both of us. I fired back:

> *I did as well. – B.*

Let's keep in touch.

Yes. – B.

And that was that.

Except for the nights and days and afternoons when I would re-member holding her close in the moonlight in Kirkwall and wishing that I could do it again.

Faulkner talked a lot about Charlie, about her Scottish pals, and, of course, about Bonnie. Late that Christmas Eve, sitting in front of the flameless fireplace that I've never actually fired-up, and probably never will, she even talked about Bonnie's death.

I wasn't aware that she'd been at the lake that day.

She was sitting right next to Charlie, on a wooden dock at Lake Moultrie, waiting for her mom and her stepdad to land his Cessna at the local landing strip, planning to meet them on the dock.

"They knew we were down there, so Chase did a couple of flyovers around the lake, and Charlie and I waved, even though I wasn't sure if they could actually see us. Then Chase winged a treetop, a huge old pine, and they flipped, banged some more trees, then crashed into the lake, not far from the shore."

"Did you see it land?"

Maybe I shouldn't have asked.

"No, but we could see the flames that rose over the tops of the trees."

I had no idea that the plane went up in flames.

Faulkner snuggled close to me on the couch, as I suppose a teenage daughter might do.

"It's nice to have a father," she said.

"Even one you don't know?" I kidded.

"Well, what I know so far, I like."

I thought to myself, *screw* the box-sender. Go ahead and shoot me again if you want, nothing could mean more to a man than a child's love.

Even though I knew it wasn't quite "love" yet. But we were working on it.

Later, she gave me my Christmas presents: a silly smiling teddy bear and an old envelope.

"Charlie agreed it was a good idea, so she sent it to me in St. Andrews."

I had no idea what she was talking about, so I took the letter out of its envelope, both of which were slightly yellowed with age:

Dear Bonnie Jean MacMillan:

It was an academic acceptance letter, sent to Bonnie over seventeen years ago, admitting her to the University of St. Andrews.

"Charlie found it in my mom's papers a few weeks ago. I guess my mom was planning to join you in Fife until what happened happened."

Meaning the pregnancy.

Beneath my usual Jersey exterior, I'd gone a bit sad-and-mushy, thinking about that lovely young girl, years ago, fully ready to leave

South Carolina behind and follow her boyfriend to Scotland, until she realized that she was pregnant, that everything had suddenly changed.

"Is it a good present? Or is it too sad?"

"It's a wonderful present, but it's sad, too."

"I know."

She changed the subject:

"OK, now, it's time for pictures! I want to see them all! Everything you've got!"

Of Markie: "She's *so* beautiful!"

Of my mom (her grandmother): "She *so* pretty."

Of my brother: "He looks like a handsomer you."

(Yes, quite the wiseguy.)

Of Angie, of the twins: "They're adorable!"

And, of course, my eighteen-year-old pictures of Bonnie. Of Bonnie and me together. At Gamecock football games, at her mom's house, hanging in the Horseshoe, studying in the library, wearing her father's hand-me-down Roger Staubach football jersey, eating pizza, smiling, always smiling, etc.

Faulkner cried, and I was helpless, but I suppose, if there is such a thing, it was a "good" cry, a "healthy" cry.

"I can actually see *it*!" she said.

Once again, I had no idea what she was talking about.

"What?"

"That you two were in love."

Which made her cry even more.

Which also made her happy. Happy to think about her own mom, back when she was the same age as Faulkner, being in love with somebody.

Being happy.

"Yes," I agreed.

Later, I slipped in a few other photos.

Irene, Wendy, Skye, and Rosie on horseback.

Wondering if she'd ever seen them before, getting a "no" on Irene and Wendy, getting a "she looks a bit familiar, but I don't think so" on Skye, and getting a "yes, I did see her once, and she's *very* beautiful," on Rosie.

I was astonished!

"When?"

"About a year ago. Maybe more like a year and a half."

"Where?"

"At the house."

I waited for more.

"I got home from school one day, and she was sitting in the living room talking to mom."

"Are you sure?"

"Yes."

"Was Charlie there?"

"No."

"What were they talking about?"

"I don't know. I didn't stick around."

It was hard to process.

"Who is she?" Faulkner wondered.

"An old friend."

Attempting to distract her, I showed her more pictures of the twins, and the "old friend" was soon forgotten.

At least, by her.

Certainly not by me.

Chapter 62

Padonia Ale House

Monday, January 7

"**I** never really liked the guy, but he could blow the crap out of anything."

I was sitting at a small table in the Padonia Ale House, watching Bob Grudin eat his nachos, smothered with chili-salsa-jalapeños-and-sour cream, regarding which he'd informed me earlier:

"My wife only lets me eat here once a week."

No wonder.

Every Monday evening, right after work, he stopped at the ale house and stuffed himself with nachos, along with a pitcher or two of peach margaritas.

He was probably around sixty, above the recommended weight, balding, with a carefully trimmed short white beard. During the day, he worked at Controlled Demolition, Inc., which imploded buildings, stadiums, bridges, towers, tunnels, and anything else under the sun.

Its main office was five miles away in Phoenix, Maryland, and Bob Grudin used to be Rex Kepler's boss.

Over a week ago, after Faulkner had flown to Columbia for Christmas, I decided to spend the next week or so dedicating an entire day to each of my primary suspects. So I could rethink everything, do some more research, and spend my time indulging in wild speculations. Somewhere in the course of my Charlie day, I started thinking about Bonnie again, and about her "missing" first husband, and about his military training.

I called up Colt and left a message:

> *I'd like a look at the military records of both Charleston McMillan and Rex Kepler.*

Such things, of course, aren't public record, but Jack Colt can get ahold of anything he wants to get ahold of.

Then I started Rex-ing across the web, Googling "demolitions" and "explosions," discovering three curiosities that especially caught my interest, always keeping in mind that I was wildly speculating:

1998 – The demolition, by Controlled Demolition, Inc., of the Villa Panamericana Housing Complex in San Juan, Puerto Rico.

2010 – The demolition, by CD Inc., of the 3K-Reactor Cooling Tower at the Savannah River Site in Aiken, South Carolina, which had more than a half-million YouTube hits, so I added a couple more of my own.

2004 – The inexplicable local explosion at a storage facility in West Co-
lumbia, South Carolina, in which a young girl was seriously injured.

The last one, most probably, was just a coincidence, but I decided to track down Bob Grudin anyway, and I managed to convince him to meet me at the ale house.

Who, between nacho bites, talked about Kepler.

About being a jerk.

About having been well-trained in the Army.

Being an expert in not only nitro and dynamite, but in various variants of RDX as well.

Being irresponsible.

Being a relentless womanizer.

Which, of course, was hurtful to hear about. Which I hoped Bonnie never knew about.

"Look, kid, I'm a by-the-booker, which you *have* to be in this racket. There's too much at stake. If something goes wrong, there's lives at stake."

"What about that storage explosion in Columbia, South Carolina?"

He wasn't prepared for that one.

"I haven't had enough margaritas to talk about that."

"All right, why not let *me* do the talking. Kepler was living in West Columbia at the time, and he disappeared right afterwards, and they found some stuff in the wreckage that implicated CD Inc."

"Whoa, we were *never* implicated in anything."

"I read you got hit with several lawsuits."

"Somebody's been doing some web-snooping."

"Did Rex do it?"

"No."

"How do you know?"

"Because he was with me in Florida at the time. We were scouting a job at the Space Launch Complex in Cape Canaveral, where we later took down their Mobile Service Structure, which happened long after Rex was out of the picture."

I was confused.

"Then why'd he take off? Why'd he vanish?"

"I have no idea, but, honestly, I was glad to see him go."

"And you have *no* idea where he is?"

"No, none."

"And you haven't had any contact with him in the past fourteen years."

"None. Look, kid, I know you said you're a friend of the guy's wife, but she's definitely better off without him. Besides, that was all a long time ago."

I didn't disagree.

"And just for the record, those lawsuits never went anywhere, although we did donate some money to the family of the injured girl, who recovered nicely, by the way. Which you probably don't know about."

I didn't.

Something else dawned on me.

"Was Rex stealing from the company?"

Grudin thought it over, carefully weighing his response.

"In my opinion, which I'll *never ever* repeat again under *any* circumstance, he was doing exactly that."

"Why?"

He shrugged.

"Because he was always bitching about me, about the company, about everything. Always jabbering about starting his own company. Where he'd be in charge, where he wouldn't have to put up with the likes of me."

Grudin laughed, then he waved to the kid behind the bar for another pitcher of margaritas.

"So what do *you* think happened to Rex?"

It was Grudin's turn to speculate.

He seemed glad to do it.

"I'd like to imagine that some bargirl's husband shot him in some filthy parking lot, then dumped him into a swamp somewhere."

He smiled, then mitigated a bit.

"I hope that doesn't sound too harsh."

I had to admit, I liked Bob Grudin, and I'd be willing to bet that he was a pretty good boss.

I stood up, shook his hand, and thanked him.

"I hope the wife can forget about that moron," he said.

I nodded and left the ale house.

When I found my rental, a black BMW, in the parking lot, I got in the driver's seat and called Charlie MacMillan.

She answered.

"It's Charlie," she said softly, with a mess of graceful Southern intonations.

"It's Bret. How've you been, Charlie?"

I wasn't sure if I needed to add my last name.

It wasn't necessary.

She told me she was doing fine, and the conversation felt a lot less awkward than I'd anticipated.

"Thanks for letting Faulkner stop in New Jersey."

"She's old enough to make her own decisions, Bret, but I'm glad she went. I think knowing her father can be a blessing in her life."

I felt certain that she got the word "blessing" from her mother, from Bonnie, and even though it seemed misapplied to the likes of me, it was lovely to hear the word.

Then we talked a bit about Faulkner, until, casually, I steered things towards Rex.

"When Faulkner was in New Jersey, we talked about both Rex and Chase."

She didn't seem surprised.

"I've been wondering," I tried, "if Bonnie ever heard from Rex again?"

"That's an odd question."

"Well, the story about a guy simply vanishing is pretty peculiar, right, Charlie?"

I could hear her thinking over the phone. I could hear her deciding to tell me the truth.

"He popped up about three years ago."

I waited.

"He wanted Bonnie to come and visit."

"Where?"

"Somewhere out of the country. I think he was wanted by the police for something, but I don't know for sure. I'm just glad she didn't get reinvolved. He's a detestable person."

"What country, Charlie?"

"I don't know."

"Any guesses?"

"Maybe the Caribbean somewhere. He was always a beach bum."

There was a pause, then a continuation.

"Why are you so interested in ancient history?"

"It sounds like it's not so ancient, Charlie. Besides, I don't want him popping up in Faulkner's life again. Or yours."

She appreciated it.

"Will I see you again, Bret?"

"Yes."

When she didn't ask when, I explained anyway:

"These days I'm wrapped up in a time-consuming writing project. How about sometime this summer? When Faulkner's back in Carolina?"

"Sounds fine."

"Take care of yourself, Charlie."

"You too."

We hung up.

Earlier, I'd decided *not* to ask her about Rosie. About the possibility that Rosie had met with Bonnie a year-and-a-half ago.

I'd need to deal with that later.

Chapter 63

The Palmetto Trailer Park

Tuesday, January 8

I t was dark, dismal, probably dangerous.

Intermittently, sketchy characters would flit in and out of their metal meth boxes as irritating rap music assaulted the outer darkness. It was Lowlifesville, USA, nine miles from historic downtown Charleston, "America's most friendly city."

Someone, clearly looking out of place, came up the lampless narrow street.

As instructed.

It was Virgil Jefferson Anderson, age seventy-two, the former mayor of Charleston, the current President of the South Carolina Senate. He was alone, dressed in an expensive gray suit, with thick-gray hair neatly coiffed.

Earlier today, I'd called him at his Charleston office and threatened to expose him if he didn't meet me here at eleven p.m.

Alone.

As he got closer, he seemed more subdued than angry or worried. As if a reckoning was at hand.

"What can I do for you, young man?"

He had a reputation for being honest. For being polite. Like a good Southern gentleman. His accent wasn't like either Charlie's or Faulkner's, it was old-school upscale Charleston.

Delicate.

"You don't look like Kurt Cobain."

He smiled.

"Yeah, that was Raven's little joke."

"Did you think it was funny?"

"No, I certainly didn't, not at the time."

"Did you love her?"

He shrugged, as if he really didn't know.

"I was married back then, and she was obviously self-destructive. She was also twenty years younger than I was, and I loved being with her. If that counts for anything."

It sounded like an honest answer.

"Tell me about it."

"Why not?"

He sounded like a condemned man who'd made his peace. Like a man who was fully ready to accept his failings, equally ready to accept the fact that his political life was over.

He told me about the opening, back when he was mayor of Charleston, of a new rehab center on Daniel Island, where he first met Raven Darrow, taking an interest in her and her problems, although, not quite yet, a sexual interest. Which happened eventually. Then she got pregnant, and all she wanted was money and drugs, so they kept it quiet.

"You let your daughter live in this dump?" I said, trying not to sound excessively self-righteous.

Failing badly.

"Yes, I had a wife and a son, and I was a coward. But I'll say one thing for Raven, despite living in this hellhole, she was a decent caretaker."

We were standing in front of #12, a complete wreck of a filthy trailer, where Charlie had spent the first ten years of her life.

"She was an addict," I pointed out.

"I know. There's no excuse. None."

He was right about that.

"Tell me the rest."

When Raven OD'd, Charlie found her dead mother with a needle still stuck in her arm. Then the mayor, now a state senator, went to Bonnie and asked her to take care of the ten-year-old.

"Why Bonnie?"

"I was an old friend of her mother's. We grew up together, and I'd watched Bonnie grow up from a distance, and I knew how special she was, even though she got herself knocked-up by some sleazeball who'd abandoned her. So I offered her some money and any kind of assistance she needed to take care of little Charleston."

"Which she did."

"Which she *didn't*."

I was confused, so he explained.

"Then I did something even *more* despicable. I drove over to her house one night, sat Charleston on the front step, rang the doorbell, and walked away. When Bonnie opened the door, she looked down at the young girl. Then she looked up and saw me sitting in my car across the street. We locked eyes for a moment. Then she looked away, took the little girl by the hand, and took her inside."

I waited for more.

I got excuses and self-pity.

"I was trying to save my marriage, but, somehow, my son found out about Raven, then Charleston, and he cut me out of his life, then he enrolled at the Air Force Academy and never spoke to me again."

"Never?"

"Never."

No wonder Chase was so screwed up.

"Later, after my wife died, Bonnie let me back into Charleston's life a little bit, as an 'old family friend,' but that ended when Bonnie and Chase got married. Later, Bonnie allowed Charlie to intern at the Senate, and now, as you know, she works for me at the State House."

"You've never told her?"

"No."

"Why?"

"Because I don't want her to hate me."

It seemed a simple enough reason.

"To be honest," he explained, "the only reason that I stay in politics anymore is to see my daughter five days a week. I know I don't deserve it, but it's been the blessing of my life, in my final years."

"I'm not a reporter," I explained, maybe feeling sorry for the guy.

"Then what *are* you? If you don't mind my asking."

"A friend of the family."

"I know the family pretty well, but I've never seen you before."

"I'm a friend of Charlie's, and I intend to tell her the truth. Whether she decides to tell anyone else is entirely up to her."

He was surprised.

"You're right, young man. I guess it's time she knows the truth."

"Does she like you?" I wondered.

Which seemed an odd question to ask, but he didn't seem to mind.

"Yes. We get along very well, but I keep myself out of her personal life. Everything that happens between us happens at the State House."

"Maybe she won't hate you."

"Maybe."

By now, he was weary and worn-out. He sat down on an old truck tire that was, for no discernable reason, lying at the edge of the road. He looked over at trailer #12, and it seemed as though he wanted to cry, cry for everything he'd done, for everything he hadn't done. But he couldn't. As if, somewhere within his heart, he knew that he didn't deserve any kind of emotional expiation.

As if from nowhere, two creeps creeped up the street, looking us over as they came. One looked a bit Hispanic, the other one was covered with so many stupid tattoos that, in the darkness of the night, it was impossible to tell *what* he was. Maybe that was the point.

They said nothing, but they were definitely checking us out. Checking out their prey, particularly the old guy in the expensive gray suit. As they got closer, I opened up my leather jacket so they could see the butt of my Colt Defender, which was sticking out of my belt.

A few days ago, after Colt got a hold of Charlie's original birth certificate, the one listing her father's real name, I told him what I was planning to do.

"You want me to tag along?" Colt offered.

"No, but thanks."

So he gave me a 9mm instead.

He knew I wasn't much with guns, but he also knew that I'd done some shooting at the range with my brother and a bunch of his cop buddies, so I wasn't completely inept.

The two punks looked me up-and-down, saw the gun, and decided not to bother.

As they walked past, I turned and watched them go. No one said a word. Then they entered one of the more dilapidated trailers and shut the door behind them.

"I should have brought one too," Anderson said, as if astonished by his own stupidity.

He looked at me directly.

"Are we done?"

"Not yet. I want to hear about Rex Kepler."

He was surprised.

"*That* idiot? He's somewhere down in Mexico."

"How do you know?"

"Bonnie told me. He called her a couple of years ago and tried to get her to come and visit, but she was much too smart for that."

"Where in Mexico?"

"I never heard."

"Did she ever hear from Rex again?"

"I believe she did."

"When?"

He thought it over, calculating.

"About eighteen months ago. He wanted her back again. I guess he'd finally realized what he'd thrown away."

"She said 'no'?"

"Yes, she said no."

I looked down at the most powerful politician in the state of South Carolina, excepting maybe the governor, excepting maybe its two senators, and he looked rather pathetic, and I felt sorry for him.

"You should get going," I said.

He stood up.

"I have a feeling," he said, "that you only want to do what's right for Charlie."

"That's right."

He put out his hand, and I shook it.

"One more thing," I said.

He waited patiently.

"What about the plane crash?"

"I'm not sure what you mean."

"I want to know the truth. Or at least your honest opinion."

"About what?"

"About what happened."

"I'm still not sure what you want."

"I want to know *why* it crashed. I want your opinion."

"I try not to think about it."

"Do you think it was an accident?"

"No."

"Do you think Bonnie had anything to do with it?"

He seemed astonished.

Horrified.

"Of course not!"

"Do you think your son did?"

He paused, then answered.

"Chase was a very troubled young man, which was entirely *my* fault."

"Did your son crash that plane?"

"I believe that he did."

He walked up the dark street towards wherever he'd parked his car. Before he completely vanished into the night, he stopped and turned around.

"When?"

I knew exactly what he meant.

"I'm not sure yet."

"Could you let me know when you decide to tell her?"

"I will."

He was grateful.

Now he could walk back into his life, which would remain the same for a little while longer, until he eventually got a call from some never-named guy whom he'd met in the darks of a low-life trailer park.

Then his whole life would change once again.

Irrevocably.

Chapter 64

Lake Moultrie

I was sitting on a wooden pier directly across from Pinopolis Peninsula, which jutted into the southern end of Lake Moultrie. It was the same pier where Charlie and Faulkner had seen the Cessna clip one of the high pines, flip over, then descend to a crash at the edge of the lake on the other side of the peninsula.

Earlier this afternoon, I'd driven around the perimeter of the huge lake, sixty-thousand acres, and it was easy to see why Lake Moultrie and the surrounding area is known as a vacationer's paradise. For South Carolinians. For anyone. With campgrounds, marinas, fishing boats, and nearby hunting. With low-lying swamps, Tupelo trees, cypress stickups, lily pads, tree stumps, grass beds, and occasional alligators (one of which, according to a brochure, was over thirteen feet long, over a thousand pounds).

It some ways, Moultrie looked like a Louisiana bayou.

It was now winter in the Palmetto state.

The afternoon was overcast, which seemed to heighten the peculiar beauty of the lake and its coastline. According to Faulkner, Bonnie loved the place, loving to get away into the wilderness whenever she could.

I suppose there are worse places to die.

Lots of them.

But I wasn't really thinking about *that* right now.

I was rereading several news accounts from *The State*, Columbia's daily newspaper, about the West Columbia storage explosion that took place fourteen years ago. The case was still unsolved. At the time, it was determined, or, at least, assumed, that both nitro and semtex had inexplicably ignited in one of the storage rooms registered to Lucas Green, which was, of course, a false and untraceable identity. The explosion destroyed the entire storage facility and much of the surrounding block, damaging several nearby warehouses.

Since the explosion had taken place early on a Sunday morning, there was only one victim, Missie Andrews, a twelve-year-old girl, who was riding her bicycle down Highcrest Avenue, returning from a Church service, when she was struck by metal shrapnel in her left leg. At Lexington Medical Center, the doctors were fully expecting and fully prepared to remove her leg, below the knee, but somehow the limb was salvaged, and two years later, she was walking normally and supposedly recuperated from the trauma.

There were no suspects, except the never-located "Lucas Green," and only a few people had been seen in the area that Sunday morning: a homeless man named Jason Ricker, two teenage boys, and a young girl, who may, or may not, have been the girl on the bicycle. Ricker and the boys were all questioned, and the investigation dead-ended.

It was eventually discovered that some of the semtex had originally been purchased by Controlled Demolition, Inc., the world's most famous demolition company, located in Phoenix Maryland.

But that fact led nowhere.

It seemed to me, and I'm sure that Bob Grudin felt the same way fourteen years ago, that Rex Kepler had stolen the explosives from CD Inc., stored them at the facility under a bogus name, and then skipped town, the country, and his marriage right after the explosion.

I got a text from Irene:

How'm I doin?

Well, I guess she was doing rather badly if she was still contacting her stalkee despite the restraining order.

I heard footsteps coming down the pier behind me.

Vinny.

He'd spent the morning, and all day yesterday, reviewing the remaining wreckage, which was still being held, by law, in a hangar at the Berkeley County Airport, as well as all the NTSB reports about the plane crash.

"I need you, Vin," I said last week, "to check out a Cessna crash in South Carolina."

"Sure."

"With no questions asked."

"None."

It's what friends do, and Vinny was my best and oldest friend. Along with my brother.

He came up behind me, sat down beside me, and looked at the lake.

"It's very beautiful."

"Yeah."

"And weird."

"Yeah."

During my last semester at South Carolina, Vinny had come down for a weekend. We drank too much, watched the Gamecocks lose to a highly ranked North Carolina basketball team, and had a great time. He also, of course, met Bonnie, whom he thought was the "greatest."

So even though it was a no-questions-asked situation, Vinny, of course, knew *exactly* who'd died here.

"I thought you were going to marry that girl," he said.

"So did I, whenever I bothered to think about it back then. Which wasn't very much. I was too young, too stupid, having too much of a good time. Totally oblivious."

"Yeah, we were both pretty oblivious back in those days," he agreed.

We stared at the dark gray waters, beneath the huge dark gray sky, and said nothing much for a while.

Then he decided to tell me what I wanted to know.

"The Cessna 175 is a hell of a little aircraft. Do you know anything about it?"

"No."

He told me.

Known as the Skylark, it's a four-seat, single-engine, high-and-fixed wing aircraft. The most popular and reliable personal aircraft in aviation history.

"When these things come down, it's almost always pilot error. Or weather-related."

"But wasn't it reported as some kind of an engine malfunction?"

"Yeah, and what's left of the engine seems to support it, although I found a bit of metal scarring."

"Is that suspicious?"

"It wouldn't be to most people, but it is to me. I wouldn't rule out some kind of small explosive. Something *very* small, something *very* well-placed. But there's no real evidence."

"Nothing? No residue?"

Vinny laughed.

"I guess you *have* been paying attention all these years. Yeah, I did spot a few possibilities for chemical residue, and I'll be checking them out. Right away."

"Anything else?"

"Some possible DNA traces on a few of the fragments, but don't get your hopes up. It's perfectly normal. It's probably from either the pilot or one of his mechanics."

"Or maybe not."

"Or maybe not."

Chapter 65

Myrtle Beach

Thursday, January 10

"**I**t's time to go."

It was a beach bar called Gamecocks on the boardwalk facing the ocean, not far from Ripley's, not far from the SkyWheel. It was almost two in the morning, the crowd was long gone, and the bartender was getting impatient.

Colt, who hadn't said much of anything since I'd picked him up at Myrtle Beach International Airport an hour ago, stood up from our corner table, walked over to the only remaining people in the bar, a seemingly pleasant lovey-dovey couple in their early thirties, then bent over and said something that I couldn't hear.

Immediately, the couple stood up, with what seemed to me a look of fearfulness in their eyes, and left the bar.

I felt sorry for them, but it was hard not to be impressed by the way Colt could clear a room. Then he walked over to the bar.

I joined him.

The bartender was wrapping things up for the night. He was probably around forty, still a good looker, with black hair and a tattoo on his right forearm.

"Bonnie."

Colt spoke first.

"How were things down in Puerto Morelos, Rex?"

Colt, of course, had done exactly what I'd asked him to do. Track down Rex Kepler. Who'd been living in a little seaport town south of Cancún on the Yucatán Peninsula, where, for over twelve years, he'd worked in a bar on the beachfront.

"He seems to think the Feds are after him," Colt told me on the phone.

Probably believing that the Feds were after him for the explosion of his stolen nitro/semtex which had somehow detonated in West Columbia, injuring a young girl.

Eventually, Rex had taken a chance and returned to South Carolina.

As Charlie had mentioned four months ago in West Columbia, he was "always blabbing about buying a beach house in Myrtle Beach."

Which he finally did.

But here in Myrtle Beach, Rex wasn't known as Rex. He was pretending to be some guy named Jack Barlow. But, of course, Rex knew *exactly* who he was, and he was more than spooked by Jack Colt.

"I don't know what you're talking about, pal," he said, rather cockily.

Colt didn't appreciate the bravado.

"I don't like your attitude."

"Too bad."

"That's the wrong answer."

Rex tried to bluff his way out.

"Look, you two Yankee assholes can get the hell out of here *right now*, or you can deal with whatever's about to happen."

Which was *definitely* the wrong move.

Colt reached over the bar, grabbed Rex by the neck, and pulled him up-and-over the bar and threw him to the ground.

I didn't even know that you could do that to another human being without breaking his neck, but Rex's neck was working well enough for his throat and tongue to fire up some pretty nasty expletives aimed at Jack Colt.

So Colt took out his taser, actually his stun gun, and zapped the guy in the neck. I'd seen it in the movies, of course, but it was rather remarkable to see it in real life. Rex twitched like a cartoon cat whose tail was stuck in an electrical outlet.

It was amazing to watch how much the human body can tolerate.

When his twitching, convulsing, writhing, and jerking was done, Rex seemed a whole lot more amenable.

Colt wasn't.

"You're going to answer every one of this guy's questions, and I better not sense any equivocations or untruths."

Rex understood.

He nodded.

Then Colt leaned over again and zapped him another time in the neck, which I assumed was some kind of insurance policy. So the two of us stood there, one more time, watching Rex flop around on the floor, with 35,000 volts screwing around with his nervous system, not to mention his electroshocked brain, and, in truth, it wasn't as disconcerting to watch the second time around.

When Rex finally settled down, Colt leaned over, grabbed him, and lifted him into a nearby chair. Then he wiped the drool from Rex's chin and saved it in a little evidence baggie.

Then Colt looked over at me.

As if to say, don't you have some questions?

So I sat down at the small wooden table across from Rex.

It's amazing how our cocky wiseass confident selves can be crushed unequivocally in a matter of moments.

"Did you have sniper training in the military?"

He seemed astonished by the question.

"Yes."

"Good answer," Colt butted in. "We've got your military records."

Rex seemed totally bewildered.

"When were you last in New Jersey?"

"I've *never* been to New Jersey. Never."

"Except to shoot me in the shoulder five months ago."

"What! Wait a minute! I don't know what you two guys are after, but I haven't fired a rifle in years. I'm just a bartender who likes the beach and pretty girls."

I was glad I didn't have a taser. I might have given him some volts myself. But I had to admit, he seemed to be telling the truth, and Colt, who was now sitting on the top of the bar, seemed to be buying it as well.

"Let's talk about blowing things up," I said.

"Sure, I used to do it for a living. But I'm sure you guys know that already."

"What about the storage facility blast in West Columbia?"

Once again, he seemed completely astonished, but for different reasons. He'd been running from that blast for over fourteen years, and he certainly didn't want it catching up to him here, tonight, in the US, in South Carolina.

Colt, who was now holding a drink of some kind, which looked like whiskey, which had apparently materialized from nowhere, must have sensed that some untruths were forthcoming, so he fired his taser again, and Rex and I watched the electricity happily sparkling across the void between the two electrodes.

"I know you stole the stuff from Controlled Demolition," I said, helping Rex along.

"OK, yeah, but I *never* set it off. Why would I? The stuff was worth over a quarter-of-a-million bucks. Besides, I've been on the lam ever since, which you guys seem to know about. Why would I do that to myself?"

It was a reasonable argument.

"Bob Grudin thinks you did it," I pointed out, misleadingly.

"Of course, he thinks I did it. That guy hated my guts, and he'd probably figured out that I was lifting the stuff. But I didn't do it. When that little girl got hurt, I packed my bags and left for Mexico."

I said nothing.

Colt said nothing.

Rex tried again.

"Look, I stole the stuff, all right? I guess that makes me responsible for what happened to the little girl, but I never set it off, and I have no idea who did."

"Could it have been an accident?"

"Maybe. Maybe faulty wiring of some kind. Or excessive heat. But it's highly unlikely."

I was done.

I looked at Colt, who knocked off his whiskey, or whatever it was, and slid off the bar. He took out his wallet and dropped a twenty in Rex's lap, obviously for the drink.

"Here's your tip."

Then he dropped another twenty in the guy's lap.

When I stood up, I opened my leather jacket so Rex could see the tape recorder.

"Don't go anywhere," I said.

Just like the tough guys say in the movies.

It felt good.

We went outside, got in my rental, and headed back to the airport. Since we were low on gas, I stopped at a deserted Exxon, where Colt pumped the gas while I went inside to pay the cashier and get myself a Coke.

As I was coming out the front door, I watched in amazement as a newish, burgundy, Silverado pickup backed itself close to the front of my rental, as Rex, carrying a shotgun of some kind, stepped into the bed of the truck and blasted both barrels into the windshield of the BMW.

Stunned, I dropped my Coke to the ground, pulled out my Defender, and walked towards Rex who'd already reloaded. I couldn't see Colt anywhere, and I was hoping that he'd ducked down, beneath the blasts, in the front seat. Rex must have assumed the same thing, so he stepped forward to fire again.

"Drop it, Rex!"

He looked at me like I was some kind of idiot, then he turned himself in my direction to blow me in half. I fired first, exactly as Kyle had taught me at the range, and I hit him somewhere in the torso, but he didn't fall down, and I knew that I'd have to shoot him again.

Colt took care of the problem.

Five shots rang out in such rapid succession that it seemed like a single staccato sound. Rex contorted, then dropped to the bed of the pickup. When I looked through the mostly missing windshield of the BMW, I could see Colt, sitting in the passenger seat, with blood all over his face.

After several hours dealing with the local cops, all of which was corroborated by the Exxon clerk, I drove the still driveable BMW back to the airport so we could fly home to New Jersey, where Colt would head back to Paterson, where I'd connect on a second flight to Cape Breton Island.

"Maybe it's time you told me what's going on," he understated.

Not needing to add, "I think I've earned it."

"Yeah," I agreed.

So I told him everything.

Almost everything.

Violating the guidelines.

"That's an interesting mess you're sitting in."

"Yeah," I agreed.

"I like messes," Colt admitted.

"Do you think Kepler was telling the truth?"

"Yeah."

"By the way, Colt, you've still got a piece of glass sticking out of your head."

"It's not the first time."

Chapter 66

The Red Shoe

Friday, January 18

I was listening to the real thing live.

Sitting in the Red Shoe, the famous pub in Mabou, close to its little stage, close to the piano, listening to my cousin Howie MacDonald's drop-dead version of Niel Gow's "Lament," which my cousin Leslee, who was also Howie's cousin, had asked him to play.

I was sitting with, and much enjoying, my second cousin (once removed), Leslee, and her husband, Gregor Lennox, celebrating today's Oscar nom as well as the forthcoming publication, by Simon & Schuster, of my new novel entitled *Novel*. "Written by Bret Buchanan," whose previous novel, *Radium Eyes*, co-authored with his wife, had won the Pulitzer Prize.

Which still seemed inexplicable.

Leslee, always my favorite of my favorite Canadian cousins, knew how much I loved the old Scottish tune, so she asked Howie, her first cousin, to fiddle the old Scottish air as I finished my pulled-pork sandwich, with BBQ sweet-potato fries. All of which was extraordinarily delicious.

Rosie, of course, was still on my mind, given that Faulkner had identified her on Christmas Eve. But it was impossible for me to believe that Rosie had anything to do with this mess, even though it seems obvious that she did. Unless, of course, Faulkner was lying, which also seemed impossible. In the meantime, I'd decided to do nothing about it, aware that questioning Rosie over the phone or by swapping emails would have been not only dreadfully awkward but entirely unproductive.

I pushed it from my mind, enjoying the fiddle music, enjoying the company.

Earlier today, the Academy had released its annual list of nominations, and there I was, Bret Buchanan, for Best Adapted Screenplay for *Aircrash*, and, naturally, all my friends and family were very excited about it. Much more so than they were about my forthcoming novel, which none of them knew anything about.

At Paramount, of course, everyone, especially Melanie, was over the moon. Especially given all the other *Aircrash* noms, best picture (which I felt had no chance); Jennifer Lawrence (a lock); best director for J.J. Onah (maybe); best cinematography for Joseph Urbanczyk (I hope so); as well as best costume design (who knows?).

In truth, I was more than glad to get lost in the shuffle, but I knew that I couldn't show up for the Oscars alone. Unfortunately, Kyle was scheduled to be mid-trial at the Passaic County Courthouse.

"Why not go with *all* your friends?" he suggested wiseassedly. "Go alone."

So where did that leave me?

Maybe Faulkner? But wouldn't that necessitate Charlie?

Charlie? Whom I was still feeling awkward about.

Rosie? Whom I was *way too* awkward about.

Skye? More awkwardness.

Wendy? More of the same.

What about Vinny? Who knows?

What about Angie? But she'd never leave the kids in New Jersey.

Maybe I should take Kyle's advice and go with *all* my friends.

Alone.

But I *did* come up with a clever scheme to, in some way, cover myself, emailing Wendy about inviting everyone to the Waldorf three nights after the ceremony to celebrate, win-lose-or-draw, with family and friends.

If possible, getting them all in the same room together.

To look for the box-sender.

During the break, Howie came over and talked for a while, and I thanked him for the dedication. When my cell vibrated, I looked at Colt's text:

The DNA matches.

I wasn't surprised.

Then another one came through:

Call me.

Which seemed odd.

I excused myself, headed for the men's room, then ducked outside, walked up the street, and sat on the hood of Gregor's green Focus.

When I called Colt, he did what he never does. He answered his own phone.

Something was up. I waited. He didn't waste words or time.

"The rifle was purchased in Georgia. Along with a 9mm Beretta."

I didn't ask, "By whom?"

I just waited.

"By Faulkner McMillan."

It was January in the Maritimes, cold as hell, so maybe it numbed the shock.

"Thanks," I said.

But he waited on the line a bit, as if he wanted to help me in some way, but since there was really nothing that he could do, he just waited.

"You all right?"

"Yeah."

"It doesn't *necessarily* mean what it seems to mean."

"I know."

Aware that he couldn't do anything more, Colt hung up his cell, and I did as well.

Then I looked upward, into the wide Cape Breton nightsky, doing what I'd come here to do.

Think.

Chapter 67

The Academy Awards

Sunday, February 24

A nd the Oscar goes to . . . "

None of it seemed real:

The limo drop-off in front of the Dolby.

The security.

The jacked-up crowds pressing to see the stars.

Reporters calling out questions about the novel.

"Is *that* your daughter?"

Walking the red carpet.

Surrounded by cameras.

Flashing everywhere.

Walking the grand staircase.

Until, finally, we were sitting in our seats.

"Peter Morgan, *Trafalgar*."

Everyone applauded. The Brit made his way to the stage, and Faulkner, who'd been holding my hand very tightly, relaxed. I'd warned her, of course, and Charlie as well, when I'd picked them up at LAX this afternoon, that there was *absolutely* "no chance" because Peter Morgan would win tonight. Besides, he deserved it.

So Faulkner wasn't really disappointed, and I kissed her on the top of the head and smiled at Charlie.

After all, they still had the Oscar post-parties to go to.

How many people get to do that?

Chapter 68

The Ritz-Carleton

Sunday, February 24

I t was midnight, and I was sitting at the top of Los Angeles.

Almost.

Halfway up.

Near the rooftop pool of the Ritz-Carlton, on the twenty-sixth floor of the sleekest hotel in Downtown LA, which is actually fifty-four-stories high. Below me, the interminable lights of the City of Mary of the Angels stretched out like a diamond-speckled-sparkled brocade into the distant black void of the Pacific Ocean in the west, into the slightly discernible Santa Monica Mountains to the northwest, beneath a sky of oddly bright and glittering stars.

I was sitting in a comfortable lounge chair, beside the hotel's spacious rooftop pool, still wearing my tuxedo. Twenty minutes earlier, we managed to get Faulkner to bed in her Club-Level suite. She was exhausted, jet-lagged, champagned, and star-struck. She hugged me, kissed me on the cheek, then fell backwards, willingly, into her huge bed.

"I feel like Cinderella!"

It made sense.

Not many college freshmen attend the Oscars, wear a Calvin Klein evening gown, then go to the after-party at Hotel Bel-Air, girl-talking with Jennifer Lawrence, Emma Stone, and Carey Mulligan.

Not to mention meeting Russell Crowe.

It seemed to me, that she'd charmed them all, with her Southern ease, with her Southern accent. So did Charlie. I did my best to protect them both from too many questions and rumors about the book that had been published tonight in New York City, inexplicably on a Sunday, which no one had actually read yet.

Even though all kinds of stuff was floating around:

"Miss MacMillan, have you read the book?"

"Have you ever been threatened?"

"Have you met Dr. MacAllister?"

"Is most of it real?"

"How does it feel to be a character in your father's novel?"

Etc.

To which Faulkner just shrugged, smiled, and said, no, no, no, I have no idea. None!

Charlie did pretty much the same, and it never became a problem. That would have to wait until tomorrow.

As far as I could tell, Faulkner conked out the moment she hit the bed.

I looked at Charlie.

"Is she supposed to sleep in that thing?"

Meaning her evening gown.

"I'll take care of it," Charlie said. "Meet me upstairs."

So I left, came to poolside, and waited.

At present, Charlie was somewhere within the pool. I was waiting again, trying not to think about the only thing my mind was capable of thinking about.

She rose from the pool before me, spectacular against the sky and the stars, dripping in her modest dark green two-piece. She picked up a white towel, pressed it against her face, then down against the dripping rest of her.

I said nothing.

What was there to say?

She leaned over and kissed me on the mouth. She tasted like Asti Spumante. Her scent was a deadly mix of vanilla, tangerine, and chlorine.

She looked down inside her top, took out a room card, and put it on the table next to me.

Modestly.

Then she walked away and went down to her room.

So I sat there and thought about how marvelously lovely the world was, and about how much of a mess we make of it.

Eventually I stood up and went down to her room.

The damp green bathing suit was lying on the plush white rug. Her evening gown, also Calvin Klein, almost matching Faulkner's, which she'd brought from South Carolina, was spread out, neatly, across a spotless white couch, as if resting comfortably after servicing the princess of the realm. Above the couch, I stared through the suite's huge window, seeing much the same awesome LA night view as I'd seen from the pool.

I sat at the gownless end of the couch, as the shower stopped in the marble bathroom. I suppose she wanted to wash off the chlorine, to be cleaner than clean, although I didn't mind the smell of chlorine on her skin.

She walked into the living room. Her hair was still damp, she was barefoot, and she was wearing an overlarge Gamecocks T-shirt.

Nothing else.

She was impossibly irresistible, so I resisted her as quickly as possible.

"I know what you did, Charlie."

"Yes, I know you know."

I figured that she did.

She stood in front of me, as if unconcerned.

"Can we talk about it later?"

Meaning "after."

There was no special pleading in her voice, but I heard it anyway, and I ignored it.

"No, we can't, Charlie."

She was now perfectly willing to exhibit her disappointment, but she didn't say a word. She accepted it stoically, sitting down in a nearby chair and waiting for all the hell in her life to break loose.

When I didn't say anything, Charlie did:

"What do you think you know, Bret?"

"I know that you sent me the box, that you forced me to write the book, and that you shot me in the shoulder."

"I didn't mean to."

"I hoped that was the case."

"It was. I'm sorry."

I believed her.

"But I wonder," she asked, curiously, "*why* you would think that I could make a shot like that?"

"It's a reasonable question, especially since you'd had no sniper training in the army, and since I didn't see any visible guns in your house last September. But earlier today, I called the senator, and I asked him a few questions, and he told me that he used to take you hunting sometimes when you were a teenager. He also said that you were an excellent shot."

"That's right," she remembered. "He used to take me to Sumter National Forest, where there are no antler restrictions, where I once bagged an 8-point buck."

"He told me."

She seemed proud of the memory.

"I should mention, Bret, that I've already read the last twelve chapters of the book," she explained, nodding across the room at a copy of *Novel* that was lying on the window sill, "and I thought it was pretty clever how you put it all on the Scot in your speculative resolution. I assume that she and her husband agreed to play along. To play the patsies."

"Yes."

"Why'd they do it?"

"To help me out," I shrugged. "Besides, they're both a little bit nuts."

It was the best answer I had, and Charlie smiled.

She seemed to approve.

Then she changed the subject.

"Aren't you going to ask me why??"

"Yes."

"Well?"

"Well, first I'd like to talk about the explosion at the storage facility."

Charlie was stunned. She'd clearly anticipated much of what we'd need to talk about tonight, but this came out of left field.

"How could you possibly know about that?"

She was impressed.

When I didn't answer her question, she stood up, walked over to the bar, and poured herself something that looked like brandy.

"You want one?"

"No, thanks."

She came back to her chair, sat down, and sipped at her drink. I think she wanted to hear my version first, my theory, my speculation, my assumption.

I gave it to her.

"I think you watched Rex knock Bonnie around one too many times, and somehow you knew about his stolen explosives, so you stole his key, rode your bike over to the warehouse district, and blew the hell out of everything. How a twelve-year-old girl knew how to do what you did I have no idea."

"I read his stupid instruction manuals! The guy was a slob, and he left them lying all around the house, so I went over there with a really long visco fuse that I'd stolen from the trunk of his car."

"Then that other little girl got hurt."

"She did, and I think that messed me up more than my ten years with a meth mom. It's why I'm still a mess, Bret."

I didn't disagree.

"It's not an excuse," she added.

"No, it's not, Charlie, but you did get rid of Rex."

"Yes."

She was proud of the memory.

"Did you know that he moved back to Myrtle Beach two years ago?"

She was horrified by the possibility.

"No."

"Did you know that he contacted Bonnie eighteen months ago, and that she rejected him again?"

"No, she never mentioned it."

Then Charlie, clever as always, put two-and-two together.

"Did he kill her?"

"Yes."

"Are you sure?"

"Yes."

"Is there evidence?"

"Yes, his DNA was found on some engine fragments, and a trace of semtex residue has also been confirmed."

"Confirmed by Vinny?" she asked.

It wasn't really a question, but it made me wonder *just* how much Charlie knew about my personal life. About my friends. But I didn't bother to try and figure it out. I just agreed with her.

"Yeah."

"He's a good friend, Bret."

"Yeah."

"I wish I had friends like that."

It sounded less like self-pity than a compliment.

"What about Rex," she wondered, "has he been arrested?"

"He's dead."

Charlie was stunned, but not displeased.

"How?"

I told her a truncated but truthful version of the truth.

"You could have been killed!"

"Maybe."

"I'm sorry, Bret."

It sounded as sincere as sincere can get.

"I'm fine."

She leaned back in her chair and thought things over.

"I know this sounds nuts, given my circumstances, but I can't tell you how happy I am that he's gone forever. Which is something that I certainly don't deserve, especially tonight. But I've always been terrified that he'd pop up again in Faulkner's life."

Uncertain how to react, Charlie stood up, leaned over, and hugged me. It wasn't a come-on. It was pure-and-simple gratitude, so I let it happen.

Then she sat down again and smiled.

"I had no idea how smart you were when I started all of this."

Which was another compliment.

"I had help."

"Yes, Jack Colt."

Again, I didn't bother to ask how she knew.

"Maybe it's time to get to the why?" I suggested.

"Well, I'm sure you already know the first part of it, Bret. The *easy* part. That I grew up loving you."

Which, I have to admit, threw me for a loop.

"You were *always* the man in our lives, even though you were never there. You were the one that Bonnie loved, despite her mistakes with Rex and Chase, and you were the mystery that she seldom mentioned, but whenever she did, it was always with love, and I felt the same way."

"I guess it's easy to love a fiction."

"*Very* easy, Bret. But after Bonnie died, after that bastard killed her, I discovered, or, at least, I *thought* I'd discovered, that you'd rejected her a few months before she died. My mind went totally off the rails because I thought she'd killed herself, and that you were the one to blame. After all, as far as I knew, you'd abandoned her at Faulkner's birth, and then it seemed like you'd rejected her once again her after Faulkner had grown up, and, finally, on top of it all, you were a damned Yankee."

"I thought you were over that stuff by then?"

"I was, but I was more than willing to make an exception. So those were my darker reasons, Bret, but there was also a part of me that wanted to see if, in some way, you might be worthy of being Faulkner's father. If, after all the rejections, you might finally do the right thing.

I'd read about you on the web, and about your wife, and you seemed like nice people, and I wondered if you might be ready to become a father of some kind."

None of which sounded unreasonable.

"Then why go through all the incredible BS, Charlie? Why not just fly to New Jersey and confront me?"

"Because something else happened, which is the second part of it, which you'll have to deal with."

Since I had no idea what she was talking about, I just sat there and waited.

"About two years ago, I came home from my internship at the courthouse, and there was this beautiful young woman sitting in the living room talking with Bonnie. She'd come from San Juan on behalf of her sister."

Just as Faulkner had told me on Christmas Eve.

"Markie was dead by then," I pointed out.

"Exactly."

Charlie continued:

"It seems that before she died, your wife asked her sister to make certain that you continued writing. Specifically novels."

I was stunned.

Disbelieving.

"That's pretty hard to believe, Charlie. Why would she do that?"

"I have no idea. Maybe she had some kind of premonition of her death."

"That's idiotic. Besides, she would have told me."

Charlie shrugged.

"I'm sorry, Bret, but you want the truth, and this is the truth. All I know is that your wife left her sister money to do what she wanted her to do. I believe it was $50,000."

"What!"

"You need to hear me out, Bret."

I did.

"She wanted her sister to do *whatever* it might take to get you moving again. She even suggested involving Bonnie or the woman in Scotland. But Rosario wanted absolutely no part of it, even though she felt obliged to talk to Bonnie about it, who also didn't want to get involved. So I excused myself, went outside to my car, and waited. Eventually, Faulkner came home from school. A few minutes later, I saw the light go on in her bedroom upstairs, so I knew that she wasn't with Bonnie and Rosario. Twenty minutes later, Rosario came out of the house, and I walked over to her, and I said, 'I'll do it.'"

"I'm still finding this hard to believe."

"Me too."

"Besides, that was two years ago."

"Yes, but the prompting, let's call it that, wasn't supposed to actually happen unless you really *didn't* write a novel."

"There was some kind of time-window?"

"Exactly. Five years. Then Bonnie died, and I discovered her email addressed to you, and I said, 'screw it,' and I did what I did."

"Did you tell Rosie?"

"No, there was no reason to tell her."

"Did you get the money?"

"No, of course not, Bret. I didn't want the money."

I stood up and stared out the window at the endless nightlights of Los Angeles. Was it really possible that Markie had initiated everything? Over five years ago? Innocently? Which, eventually, had motivated this screwed-up naked idiot in the Gamecocks t-shirt sitting in the white chair across the room?

I walked to the bar.

It was Hennessey White. I poured myself a glass, carried the bottle over to the couch, put it on the table between us, then sat down.

"It's no excuse, Bret, but it got me thinking."

"Would you have done it," I wondered, "if Rosie had never come to Carolina?"

"I have no idea, Bret. I've been a basketcase ever since that plane went down."

"You hide it well."

"I'm good at it, Bret. I learned to hide things when I was a little girl."

I understood and nodded.

"What happens next?" she wondered.

I looked at her again. Closely. Her short hair was still damp, her face was still perfect.

"Tell me where the gun is."

"What gun?" she asked.

She was lying.

For the first time.

She was a lousy liar.

"The Beretta you bought in Georgia when you bought the Remington 700 with Faulkner's doctored ID."

"Faulkner *never* knew about that," she clarified.

Which I'd already assumed.

"Tell me where it is."

"In the night table by the bed."

"Were you really planning to shoot yourself in a room right next to Faulkner?"

"No, I planned to get up early tomorrow, go to the ocean, reread Chapter 38 a few times, then do it on the beach.

[Chapter 38 is about our day together on Sanday Island and our night together in the Kirkwall Hotel.]

How do you respond to something like that?

It was nothing but sadness.

Depressing sadness.

"I can't face her, Bret," she admitted, with more emotion than she'd shown all night. "Not after everything I've done."

I got up, walked into the bedroom, opened the drawer, and pulled out the 9000D. Removing the clip, I walked back to the living room, tucking both the gun and the clip inside my tux jacket. The 9000D is compact and lightweight, exactly as described on the web, which I'd checked out after Colt told me about the additional purchase in Georgia.

"How did you know," she wondered, "that I didn't plan to use it on you?"

"I didn't. I just assumed it."

"You were right."

I sat down and looked at her directly, into her deep brown, pretty, but confusedly demented eyes.

"You've got some real problems, Charlie, but I don't think you're about to kill anyone."

"I appreciate that, Bret, but I could have definitely blown a bullet through Rex if I'd ever had half a chance."

"Why don't we keep that between ourselves?"

"Why?"

"Because I'd like to keep the police out of this, Charlie. Out of all of it."

"But surely you're going to set the record straight, right? You can't leave people thinking that Skye MacDonald did everything."

"I'll set the record straight, Charlie, but I'm not planning to press charges about getting shot, and I don't think the Wayne police will bother about it either."

She thought it over.

"What about the explosion? In West Columbia?"

"It's long past the statute of limitations, and the little girl's recovered, and she's moved on with her life. Even if she does file a civil suit, you were only twelve years old at the time, there was no intentionality, and you were responding to a high-stress domestic-abuse situation."

I sounded like my brother.

Charlie seemed confused.

"But I deserve to be punished, Bret. I'm sorry for what I've done, even though it's brought you and Faulkner together."

"It also got me to write a novel, even though it really isn't a novel."

She smiled.

"And we slept together, too. That was nice."

"Yes, that was very nice."

Which I admitted a bit too readily given my lingering guilts, religious and otherwise.

"Soon everyone will know about it, Bret."

"Yeah, but I suppose we can live with it."

She laughed.

Then she started thinking about her future, about a future that she'd been assuming would terminate a few hours from now on the beaches of Santa Monica.

"I'll lose my job, of course," she said, matter-of-factly, "and everyone'll think I'm nuts. But I guess I am."

"You need to get some help."

It seemed as though she'd never even thought about it before.

"Go away somewhere?" she said.

"Yes, go away somewhere and get some help. Get yourself straightened out."

"I'm not sure that it's possible."

"I have a feeling that it is."

She stood up, gently pushed her evening gown aside, sat down next to me, and wrapped her arms around me.

"I just want to be close," she said. "That's all."

Which was fine with me.

Somehow I felt that I owed it to Bonnie to do whatever I could to help her messed-up daughter.

"I wish my Bonnie was here," she said, just like a child, "then none of this would have happened."

She was right about that.

"But I wouldn't know that I have a daughter."

"Yes," she said. "And thank you."

Meaning, I suppose, the hug.

Then she stood up again and sat back in her white chair.

"I'd like some more brandy," she said, as she poured herself another glass.

"Actually, you might be *needing* it," I said, as if preparing her.

She stared at me with curiosity.

"There's more?"

"Yes."

She waited.

"What if I could tell you who your father was, Charlie? Could you handle it tonight?"

She was stunned, but she answered anyway.

Without hesitation.

"Yes."

I believed her.

"Are you sure?"

"Yes."

"Your father is Virgil Anderson."

She was shocked, confused, pleased, and angry all at the same time.

"Is it possible?"

"It's definite."

"How could I not see it after all these years? It was right in front of me."

She worked a few things out in her head.

"That means Bonnie married my father's son. Who was also my own brother!"

"That's right."

"Bonnie must have known."

"Of course, she did."

"Then why didn't she tell me?"

"She left it up to your father."

"Then why didn't *he* tell me?"

"Because he was afraid that you'd hate him."

She didn't respond.

It was complicated, and she was thinking it over.

"Would you have hated him?" I wondered.

"I don't know. I don't think so, but I really don't know."

"Look, Charlie, the guy's been a total coward, but he's also been wracked with guilt for twenty-eight years, and I believe he loves you more than anyone else in the world."

"That would be nice. He's always been kind to me, always the perfect gentleman."

She was trying to convince herself.

"Does he know that *you* know?" she wondered. "Does he know that you're telling me?"

"Yes. I've also told him what you've done. I gave him a copy of the book, and I told him to substitute you for Skye."

"This is too bizarre."

"Well, *you* started it, Charlie. I was just sitting in my log cabin reading Dante and minding my own business."

She laughed.

"You're right, Bret, I did start it, but if anything good comes of this mess, your wife should get the credit."

Which was beyond bizarre.

Which was something that I still needed to process.

"Why don't you put on some clothes, and I'll take you to meet your father."

"He's here?"

"Yeah, three floors below."

She stood up immediately, vanishing into her bedroom.

In no time she reappeared, looking like she was ready for a Senate hearing, dressed in a knock-out charcoal business suit, with a two-button blazer, and a light green blouse.

"Calvin Klein?" I said.

She smiled.

"How could you possibly know that?"

"Lucky guess."

"How do I look?"

"Great. You *always* look great, Charlie."

She liked that a lot, but there was something else on her mind.

"When you set the record straight, do you have to mention the thing in your pocket?"

Meaning the Beretta 9mm. Meaning the fact that she was ready to kill herself tomorrow morning.

"Yes, Charlie, it'll be the truth and nothing but the truth."

She nodded.

She didn't dwell on it.

"All right, Bret. I was just thinking about Faulkner, but you're right. Just tell the truth. Besides, everyone's going to think I'm nuts anyway."

"You *are* nuts, Charlie, and you need to do something about it."

"I will. I promise."

We left the suite and rang for the elevator.

Tomorrow, when the sun comes up, I'll have to deal with Cinderella.

My daughter.

There's a lot to tell her.

Chapter 69

Rockefeller Center

R ather furiously, I was working on the re-resolution.

Yesterday, I'd met with Faulkner in her room at the Ritz-Carlton, and I did my best to try and explain that her sister/aunt had shot me in the shoulder.

Along with all the rest of it.

She took it remarkably well.

It seemed to me that now that Bonnie was dead, no one in the world knew Charlie better than Faulkner, who loved her like a sister, who loved her like a niece, who also knew that something wasn't on the up-and-up. That there were issues. That, despite her functionality, Charlie was a bit unbalanced.

Wearing jeans and a black St. Andrews sweatshirt, Faulkner sat on the couch in her suite and listened carefully and didn't say much, except for asking, a couple of times:

"Is she all right?"

I assured her that she was. That Charlie was with her father, which also took some explaining, and that Charlie had agreed "to go away for a while," that she'd agreed to get some help.

"Will I see her before she goes?"

"Of course."

I also explained how her own life might change at school. How some of her fellow students will read the book and know what her aunt has done. I told her that I'd already contacted the Dean of Arts and Divinity, as well as Beaton MacMaster (my private investigator) to prepare them for what was coming.

"It won't be easy being a *real* character in a novel."

She seemed unconcerned.

"My friends will protect me."

I believed that they would.

"Besides," she decided, "if Kate Middleton could survive four years at St. Andrews, I'm sure I'll be able to handle it."

"Well we certainly don't have royal connections," I pointed out, "or royal resources."

She smiled.

I marveled at her equanimity. She was really-and-truly a "Buchanan." Whatever was going on within, she seemed as calm as calm could be on the outside.

"Maybe," I started thinking aloud, "I should fly back to Scotland with you this afternoon?"

"It's not necessary. I'll be fine. Besides, you have to finish the book. With the *real* ending. Right now, all I want to do is help Charlie, and I wonder if I should take a leave of absence."

"She needs to do this on her own, Faulkner. At least for now. Besides, I'm sure she'll want you to continue with your life, continue with your studies, but you can talk it over with her."

"Can I see her now?"

"Of course. She's waiting in the room next door."

We stood up.

I didn't know exactly what to say, even though, despite our rather ridiculous circumstances, there'd been no sense of awkwardness between us.

"I'm sorry about everything, Faulkner."

"It wasn't your fault. Besides, now I've got a father!"

"Why don't you spend next summer with your father?" I suggested. "In the most beautiful place on earth."

"Where's that?"

"New Jersey."

She laughed.

"Why not?" she decided.

Then she reached her arms around my neck and hugged me.

Later, I flew back to Newark, perfectly content, hoping to beat the coming storm. Kyle picked me up, as always, drove me to the log cabin, and I grabbed whatever I needed. Then I moved into Vinny's basement, out of sight, with Jenny's blessing.

What did Charlie say? "I wish I had friends like that."

Immediately, I began writing the new appendix, moving at a fast clip, actually enjoying it.

But I needed to take a break at 3:00 to watch the presser scheduled at Simon & Schuster at Rockefeller Center. Which was an attempt to deal with, to fend off, the countless problems, questions, and accusations about the book.

Wendy, as always, was doing her best to help me, to protect me, to keep me out of it, so she'd arranged for me to watch it live through a security camera at the back of the small conference room.

At two-fifty-five, my timer went off, and Vinny came down the basement stairs with popcorn and Snapples, just like it was a Giant's game. Somehow he directed Wendy's S&S feed onto his huge football flatscreen, and we sat down on his leather couch and waited.

"This should be fun," he decided, placing the huge bowl of warm popcorn between us.

Suddenly, it was lights and action.

The screen went live.

The conference room was packed with multifarious literary types, academics, and reporters. Both ABC and Fox had set up cameras in the rather non-descript room, with its small stage, small wooden panel-type table, and a handsome wooden podium with an S&S logo on the front.

At first, as Vinny and I watched over the backs of the murmuring audience, the stage was empty. Then Camilla and Wendy came out, both looking very business-casual, like attractive young professionals. Wendy sat down in a chair at the panelist table behind the podium, as Camilla stepped up to the microphone, placing her notes on the podium in front of her.

"Good afternoon. I'm Camilla Nelson, Chief Acquisitions Editor at Simon and Schuster. Thank you for coming."

I was certain that Camilla wasn't *really* thankful about any of it and that she would have preferred to be anywhere else on the face of the planet rather than standing at the S&S podium, preparing to defend the indefensible. Immediately, hands shot up and numerous members of the audience started calling out "Miss Nelson!" "Miss Nelson!" hoping to be recognized.

Camilla ignored them all.

"First, I'd like to read a prepared statement. Then I'll do my best to answer any questions that I'm capable of answering. Sitting behind me is Wendy Parks of the Parks Literary Agency, who represents Mr. Buchanan."

Everyone waited.

"Wendy looks great," Vinny pointed out. "You sure you didn't blow that one?"

I ignored him, just as he expected me to. I was fully prepared to put up with his inane running commentary.

Camilla began her statement.

"There've been numerous and reasonable questions asked about the novel entitled *Novel* which Simon and Schuster published two days ago. Most of the questions relate to the fact that many of the characters in the book are based on real people, and that the novel actually uses their real names. Simon and Shuster, of course, was unaware of this fact when we initially purchased the rights to the novel."

"There she goes!" Vinny yelled out. "Throwing Wendy under the bus!"

I wasn't surprised.

Camilla was always a bit officious and self-serving, and when it came to *Radium Eyes*, she was more than a bit proprietary. She'd always respected and admired Markie, but she always treated me like a tag-along until the Pulitzer walked in the room. These days, however, I'm sure she was kicking herself for cutting the *Novel* deal with Wendy last September.

"There've also been questions about the reality of the novel, particularly the fact that it seems to implicate Dr. Skye MacDonald of St. Andrews Scotland of various crimes. I'm here today to clarify and make reparation."

"What the hell does that mean?"

"Eat your popcorn."

"First, Dr. MacDonald and her husband willingly agreed to serve as, shall we say, the villains in the novel. They did so as a kindness to the author, and they also signed a notarized statement, dated October 31 of last year, to verify their consent and their approval. Second, the book also implicates Dr. MacDonald's younger brother, Braden MacDonald, but, as some of you in the press have already ascertained, Dr. MacDonald does *not have* a younger brother. He is, in fact, a fictional character, a fictional creation, and maybe we would all do well to remember that we're talking about fiction."

Which prompted more than a few ugly grumblings in the crowd and yet another observation from the air crash specialist.

"She's over-pushing her luck on that one."

Camilla pressed forward:

"Third, there will be an explanatory appendix added to the novel which will answer many, if not all, of the questions that you – and I – have about the novel."

Accelerated grumblings.

"We expect to publish the *completed* book within two months, and we plan to exchange the revised copies of the book for any already-purchased copies of the first edition. I want to be perfectly clear about this: *anyone* who has purchased a copy of the book will be able to exchange it for a copy of the completed second edition of the novel."

"That's pretty clever, Bret! I like it!"

"As far as I'm aware, this is entirely unprecedented in the history of American publishing. Simon and Schuster wants to emphasize that our primary concern, as always, is our customers. The readers who purchase our books."

The entire audience, even Vincent Erickson, PhD, popcorn enthusiast, seemed a bit stunned.

Yet hardly satisfied.

"Now I'll take your questions."

Which looked like first grade, when the teacher tosses out a softball question and every hand in the room shoots up.

Camilla acknowledged a scrawny-looking pencil-neck in a tweed jacket who stood up, with his back to me and Vinny, and got right to the heart of the matter.

"But is it *really* a novel?"

"I believe it is."

"Cammy's gonna need," Vincent observed, "a bit more conviction than that."

Mr. Scrawny also sensed her weakness, and he refused to give up the floor.

"But it's full of *real* people?"

The inquisition was underway.

"That can happen in fiction."

"No. *That's* called 'non-fiction'," he said defiantly.

Camilla seemed down for the count.

Then an older guy, with an air of self-important oldness about him, stood up. Needless to say, he had a professorial beard, professorial glasses, and professorial condescension.

"This whole thing reeks of fraud. Or a hoax of some kind. Why isn't the author here to defend himself?"

"Mr. Buchanan was apparently delayed in Los Angeles. Isn't that right, Wendy?"

Vinny and I couldn't see the eyeballs in the room, but we could hear them all shifting and locking on Wendy.

My surrogate.

"Yes."

Scrawny was back.

"This is bullshit!"

Everyone seemed to agree.

Camilla gave it another try.

"I'm sorry that I can't answer your specific questions, but I'm sure they'll all be addressed in the forthcoming second edition."

Which didn't fly that well.

"Which, of course, means," Scrawny *j'accused*, "that you've been selling an incomplete book. An *unfinished* book!"

Camilla offered no response.

"She should get the hell out of there," Vinny suggested.

Another blowhard stood up, even *more* professorial than the other one, most probably a literary theorist, an obvious salad-eater with a bow tie and a man bun.

"Wasn't that his daughter at the Oscars? And wasn't that other woman the one called Charleston in the book?"

"Yes."

"Well, young lady," he continued, "it does make you wonder about everything, doesn't it? About Buchanan's Oscar nomination. About whether it was justified. Not to mention his Pulitzer, a novel he supposedly wrote with his wife."

Wendy looked down at her cell on the table in front of her. She touched it, and Vinny's screen went black.

"What the hell are you doing, Wendy!" Vinny yelled at the void on his screen. "Things are just getting good!"

"She's protecting me, you idiot. She doesn't want me to hear anything negative about Markie."

"Yeah, all right, I get it. You want some more popcorn?"

"Sure."

"This is a blast, right?"

"I guess so, for us anyway, sitting down here in your bomb shelter, but I feel sorry for Wendy and Camilla."

"Camilla's just a cover-her-ass type anyway."

"Yeah, but she got blindsided."

"Yeah, I suppose she did."

Then the image and sound were back.

Camilla, far less successful than Sutpen had been in Haiti, was still attempting to subdue the natives.

"I think we can all see that I can't properly answer your questions, especially those about the nebulous lines between fiction and non-fiction. We'll just have to wait and hope that the forthcoming Appendix will resolve all your questions. I'm certain it will. In the meantime, are there any other questions relating to different topics?"

"Yes."

A young kid popped up, probably a grad student at NYU-Columbia-Fordham-City College, etc. He seemed genuinely confused.

"I don't understand why, in the book, Skye MacAllister went to the Oscars given that she was the one who set everything up. It doesn't make sense."

Camilla was visibly relieved by the stupidity of the question. Everyone else in the room shook their heads, most probably rolling their eyes as well.

Why should anyone care about anything as insignificant as the damned plot?

"I suppose," Camilla suggested, politely, "that she fully expected to be exposed eventually, so why not go to the Oscars before everything finally hit the fan? But that's just my own opinion."

The kid seemed satisfied.

I liked him. It seemed as if he was the only one in the room who'd actually thought about the novel.

About the story.

About the plot.

"I have a theory," he began, as everyone in the conference room groaned out loud, but he seemed impervious. "I think that the novel is actually telling us what *is* and what *isn't* true. And that it's using italics to do so. As a marker."

The crowd seemed slightly interested.

"I think that every section of the story that moves into a non-reality is introduced with a completely italicized sentence that might, at first glance, seem completely random. Is that the case?"

Camilla was entirely befuddled. She turned to Wendy.

So did everyone else.

"I think you're a very smart young man, and I believe that the author hoped that careful readers like you would understand. Would get it."

Which, of course, meant that nobody else in the room got it.

Including the guy sitting next to me on the basement couch.

"Wait! Is that for real, Bret? Don't tell me I've got to read the stupid thing all over again."

I was worried about Wendy. In defending me, she'd hopped on her high horse, and I was afraid that the crowd would get ugly, rush the stage, and pull out the tar-and-feathers.

Camilla took over.

"Which, I must remind everyone, is taking place within the world of the novel, which is, of course, fiction."

Which left everyone either confused, or doubly-condescended to, or both.

Nevertheless, Camilla pressed forward, boldly:

"One final question."

Which pleased absolutely no one.

The young Pencil-Neck, once again, proved to be the quickest on the draw, rising from his seat.

"I'm especially disturbed that no one's even mentioned the author's absurd stylistic ticks. Every other sentence begins with 'which'; the whole book's a morass of fragments and adverbial dependencies; and he seems to have lost his thesaurus, believing that there are no viable synonyms for the word 'lovely.'"

"Which is true," Vince concurred.

"Which is," I agreed.

"I've highlighted," Scrawny continued, with visceral disgust, "at least thirty instances of that childish word within the overall text."

"Get a life," I suggested.

"Yeah, but *what's* the deal with you and 'lovely' anyway, Bret?"

"It's a lovely word."

In the heart of New York City, Camilla had had enough.

"Personally, I found the text perfectly readable, and I'm afraid that I'll have no response to someone's stylistic preferments."

"Go girl!"

I much agreed with my couchmate, enjoying Camilla's condescending dismissal, much appreciating her use of the word "preferments."

"Well," Camilla said, deftly extricating herself, "that's all we have time for today. Thank you for coming."

There was a uniform rising of the mob. Literally. They all rose from their seats, babbling their dissatisfactions with anyone who would listen, and, occasionally, shouting out unpleasantries at Camilla and Wendy, who were ever-so-gracefully exiting the stage.

"This is bullshit!"

"Buchanan's a fraud!"

"You ladies should be ashamed of yourselves!"

"This is some kind of hoax!"

"I hope no one buys the stupid book!"

Etc.

The screen went black.

"I'm pissed too, Bret. I'd like to watch three more hours of whatever-the-hell-that-was!"

"Personally, I think Wendy did fine," I pointed out, ignoring Vinny.

"Yeah, she did, Bret. Very well done."

"What's for dinner?"

"Jenny said you wanted gyros from Zorba's."

"Yeah, cause I don't want her cooking for her new tenant. It's bad enough that she's hiding the Unabomber in her basement."

"She's actually enjoying it. She likes giving the reporters false leads. She told one yesterday that you were in Amsterdam consorting with prostitutes."

"She's the best storyteller in the family. And speaking of such things, I need to get back to my Appendix."

"Yeah, I'm waiting for that with bated breath."

"Go upstairs and leave me alone."

Which he did.

A Wendy email dinged:

As the Wendy in the novel said: You don't make things easy.

I laughed and e-ed her back.

As the Bret in the novel replied: I'm sorry. (Which I really am.)

Chapter 70

The Algonquin

Wednesday, February 27

T his time, in the real world, we were having a drink at an isolated table in the main dining room.

I handed her the manuscript.

"I also emailed you a copy, and I'll send you the last five chapters next Tuesday."

She knew what it was.

The Appendix.

The "re-resolution."

Or, at least, most of it. Chapters 60-69.

"That was fast!"

"I'm *supposed* to be a writer, right? Writers write, right?"

She laughed, sipping her Manhattan.

"I thought of ordering a Martini," she said.

"Just to give me a hard time?"

"Of course."

While it was nice to be kidding around with Wendy, it was time to bring up what we both knew I'd *have* to bring up.

"I got the note yesterday. In the mail."

When she didn't offer any help, I pressed forward:

"I know that you mailed it, Wendy."

She shrugged.

"Markie never said that I had to pretend that I didn't."

"Tell me about it."

"It was about a month before she died, and she called me from Malibu, and she said, 'I'd like you to do me a favor,' and I said sure."

"Do you know what's in the letter?"

"No, but I've got some guesses, and I'm naturally curious."

She was fishing, just like me.

"I'll tell you when we visit Dutch Shultz," I offered.

She seemed fine with that.

"I can wait some more."

"Didn't you think it was odd?"

"Of course, I thought it was odd! But you two were always up to all kinds of silly stuff, so I did exactly what she asked."

"Which was what?"

"To mail it out on the publication of your first novel. Which was Sunday, so I dropped it in the mailbox that night."

I thought it over. So did Wendy.

"Thanks."

"No problem," she said. "I hold no brief for myself."

I laughed.

She was quoting Rosa Coldfield from *Absalom, Absalom!*.

"Somebody's been reading *Absalom*. Good girl!"

"Yeah, it's a pretty tough sled."

"Yeah, but it's worth it. Right?"

"Yeah, but I'm still floundering around in Chapter Eight. Page 400."

I waited for more.

"I can see why you like it so much, Bret. It's got the scope, the story, the style. Not to mention, Judith."

Referring to Thomas Sutpen's daughter, Judith.

I wasn't exactly sure what she meant.

"Judith?"

"Of course, you're in love with her, right?"

I'd never thought about it before.

So I thought it over now.

"I guess I am."

"Why not?"

"Yeah, why not?"

"I'm sure she's not your only fictional love-crush."

I thought about it some more.

"I guess I've always been in love with Jane Eyre."

"What about Anne Elliot?"

"Yeah, her too."

"Without a doubt, you're the most ridiculous person I've ever known."

"Is that a compliment?"

"Yes."

"Well you're one of the best people I've ever known, Wendy."

"I hold no brief for myself."

I laughed again.

It seemed like a good time to leave.

"I better get going, Wend."

She understood.

Perfectly.

"But not to New Orleans, as it says in the bogus resolution?"

"No, not to New Orleans, but away for a while."

Which she understood, even better than me.

"I appreciate *everything*, Wendy."

"I did it for Markie."

She smiled, then added:

"For you, too, of course."

"So what's the DP for the day?"

"I had several prepared, but I think I'll go with 'Godspeed'."

Oh, seek, my love, your newer way;
I'll not be left in sorrow.
So long as I have yesterday,
Go take your damned tomorrow!

We laughed.

"Is it too much woe-is-me?" she wondered.

"Not at all, to hell with Bret Buchanan."

"Exactly."

"Exactly."

"As a kind of literary déjà vu, you can kiss me goodbye, but don't you dare say anything nasty about my Manhattan!"

I did, and I didn't.

She tasted marvelous.

Chapter 71

The East Beach

Thursday, February 28

"Did mom know?"

"No."

"Good."

He was, as the expression goes, processing everything, specifically that his long-dead, much-admired-from-a-distance father had been a scumbag, had betrayed our mother, had blasphemed their marriage, had corrupted our family.

"You OK?"

"Yeah."

"Was I right to tell you?"

"Yeah."

"Should I have told you sooner?"

"I don't know, Bret, ask Fr. Ferguson."

"I've asked him a bunch of times, but he's been no help at all. Basically, he just keeps saying man up and make your own decision."

Kyle smiled.

"Yeah, I've heard plenty of that myself."

We sat together on one of the white wooden-plank benches at the east beach, staring over the hard winter sand at the black lake in the dead of winter.

It was cold, leafless, dead, forbidding, and beautiful.

"Why do you think the old man kept those emails?"

"Maybe because he was an idiot."

"Maybe because he didn't care?"

"Maybe because he was planning to leave mom?"

"And leave us all."

We knew that we could never *really* know, and that all those maybes were about as far as we could speculate, but they served as an appropriate ending to such an ugly subject.

I handed my brother the updated re-resolution.

Chapters 60-70.

"I'll be adding a few more chapters next week, like this one. Wendy's expecting the second edition to be published on April 12."

"What do you mean 'this one'?"

"Chapter 71. Me telling my brother that our old man was a bastard."

He understood and smiled.

"You good with that?" I checked.

"Sure, why not?"

"Yeah, why not?"

"What about your sins of detraction problem?"

"I still haven't figured it out yet, but let's face it, the cat's out of the bag. Right?"

"Right."

He looked down at the manuscript in his hands.

"I'm sure it's all here in the real ending, but what tipped you off about Charlie?"

I thought it over.

"Maybe everything *isn't* in there," I realized.

"Maybe it *should* be."

"Or maybe I should drop it in *this* chapter, when my clever-ass brother asks me a clever-ass question."

"It can't be that clever if I haven't even read the new ending."

"Good point."

"Tell me anyway."

"It goes back to the very first day, when I was sitting there, with the bullet hole in my shoulder, waiting for the EMTs, and thinking about the guidelines. About how the box-sender had used a couple of linguistical phrasings that sounded rather odd. Like 'private investigatorial assistance.' I mean, *who* writes like that, right?"

"Maybe a foreigner? Maybe one of the Scots. Maybe Skye or Gordon or Heather?"

"Yeah, I thought about it a lot. But Charlie's got a definite formality about her, which made me wonder. But it was really the word 'explicitly' that set me off. I didn't pay too much attention the first several hundred times I reread the guidelines, but when I went to Canada to think things over, I was thinking about my night with Charlie in Kirkwall, and I remembered that she used the word 'explicitly' when we were lying in bed talking about Bonnie's plane crash. Which sounded a bit awkward, a bit off. Like she *liked* the word. Like she *liked* to use it. Even if it wasn't the most appropriate place to use it."

"That's not much to hang a shooting on, Bret."

"No, but it got me thinking hard about Charlie, which led me to thinking hard about Rex, which led to all the rest of it."

"Colt would be proud."

"Actually, Colt did pretty much everything. I'm just a hack writer."

He smiled again.

"What's next for the hack in the family?"

"I'm planning a little trip."

Chapter 72

New York Times

Sunday, March 3

THIS WEEK	HARDCOVER FICTION	LAST WEEK
1	*PASS CHRISTIAN* Margaret McMullan. (Knopf.) Post-Katrina complications on the Mississippi Gulf.	1
2	*CITY OF NIGHTMARES* Michael Connelly. (Little, Brown.) Harry Bosch attends the funeral of someone he knows is alive.	3
3	*MURDER IN NASHVILLE* W. E. Reab (Scribner.)	4

A Nashville mystery begins with
a kidnapping at the Grand Ole Opry.

4   *OXFORD*   12

John Grisham (Doubleday.)
A disbarred lawyer investigates
a murder at Rowan Oak.

5   *NOVEL*   —

Bret Buchanan (Simon & Schuster.)
A threatened novelist is forced to
write a novel.

Chapter 73

Hotel el Convento

Sunday, March 3

"**I**'m back at *el Convento*. Can you come?"

"Yes."

"Tonight?"

It was almost midnight.

"Yes."

I waited alone on the sun terrace beneath a soft moon above Old San Juan which lay out before me: the cathedral, the rooves of the houses, the winding streets, the beach, the bay, the Atlantic Ocean, and the black-night sky.

The hotel, over 350 years ago, was once a Carmelite convent. These days, everything about the place was lavish, yet tasteful and lovely. With mahogany-beamed ceilings, lots of wrought-iron, wood-crafted furniture, old-fashioned window shutters, and terra-cotta Andalusian floor-tiles.

I heard her coming onto the terrace. She was wearing a white skirt with a white blazer with classic white Mary Janes, which seemed a rather odd-yet-perfect combination.

She looked beautiful.

When I stood up, she walked over to me.

Close.

"Can I kiss you first?" she said.

I was surprised but pleased.

She did so tenderly.

I wished that she'd do it again.

"Do I taste like Markie?" she asked.

"You taste *como el cielo*."

She seemed equally pleased and amused.

"Does that work in Spanish?" I wondered.

"It works for me."

When we sat down, I poured her a glass of red sangria, and I told her why I was back in San Juan.

"You're not going to believe this, Rosie, but I got a letter in the mail from Markie. A couple of days ago."

She was much less surprised that I'd expected, given the fact that her sister had died over five years ago.

"What did it say?"

I took the envelope out of my jacket, and I handed it to Rosie, who opened it and read it out loud:

> *Dearest Bret, If you find yourself loving Rosario, nothing would please me more.* Nada! *But if not, I hope you'll find*

someone to give you love and comfort. Con mi amor eterno,
Marquita

Rosie opened her small white-leather clutch, pulled out a similar envelope, and handed it to me.

Which I opened and read out loud:

My dear dearest Rosie, If you find yourself loving you-know-who, nothing would please me more. Absolutely nothing! Con mi amor eterno, *Marquita*

I looked over at Rosie.

"I guess I'm you-know-who."

"Who else?"

"What the hell's going on, Rosie? What am I missing?"

She told me.

"Two months before the car crash, Markie was diagnosed with terminal lymphoma."

I was stunned, to say the least.

Shocked.

Maybe even, selfishly, a bit hurt.

"Why didn't she tell me?"

"She intended to, of course, but she wanted to put some things in order. Then that rotten drunk killed her on Pacific Coast Highway."

I guess I'd been slow on the uptake.

I tried to spell it out for myself:

"First Markie makes plans to make sure that I write my first novel. Then she makes plans for you and me to be together."

"I guess so, Bret. I knew nothing about the second part of it until her letter arrived in my mailbox yesterday."

She nodded down at the note in my hand.

"What about the first part of it?" I asked.

"When Markie called me and told me that she was sick, I immediately flew to California. One day, while you were off teaching at USC, she told me that she was worried about what would happen to you after she died, and that she'd concocted a ridiculous plan to make sure that you kept writing. At the time, I was way too upset to think about anything so absurd, so I just nodded and shrugged and forgot about it. Then three years after we buried her, I got a letter in the mail postmarked from New York City, which I assumed came from her agent, and it said that she wanted me to 'shake you up' and that it might be a good idea to get one of your old girlfriends involved."

"Did the note say how?"

"No, it was very short, and it lacked specifics, but it said something like, 'he's stubborn sometimes, so you might need to trick him into it.' Which, again, sounded a lot like Markie. But it also sounded preposterous. Part of me wondered if it was brought on by the disease. Another part of me thought, 'Oh, hell, it's just Markie being Markie.' Then she sent me money! $50,000, which is still sitting in Banco Popular."

"Eventually, you decided to visit Bonnie."

"Yes, on the fifth anniversary of Markie's death, I was standing at her grave in Santa María Magdelena de Pazzis, and I was feeling terribly guilty about what we'd done the night of her burial. Then I also started feeling guilty about *not* doing what my dead sister had asked me to do. So I went to see Bonnie MacMillan."

"What happened?"

"Not much. I felt like a fool on a fool's errand. Which it was. Bonnie, of course, said she'd do *anything* she could to help, but since neither of us had a clue about *what* we should do, it should have ended right then and there. I should have flown back home, donated the money to cancer research, and hoped that you'd eventually write some stupid books on your own."

"Then Charlie stepped forward."

"Exactly. She seemed lovely. *Very* Smart. *Very* confident. She said, 'I'll take care of it,' and I thought, 'why not?' Of course, I had no idea that she was a bit unhinged."

"She's good at hiding it."

Rosie took a drink of her sangría. Her lips went wet, stained with purple, even though she was completely unaware and pensive.

"Did I make a mess of everything, Bret?"

"No more than anyone else under the circumstances. I'm sure that Markie knew it was perfectly impractical. Nothing but a long shot."

"Yet, oddly enough, it worked."

"It did. Like "*L'Ange gardien.*"

Rosie remembered, completely amazed.

"Yes! That was one of Markie's favorite short stories. André Maurois, am I right?"

"Yes, do you remember the story?"

"Yes, something about a talented but impulsive French politician who marries a woman who keeps him under control. Then, when she gets seriously ill, she becomes fearful for her husband's future, so she arranges to have letters sent to him after her death whenever he's in need of her help."

"Exactly, there were three of them. One when he's about to make a political blunder, one when he's about to marry a sketchy woman, and the final one when he meets the right woman."

We sat in the moonlight together and marveled at Markie.

And Maurois.

"Where the hell did she get that from?"

"Jack Burke."

Rosie was re-amazed.

"That writer that the two of you always liked so much?"

"Exactly."

"Tell me about it, Bret."

"In the last book of the Burke trilogy, entitled *Portugal 1982*, Burke's dead wife similarly imitates the story by Maurois."

Rosie thought it over.

"My sister was incredible!"

"Yes, and so are you, Rosie."

She looked at me in the San Juan moonlight.

"Do you think," she wondered, "that you and I could really love each other, Bret?"

"I think we need to find out. Besides, Markie's not giving us much of a choice, is she?"

She smiled, agreeing.

"Besides," I added, "I don't want any more promptings. One bullet in the shoulder is more than enough."

She laughed.

I wanted to kiss her again.

She beat me to it.

Chapter 74

Re-Ending

Monday, March 12

Nine days later, on the balcony of Rosie's Isla Verde condo, I stared at the beach, the Caribbean, and the blue-blue sky. Then I started working on my first fictional novel.

About the Author

William Baer, author of over forty books, has been the recipient of a Guggenheim Fellowship, a Fulbright (Portugal), a fellowship in fiction from the National Endowment for the Arts, the T.S. Eliot Award, and the Jack Nicholson Screenwriting Award. His various books include *Times Square and Other Stories*; *Advocatus Diaboli*; *Psalter: A Sequence of Catholic Sonnets*; *The Heretic*; *The Dark Knight of Assisi*; *The Gravedigger*; *Classic American Films*; *Luís de Camões: Selected Sonnets* (translations from the Portuguese); the Jack Colt mystery series (*New Jersey Noir*); and the Deirdre mystery series. He is a graduate of Rutgers, NYU, South Carolina, the Johns Hopkins Writing Seminars, and USC Cinema. He was also the founding editor of *The Formalist*, the director of the St. Robert Southwell Summer Workshops, and the film critic and poetry editor at *Crisis*.

His other writings have appeared in a wide range of literary, religious, and/or cultural journals including *The American Scholar*, *Chronicles*, *First Things*, *The Hudson Review*, *The Kenyon Review*, *London Magazine*, *Modern Age*, *National Review*, *The New Criterion*, *Ploughshares*, *Poetry*, *Quadrant*, *The Southern Review*, *The University Bookman*, *The Virginia Quarterly Review*, and *The Wanderer*.

He lives happily in a log cabin in northern New Jersey and loves pizza, books, sports, and chocolate.

Also by the Author

Catholic-Themed Novels by William Baer:

Advocatus Diaboli

The Heretic

Jacinta

The Dark Knight of Assisi

Selected Other Novels:

New Jersey Noir

New Jersey Noir: Cape May

New Jersey Noir: Barnegat Light

The Gravedigger

Novel

Murder in Times Square

Murder in Nashville

Annie Oakley Mystery

Mary Pickford Mystery

Central Park

Companion

The Sweet Science

Equinox

Selected Other Books:

Times Square and Other Stories

One-And-Twenty Tales

Psalter: A Sequence of Catholic Sonnets

Formal Salutations: New & Selected Poems

Classic American Films: Conversations with the Screenwriters

Elia Kazan: Interviews

Luís de Camões: Selected Sonnets (translations)

Writing Metrical Poetry

Conversations with Derek Walcott

www.ingramcontent.com/pod-product-compliance
Lightning Source LLC
Chambersburg PA
CBHW061543190726
48289CB00004B/1141